TIME *Blinked*

A Time-Travel Baseball Novel

TIME *Blinked*

George W. Young

CELESTIAL ECHO PRESS
ROSLYN, PA, U.S.A.
2021

Cover art and design: Don Dyen
Editing: Gemini Wordsmiths, LLC

Published by
Celestial Echo Press
An imprint of Gemini Wordsmiths, LLC
P. O. Box 1191
Roslyn, PA 19001
celestialechopress.com

To my wife, Lee, without whom none of the

last 35 wonderful years would have been possible.

Praise for TIME *Blinked*

Baseball stories are part of our collective soul. And every now and again, if we're lucky, a book comes along to remind us that life renews every April. *TIME Blinked* is one of those books.

And who among us hasn't wondered, what would it be like? What would it be like to face Vida Blue? Or stand at the plate at Yankee Stadium? Or be chewed out by Connie Mack, given a high five by Billy Martin, or hear Earl Weaver yell, "Ford's done; warm up!" *TIME Blinked* brings that "what if" to life.

There was a time when even the most disastrous of days could be redeemed by nine innings and a hot dog. *TIME Blinked* brought me back to those days. To the days when "what if" seemed like a perfectly reasonable thought, and my dribbler up the first base line didn't end with a slow walk to the dugout, but cheers from the crowd as it brought home the winning run and the World Series.

~Daniel Ogawa, Documentary Producer - KQED/PBS

George W. Young has written a fast-paced baseball thriller that grabs your attention like a high and tight fastball. And he knows the rhythm of the game, its subtleties, and its subterfuges, which makes *TIME Blinked* about baseball — but also so much more.

~Robert Brancatelli, author of *The Gringo, Laura Fedora,* and "The Brancatelli Blog"

With *TIME Blinked*, George W. Young has fashioned an entertaining, fast paced, and singularly detailed love letter to baseball in the spirit of Bernard Malamud's *The Natural* and Ron Shelton's *Bull Durham*.

~Gino Caputi, Host / Fabulous Film & Friends

A tip of my (baseball) cap to this skilled debut author, who brings his Triple-A game and creates a probable major league best seller. Between the subplots of scandal, time travel, mysterious death, and of course baseball, Young humorously ties emotion to devotion and recalls memories of a Black Sox-like scandal in a more modern day. Young demonstrates his knowledge of the game artfully and evokes the intense thrills of the game.

~Mike Morsch, author of *The Vinyl Dialogues* book series (vinyldialogues.com)

Foreword

Growing up in the 1950s, baseball truly was *America's pastime*. The NBA was less than a decade old, and football, in terms of television exposure, was the new kid on the block. The sports icons were players like Babe Ruth, Lou Gehrig, Ted Williams, Mickey Mantle, Willie Mays, Jackie Robinson, Warren Spahn, Robin Roberts, and Bob Feller.

And so, like many boys in my Baby Boomer generation, I grew up with little on my mind other than baseball.

I wasn't that kid who could rattle off the batting averages of my favorite players, nor identify players merely by the numbers on their backs. But I was that kid who fanatically collected baseball cards and gleefully engaged in flipping them, an early and acceptable childhood form of, let's face it, gambling. At some point in time my mother committed the supreme act of infamy—she audaciously and without warning invaded my room when I was out (playing ball, perhaps?) and disposed of my beloved collection. It wasn't particularly valuable at the time—I had too many Luke Easter and Frank House cards, and not nearly enough Duke Snider, Willie Mays, and Mickey Mantle cards, the immensely talented trio who provoked endless arguments about who was the best center fielder in New York. But that shoebox I kept my collection in held my treasure, the only treasure I had.

Those were the days before television demanded important games be played at night, when the audience was larger, and so I sneaked a tiny transistor radio into class, and with the help of a single earphone listened to the games during French class—which probably accounts for my atrocious foreign language skills.

I wasn't simply a fan. I was also a kid who played baseball seriously from the time I was eight years old. My parents, city-dwellers, felt it their duty to get me out of the hot, dirty city every summer from the unconscionable age of only four, for two months every summer, first at a camp in Massachusetts and then Maine. I don't remember any of those years until the age of eight when I began to play baseball. It turned out I had a knack for the game, especially hitting. The counselor in charge of baseball determined I had a natural swing, using my hips to turn on a pitch rather than my arms. He likened my swing to Ted Williams'. I knew who Williams was, of course, and I was flattered to be compared to one of the all-time greats, but the truth was I swung the bat the way I swung the bat.

I was good enough at nine to play on the "9 and under team" as well as the "12 and under team." But certainly not good enough to fulfill my dream, the same dream as George W. Young's protagonist, Bobby, of playing in the major leagues.

My love affair with baseball continued into adulthood. I became a freelance writer and wound up writing a quickie paperback bio of Darryl Strawberry (under the pen name Walt Saxon). Soon after that, I was asked to work on a revision of the classic Charley Lau's *The Art of Hitting .300*. By that time Lau had passed away, and so I wound up working with Tony La Russa and Walt Hriniak, one of Lau's disciples. I'll never forget standing in the middle of my tiny bedroom, my phone in one hand, a bat in the other, as Hriniak instructed me how to hit. That job led to my being asked by my friend George Robinson to work with him on a book about baseball's worst teams of the 20th century. We called it *On a Clear Day They Could See Seventh Place*, and we even got to spend a couple days up in Cooperstown, going through their archives to research ten remarkably bad teams. By then, I was a full-blown New York Mets fan and Robinson generously allowed me to write about the 1962 Mets, a team which clearly earned the right to be the worst team of the 1960s.

I never fulfilled that dream of playing major league ball— although I did get an opportunity to visit the clubhouses in Yankee Stadium and Veterans Stadium when I wrote an article about umpires and one on trainers for the *2020 Official MLB NLCS Program*. But over the years I've devoured books about baseball, which became a way to keep the dream somewhat alive.

Which brings me back to George W. Young's wonderful novel, **TIME** *Blinked*, in which George makes real the fantasy of practically every boy in my generation: to make it to *The Show*. I followed Bobby's journey with him, so eager to see where it led him. So, thanks, George, for making a dream *almost* come true. And damn you for reminding me of dreams unfulfilled.

~Charles Salzberg, Shamus Award-nominated author of the Henry Swann Detective series, *Devil in the Hole,* and *Second Story Man* (charlessalzberg.com)

*"A lot of life is being in the right place at the right **TIME**."*
-Anonymous baseball fan

Part One:

The Exhibition Season through June

TIME blinked.

  TIME blinked in 2020 — or was it 1975? Perhaps both.

  April of those years coincided with a paradigm shift in the fortunes of a baseball team from Philadelphia, and a young man who could not find his way home.

  TIME blinked.

****

  TIME sprinted along the continuum in April of 2020 during one of its daily journeys around Earth. As *TIME* flew by Northern California, it passed a baseball game between the American League's Oakland franchise, which had been in Philadelphia until 1956, and the National League's Philadelphia club.

  The two teams engaged in their annual charity game were in the same "throwback" uniforms they wore the last time both played professional baseball in the City of Brotherly Love *and* were competitive in the same year: 1913.

  1913. The Philadelphia teams from the National and American Leagues fought for their respective pennants and the right to appear in the World Series. New York's ballclub eventually prevailed in the National League, but Philadelphia took the American League pennant and went to the October Classic.

  Philadelphia defeated New York four games to one in the 1913 World Series. It was the closest the two franchises from Philadelphia would come to playing each other in a crosstown World Series.

  Beginning in 1970, to commemorate that near-historic season, ownership of the Philadelphia and Oakland ballclubs hosted an annual charity game just prior to the start of each Major League Baseball season. The money raised would be donated to a different cause each year, the winner choosing the lucky recipient.

  Then in 2020, Colin Marko, the National League's Philadelphia team president, added something new: a home run contest between the top college players in the local area. The winner would get an opportunity to bat against Oakland's starting pitcher at the beginning of the charity game. Colin thought it good for attendance, which had lagged for the charity event in recent years.

Marko commissioned this All-Star-style home run derby to be held at his team's ballpark in Philadelphia a couple of days prior to the 2020 charity game.

CHAPTER ONE

The Changeup

"I'm going anyway."

"You'll never get past security. You think you're the only good college baseball player who got passed over for this home run publicity stunt?"

"Don't care. I led the Middle Atlantic Conference in extra base hits two years in a row."

"A Division III school? Surprised that didn't get their attention."

Bobby Young, still in his baseball practice clothes, sat on his dormitory bed at Ursinus College. His long black hair hung down. His eyes traveled to the floor. His older brother, George, a slender clone, sat across from him on the roommate's bed.

"Did they take anyone from the MAC?" asked George.

Bobby looked up. "Jeff Mills from Widener."

"Yeah, I'd be upset if I were you."

"Not helping."

"Nope. And we gotta get going. Come on. Campus is as empty as you'd expect before spring break. Mom, Dad, and Kathi are expecting us. Can still beat the traffic."

Bobby didn't move. George walked over and picked up his brother's travel bag and slung it over his shoulder. Before he could take another step, Bobby looked up at him, frustrated.

"This was it. This home run contest with our Philadelphia team. You know it. I know it," he said. Bobby lifted his head and yanked back his hair. His face a combination of exhaustion and resignation. He showed George his right hand and counted on his fingers. "Didn't get drafted out of high school. Walked away from the scholarship at Arizona State because I didn't want to be away from home. Skipped the last season of summer baseball. Refused to play in Mexico last year because, again, I didn't want to be away from home. I rolled up a pretty good reputation as a head case. And here I am with three years of varsity ball at 'Where Did You Go to College?' University."

George tossed the travel bag onto the cheap area rug that divided the room.

"Are you joking? A home run contest for an at-bat in one exhibition game is your ticket to the 2020 National League?"

Bobby's head dropped again. "Yep."

"Really?"

George laughed that barking hyena laugh that Bobby loved so much. Soon they were hysterical. The R.A. came by, knocked on the door, and interrupted them.

"Locking up, you two. Let's go!"

****

Out in the parking lot, George closed the trunk of his 1965 Mustang Fastback. He got into the driver's seat. Bobby took his place riding shotgun, and stared at the floormat.

George started the car but switched it off. He turned to face Bobby.

"When's the contest?"

"Saturday," Bobby said, and the words died on the car's floor.

"Then we've got two days to MacGyver our way into the competition."

****

Two days later, George stood next to his Mustang. He wore a thundercloud-gray Armani suit. An iPad tucked under his arm completed the look.

"Where did you find *that* outfit?" Bobby asked, coughing on a laugh.

"I'm sorry. Did you miss my summer stock turn in *Glengarry Glen Ross*?"

"Yes, I did," said Bobby, a smile turning up a corner of his mouth. George stared at him until Bobby paid attention.

"I'm your agent from the time we hit the pavement in the parking lot of the ballfield," said George. "Got it?"

"You're going to get us past the check-in as my agent?"

"Yes," said George, unlocking the driver's side door. "Using this suit and the letter I've got from Colin Marko, personally inviting you to the contest."

"Oh, now we know Colin Marko?"

George adjusted the jacket of the Armani suit, sitting on the coattails and straightening his shoulders.

"Colin? We go waaaaaaaaaay back."

George barked like a hyena and put the Mustang in gear. Next stop: Philadelphia's National League ballpark for an encore performance of *Glengarry Glen Ross*.

****

George handed Bobby an ID card as they pulled into the parking lot of the ballfield, one of the three sports venues in the complex that included the outdoor stadium for the Philadelphia pro football team, and the indoor dual-purpose rink and court, where both the pro hockey and the pro basketball teams competed.

"Who the heck is Dave Moss?"

"One of the characters in *Glengarry Glen Ross*. If you had gone to see the —"

"Why can't I be Robert Young?"

"Oh, come on. Where's your sense of theatrics? Just play along. It'll make my job easier to get you into the contest."

"How does that make any sense?"

"Again, it appeals to *my* sense of theatrics, which is all we have right now."

Bobby tucked the ID into a back pocket. He slumped into the confines of the bucket seat, making no effort to leave the car.

"What if I win? Who do I get to be then?"

"You win, and you can be whoever you want. I'd suggest, though, in order to make Homeland Security happy, that you may want to use your real name for the airline ticket. Should it come to that."

Bobby said nothing. He squeezed the sides of the car's bucket seat. George shifted and faced his brother, pointing a finger at him.

"Game's in Oakland this year, bucko. You win, and you *have* to leave home. Either that or you don't answer another knock at the door of opportunity. And I don't believe any more of them will be coming your way."

They exited the car and approached a security guard at the VIP entrance to the ballpark, a young man with a name tag that read, "Cecil III."

"Name?" asked Cecil III. George stared at the tag.

"I don't think we'll come up with anything better than Cecil the Third," quipped George, handing him Dave Moss' ID.

"Funny," said Cecil III, his voice expressing zero emotion.

"Are you the King of the Ballpark?"

Cecil studied the ID.

"My grandfather was security for Philadelphia's ballclub fifty years ago."

"What about your dad?"

"Dentist."

"So, security skips a generation?"

"That's funny, too," said a stony-faced Cecil. Bobby rolled his eyes and set the equipment bag down on the gray cement.

Cecil handed the ID back to George.

"You're not on the list, Milton Berle."

"You're right," said George, handing Cecil a piece of paper. "Special invitation from Mister Marko. You should come in. You don't want to miss a Dave Moss home run display. Milton Berle? How old are you?"

"Grandfather was a big Uncle Miltie fan."

Cecil took the letter and pulled out his cellphone. He photographed it and uploaded it.

"What are you doing?"

"Sending it to Mister Marko."

George's expression didn't change. Bobby glanced around to see how close they were to the Mustang. He grabbed the wide strap and slung the equipment bag over his shoulder and turned in the direction of the car.

Cecil's phone chimed.

"Go right in, Dave Moss," said Cecil. "You too, Milton Berle."

As they walked into the stadium, the brothers heard Cecil's laugh behind them, and they turned back.

"Mister Marko says you better be good!" Cecil shouted.

"Yes, he'd better be," said George, more to Bobby than Cecil.

****

Inside the park, an assortment of young athletic men, some tall, some rangy, some squat and muscular, roamed the area between dugouts. The PA system, crystal clear in the spring air, announced a name every few minutes.

Hope soon turned to disappointment as most returned from the batter's box with nothing to show for their effort. The pitching machine had been set to a big-league fastball speed of 95 mph. Most couldn't even turn on the ball.

"Dave Moss! You're up!" The PA clicked on and off.

Bobby exhaled and stretched by lacing a bat around his hips. George shook his hand.

"Life is—"

"Yeah. Yeah. Yeah. A series of moments. I got it," Bobby interrupted. "I got this."

"You seem a little *too* relaxed. You been drinking?" asked George.

"Not yet, but give me a few minutes."

Bobby stepped in and signaled he was ready. The machine delivered.

I really hope those minor tweaks to my launch angle that Coach made help. ...

Every head in the stadium looked skyward as the baseball, now the size of a pellet, shot into the air and dropped into the kids' amusement park in left-center field. Another pitch from the machine. Bobby, like an expert archer, placed this one right next to the first home run. Two more deliveries. Each home run duplicated the first, but a little further and higher. Bobby raised his arm, pointed upward, signaling a break.

"What the hell?" asked one of the field officials.

"Switching," said George, loud enough for the official.

Bobby shifted to the lefthanded side of the plate after one pitch by the machine zipped by and rattled into the cage. He set himself.

Another exact meeting of the bat with the ball, but this time the upper deck in right field received the batting practice offering. Then another. And another.

Except for the ball that Bobby allowed to pass by, every pitch found its way into home run territory.

George strutted to the front of the dugout and watched as Bobby lifted several more home runs over the stadium wall. Not ten feet from him, Colin Marko, accompanied by two security guards, enjoyed the last part of the performance as well.

"When you're back from Oakland, Dave," said Marko, offering his hand as Bobby exited the batter's box, "we'll need to extend that one-day contract a little, if that works for your, uh, agent?"

"Mister Marko," said George. "I think we'd better tell you something."

Colin Marko smiled and let go a laugh once George divulged Bobby's real first and last names.

"Not a bad stunt there. The fake on team's official letterhead? That was good, too. Guess you can do anything on the internet these days," said Marko. He let go of Bobby's hand and walked the brothers back to the dugout.

"Decided to let you have one swing of the bat, and when you whiffed, the cops were on standby to have the two of you arrested," said Marko between laughs. "I think that first one went about five hundred feet. Thought you might be worth another couple of hacks."

"Mister Marko?" asked George. "Do you think I could accompany my brother to Oakland?"

"Sure," replied Marko. "Just don't expect us to pay for *your* trip."

****

A few days later Bobby fidgeted in his seat while on the plane to Oakland, California. He had never traveled further west than

Pittsburgh, Pennsylvania. Next to him sat his brother, who had convinced their parents to front the money so both could attend the game.

CHAPTER TWO

Just Another Day at the Ballpark

Game Day, April 5, 2020. The last note of the Star-Spangled Banner rang out and former Philadelphia relief pitcher, Kenny "Gotcha!" Gottschalk, tossed the ball to the Oakland catcher.

Gottschalk, looking like he could still throw a 95-mph fastball, trim in his throwback uniform complete with number 99, left the mound and walked toward the Philadelphia dugout to the appreciative applause of the crowd. He stopped at the top of the steps, took off his cap, and waved it at the crowd before disappearing into the clubhouse.

The umpire, also outfitted in 1913 garb, bellowed to Oakland's starting pitcher.

"PLAY BALL!"

****

TIME crested the bleachers of the baseball stadium in Oakland.

Bobby stood paralyzed in the on-deck circle. The events of the last two days landed on him like the rough touchdown of the Airbus 310 that brought him to the Oakland Airport just 12 hours ago. His home in Stratford, New Jersey, felt every bit of 2900 miles away.

TIME traversed the air space from center field toward the stands behind home plate.

The umpire lifted his face guard, turned, and hollered in Bobby's direction. "PLAY BALL!"

Bobby dropped the bat. The sound, as it thudded to the turf, shocked him out of his stupor. He picked up the bat, stepped from the on-deck circle and walked toward home plate, careful not to look into the stands, now filled to capacity. Seated in the front row behind home plate, George jumped to his feet and yelled his brother's name.

At precisely the same moment, *TIME* blinked.

What appeared before *TIME* in 2020 looked exactly as it did 45 years earlier in 1975. Not just the same teams in the same throwback uniforms, but the numbers for every player on the field in 2020 were in the identical positions as 1975. The umpire behind the plate and the umpires in the field positioned to the inch of where they stood back then. The field judges young and slim. The crew chief behind the plate, stout and grumpy.

The noise at the same level. The colors in the stands identical. The number of people in attendance. The concessionaires. The crowd chants. *All exactly the same.*

And the entreaties from a young man, encouraging the player leading off the inning, identical, though 45 years apart.

"Come *on*, Bobby," shouted the voice from the stands in 2020. "Hit one out for Dad!"

"Come *on*, Bobby," shouted the voice from the stands in 1975. "Hit one out for Dad!"

TIME blinked.

2020 and 1975 blurred for an immeasurable moment. The ballparks snapped together like the last connection in a thousand-piece jigsaw puzzle. A perfect fit.

****

The first batter in the 1975 game, Bob Randolph, the team's catcher and a fan favorite, but *not* the normal lead-off hitter for the club, was listed at the top of the lineup card. Everyone knew it but Randolph. The Philadelphia manager, Brian Murtaugh, inserted the catcher at the request of upper management. Murtaugh walked along the dugout and informed Randolph of his new slot in the lineup.

Randolph grabbed a bat and headed to the dugout steps.

"Come *on*, Bobby," urged the voice from the stands. "Hit one out for Dad!"

But the fan was Bob Randolph's brother, Rod.

In 2020, Bobby Young closed in on the batter's box. In 1975, Bob Randolph reached field level, and looked out at home plate.

Once more *TIME* heard, "Come *on*, Bobby! Hit one out for Dad!"

However, *TIME* did not see a Bobby in 1975.

TIME did see a Bobby. In 2020. *TIME* blinked. Again.

After the blink, *TIME* set things "right." The missing player from 1975, due up at bat, appeared. Bobby Young, 20 years of age, put his left foot into the batter's box at home plate in Oakland. He stepped in with his right.

In 1975.

To face Vernon Santiago, the ace of the Oakland pitching staff.

****

George, whose seat was just behind home plate, had a clear view as his brother approached the batter's box. The umpire leaned out to his right and shouted something into Philadelphia's dugout, blocking George's view for an instant.

The umpire turned and motioned to the pitcher. He noticed there was no batter. He turned back to the dugout, and shouted at Ben Rodriguez, Philadelphia's manager.

"Ben! Get me a batter!"

Rodriguez stood on the top of the dugout steps, arms across his chest.

Bobby Young had disappeared.

****

In 1975, Bob Randolph hustled past the on-deck circle, and sprinted toward the batter's box, but saw someone standing in it already.

"Hey skip," said Randolph, turning back toward Brian Murtaugh. "I'm not leading off. Looks like—"

Randolph paused.

"Heck, I don't even know who that is," said Randolph, in Murtaugh's direction.

"Randolph, get in there," shouted Murtaugh, a soft-spoken, gray-haired garden gnome in his 60s. "I ain't going to ask you again. This is for charity. It ain't—"

Now Murtaugh paused. Someone wearing number 17 stood in the batter's box. Murtaugh pushed his paunchy body to the top of the dugout steps and out onto the field. He limped just past Bob Randolph.

Vernon Santiago checked his sign from catcher Pat Houston. He eased into his windup and delivered.

Unable to call a time-out before the pitch, Murtaugh, with Randolph close behind, froze at just a step or two onto the field. Both were treated to the knowing sound of a clean, solid connection of bat with baseball.

Murtaugh stepped back and collided with Randolph, who steadied the manager.

Every head in the stadium lifted up and watched the flight of the baseball that blasted off the bat of one Robert Wendell Young. It was a home run of Satch Remington proportions (ironically ensconced in right field for Oakland), though Satch's would have disappeared into the confines of the upper deck opposite of where Bobby's now headed. Left field, but still upper deck.

Bobby's shot continued on its upward trajectory until it became obvious to the fans seated in the nosebleed section the projectile would make it to them. They piled on each other in an attempt to snag the souvenir. The ball landed, clattered, and echoed around the seats like a pinball on a score-raising run. It came to rest on the very top step, and the wrestling match for the souvenir intensified. Punches were thrown. Arms pulled back. The mob gang tackled the eventual winner, but security arrived to rescue him.

Another ten feet higher, and the baseball would have landed in the stadium's parking lot, a feat never accomplished in its nine-year history.

Bobby hadn't moved from home plate. Once again, the umpire roared in his direction.

"Run, rookie!" he shouted, his face a combo of shock and amazement. "Or it's DQ'ed."

Bobby took off, not noticing Vernon Santiago glaring at him from the pitcher's mound.

"Who the hell are you, rookie?" Santiago shouted, his hands on his hips. Vernon's body language shifted forward as he watched Bobby's home run trot.

Bobby rounded first and headed for second. He hit the bag and made for third. He saw the back of the shortstop. The name on the top of the uniform, over number 19, read "Rausch." Bobby slowed and looked toward the mound where the pitcher had turned his back.

"Santiago," it read.

Vernon Santiago? Bobby asked himself.

"Hurry up, rookie," snarled Lou Rausch, who stopped just short of bumping chests with Bobby. "We have a game to play and it's only one to nothing. Won't stay that way for long."

"Lou Rausch? Is this a joke?" asked Bobby, who knew enough baseball history to remember that Oakland won the World Series three years in a row from 1972 through 1974.

That can't be Lou Rausch on this team. Not from a half century ago.

Bobby slowed to a walk, but quickened his pace when Rausch and Mel Stack, the Oakland third baseman, closed in on him. The field umpire hustled over to the three, extending his arms to keep the Oakland players from Bobby, who broke free, rounded third, and headed for home.

"If that catcher's uniform says 'Houston,' someone is playing a very elaborate practical joke on me," he whispered to himself as he trotted down the line. "Probably Kris or John Perelli. But how would those two lunkheads pull off something like this? They don't have the brains. Let alone the time."

Bobby touched home and turned to the catcher.

"Pat Houston?" he asked. "My name is Bobby Young, and I'm a huge fan, but aren't you about seventy-five years old by now?"

Bobby extended his hand and grinned. Houston removed his face mask. Vernon Santiago charged home plate. Murtaugh and Randolph had stopped to watch the flight of Bobby's home run into the right field upper deck. They spotted Santiago charging from the mound, as did the Philadelphia bench, which emptied.

Followed by the entire roster of the Oakland team.

****

In the visiting owner's box, the Philadelphia team President, Garrett Revenell, and the club's General Manager, Wade "Sleepy Hollow" Simmons, watched the majestic flight of the ball. They jumped from their chairs and hustled to the window that looked out over the field. Simmons, displaying an energy not seen in him since the '60s, kicked over his chair. It stood upside down, its wheels spinning in the air as the ball rattled around the cheap seats.

As Bobby rounded first, Revenell took note of the "17" embossed on the back of his uniform.

"Hector?" asked Revenell, turning to Hector Enriquez, the team's Director of Scouting. "Find out who this number seventeen is."

"I'm on it."

He picked up the phone and started making calls.

"Wade," said Revenell to Simmons. "Get down there with a one-day contract, if this kid's not already under one. Hector and I will find out who the heck this number seventeen is. And bring him up here pronto. Don't want anyone talking to him other than us."

Simmons, who would give Ichabod Crane a run for his money in an Ichabod Crane lookalike contest, defied the laws of inertia as he made his way from the window out of the owner's box.

****

In the rugby scrum of a baseball fight, Bobby Young dropped to the ground behind home plate and found an opening in the jungle of legs around him. He bear-walked toward daylight and to the righthanded batter's side of home plate, which put him opposite Brian Murtaugh and Bob Randolph.

Murtaugh and Randolph tried separating players, but the only progress they made shoved them further into the moving pile.

Bobby stood, searching for safe harbor from the ongoing battle, and ran right into Ichabod Crane's doppelganger. The collision resulted in Wade Simmons, who had just gotten to home plate on Garrett Revenell's orders, hitting the ground.

"So sorry," said Bobby, who helped the wraithlike Simmons to his feet.

Simmons gained a standing position with the uncoordinated movements of a marionette whose strings had gotten tangled backstage. He took Bobby by the elbow and led him through the Philadelphia dugout to a private elevator.

"Mister Revenell would like a word with you," said Simmons, spying a smile crossing Bobby's features.

"Revenell?" asked Bobby.

"Yes, the owner of the team. I'm Wade Simmons, the general manager of the club."

Simmons attempted to exit the elevator when it arrived at the floor of private boxes, but found himself restrained by the much larger young man.

"What's the joke?" asked Bobby, surprised by his own move to hold Simmons. "Colin Marko owns the team. The Revenells—"

"Security!" barked Simmons.

Three uniformed officers ran down the hallway but were cut off by the closing elevator doors. As soon as the doors shut, Bobby hit the emergency button.

"I know my history," said Bobby into the bloodless face of Wade Simmons. "The Revenells last owned the team shortly after Philadelphia's World Series victory in 1980. Someone bought it from them and had it for most of the '80s. Then—"

"What?!" shouted Simmons as he slid free of Bobby's grip. "1980? *It's 1975.* Who in hell are you? *It's 1975!* What are you trying to pull? That pitcher you just hit a 500-foot home run off, Vernon Santiago, is the number one starter for the World Series champions the last three years in a row."

Bobby dropped his arms and Simmons immediately pulled out the emergency button. The elevator doors slid open and Garrett Revenell greeted Simmons and Bobby. The security guards were nowhere to be seen.

"Mister Seventeen?" asked Garrett, dressed in a black Brooks Brothers suit with a red, white, and blue tie, the team colors. "I'm Garrett Revenell. Helluva shot."

"Uh, thank you," said Bobby, reverting back into a shy 20-year-old, still processing the information imparted to him by Simmons. He exited the elevator following Garrett and Simmons. The three walked down the sloped hallway toward the owner's box, Bobby's cleats crunching on the bare concrete floor and echoing into the distance.

Garrett motioned them into the owner's box, which more closely resembled an office than any sort of sports complex luxury seating. A bay window opened up to a view of the field from the first base side. The left and right sides of the room, as one stood at the back of the box, displayed beige walls with no artwork. Oakland team owner, Stephen Cartwright, spared every expense.

Garrett made his way to the left side, where a standard-issue, metal office desk allowed just enough room before the wall to let the owner of the visiting team sit in a stiff-backed black chair. A blotter and a white legal pad dominated the top. Next to the pad, a pencil cup made from an Oakland Lions embossed mug, and a desk phone. Bobbly examined the almost-bare desk.

I haven't seen a desk without a computer or tablet in . . . well, forever. Does this Revenell have his cellphone in his jacket pocket?

"Sit down, Mister Seventeen." More of a command. "What is your real name, by the way?"

"Robert Young."

"OK, Marcus Welby. Where are you from?"

Bobby didn't get the reference to the TV star of the '50s and '70s.

"Stratford, New Jersey. Nine Hillcrest Road to be exact. Mom and Dad have been there since 2000." Bobby's resolve faded. The last sentence came out as a whisper.

"Uh, 2000? All right," said Garrett, who coughed and stared straight ahead. "Local boy . . . to Philadelphia, not Oakland. Where do you play your school ball? What position?"

"Played at Sterling High and now at Ursinus College. Second base and right field. I also pitch."

"High school?" Garrett's voice cracked and he looked at Hector Enriquez, who entered the room holding a memo pad.

"He's at least eighteen, Garrett," said Simmons.

"I'm twenty." Bobby choked out the words. "I signed a one-day deal back in Philadelphia with Colin Marko. I—"

"*Who?*" asked Garrett, his voice rising a couple of octaves. "Been approached by any of our scouts?"

"Haven't been scouted," Bobby replied. "What gives? This is stupid. Who are you guys?"

Garrett pressed his lips together. Simmons noticed him trembling.

"Garrett."

"Shut up, Wade," shouted Revenell. Bobby sat back in his seat. Hector, who had been looking through his pad for a number, turned away from the desk phone, and held up his hand in front of Garrett. Hector's gesture caused the young owner to push himself into his chair as deep as he could.

"Let's start from this point, Garrett, Wade," said Enriquez, a former Major League pitcher. At 6'5" with hair already white from stress, his trim build gave him the appearance of still being able to throw a pretty good fastball. "I've got the information … OK, I have no information."

Garrett stopped trembling, extricated himself from the confines of the chair, and leaned forward at his desk. He pressed his lips together again and Hector took his cue.

"Sterling Regional High in Somerdale, New Jersey, had no one on their roster named Robert Young or Bobby Young. Same for Ursinus College, a small school about an hour from Philly." Hector moved across the room and away from Garrett. "The owners of number nine Hillcrest Road in Stratford are the McGlaughlins, who say that the family has owned the house since the post-World War II development opened in 1962."

"Yes, there *was* a McGlaughlin family in the neighborhood, but they lived on Overhill and moved when both parents died in 2010," Bobby interrupted. He lifted his right hand, raised two fingers to indicate the number of parents. His arm shook with the effort.

Garrett hurled the Oakland Lions coffee mug—still filled with coffee—across the room where it smashed into the opposing wall. Shards flew in many directions, and a couple ricocheted off the jersey of Brian Murtaugh, who had hustled up to the owner's box from the field.

"Enough!" shouted Garrett, his eyes squeezed shut. "Gentlemen, the Quakers are headed in the right direction, thanks in large measure to the efforts of the two of you and Brian Murtaugh. We've made some good decisions the past couple of seasons and can consider the 1975 Philadelphia Quakers a contender."

Bobby leapt up.

"The *Quakers*?" Bobby's voice broke. "Now you're messing with me. The Quakers! What in God's name is going on here?"

Garrett Revenell clacked his teeth together. Hector shifted his weight from side to side, and Simmons took on an even more funereal aspect, if possible. Brian Murtaugh coughed.

"What's with the surprise?" asked Murtaugh. "Been the Quakers since 1883."

"No, they, uh, *you*, haven't. Since 1890, they used to be … their nickname, the —"

"Nickname?" Garrett unclenched his mouth and shot the question out at Bobby.

"I don't know for sure, but they weren't the Quakers when they played in the 1915 World Series. That I do know. So, for a —"

"1915 World Series? OK that's enough, *time traveler*," insisted Simmons. "The Quakers have yet to see a World Series. Buncha second place finishes, including 1964 most recently, but Philadelphia's *Quakers* have yet to sell a ticket to a game in October."

Bobby jumped out of his chair. It crashed behind him. Garrett pressed himself back into his chair and Hector moved his imposing frame between Bobby and Simmons.

"What? Now you're going to play bodyguard?" Bobby shouted. "Who played the Red Sox in the 1915 World Series?"

"The National League's New York Stallions," said Simmons. "Went to seven games. Babe Ruth won it with a three-hit shutout. Oh, and the Babe hit a home run."

Bobby squared up to Hector, who had the young man by five inches, but Bobby didn't back away. He slapped the palm of his right hand on Hector's chest.

"New York *Stallions?* The *Stallions* played the Boston Red Sox? Who are the *Stallions?*"

"Who are the *Boston* Red Sox?" asked Hector as he pushed away Bobby's hand. "The Red Sox are in Washington, D.C." Bobby raised his hand again.

"Washington, D.C.? But they used to be the—"

This time Hector slapped the hand away.

"You wanna go, tough guy?"

Bobby directed a left hook toward Hector's ribcage but the older man rolled with the punch, then delivered a left jab that Bobby deflected with his forearm. Simmons, Murtaugh, and Revenell got between the two.

While Simmons' cadaver-like body pushed Hector back an entire inch, Murtaugh and Revenell restrained Bobby by clenching his shoulders and holding on.

"Yeah, and what about 1950? New York. Four-game sweep over the, uh, Quakers. Did you all forget that?"

"Second place," said the deadpan Simmons. "Quakers lost a playoff game to the Brooklyn Zephyrs, who, as you pointed out, tanked in the World Series. And the American League team in New York is the *Titans.*"

Bobby shoved the two men away and caught a breath. He looked down, his head in his hands.

"Quakers. Titans. Red Sox in Washington," Bobby mumbled. "The Brooklyn *Zephyrs?*"

Bobby inhaled sharply, and then let it all out in a loud *whoosh.* "Geez. In almost a hundred years, this team, the uh, Quakers, has *never* gone to the World Series? Maybe you should think about a name change. What a joke."

Hector exhaled. "Sit down everyone."

Hector didn't oblige his own request, but went to Garrett's desk and picked up a booklet. The glossy cover reflected the overhead fluorescent. Hector walked over to Bobby, who shifted into a boxer's defense, with his hands balled into fists in front of him.

"Settle down, Bobby," said Hector. "Take a look."

Bobby looked at the booklet. A picture of pitcher Apoulos "Paul" Skountzos, the team's ace and perennial all-star, graced the cover. The headline read,

"The Philadelphia Quakers' 1975 season—is this THE YEAR?"

Below the photo, the caption read, "Paul Skountzos, 1974 Cy Young Award Winner, and the anchor of a promising Quakers' staff."

"Quakers." This time Bobby did not state the name as a question.

"Since 1883," snapped Simmons.

"OK, Wade," said Hector. "I think the kid gets it."

"Yes, I get it, all right," said Bobby. "You guys need some help, and have for a while. You still can't beat Pittsburgh. Not yet, and not in 1975. Didn't happen."

Everybody in the room fixed their gaze at Bobby, who hit every word in the last couple of statements as though he were slamming each batting practice pitch into the bleacher seats. His eyes focused, his voice sharp. The comments had flown out of him and they continued. His demeanor changed from resignation to anger.

Gregory Revenell, Garrett's uncle and co-owner of the team, walked into the box. His dress matched that of his nephew. He joined Garrett at the desk.

"Don't let me interrupt," he said, his voice clear and strong.

"Pittsburgh's teams in the '70s were loaded," said Bobby, clearing his throat. "The Quakers, OK, *Quakers* of the same time, had the bats, but Pittsburgh always had better pitching."

"Of the '70s?!" Garrett shouted the question. "Anything else we should know, genius?"

"Cincinnati had the best team in baseball," he said. "Look, I remember some things, but nothing real specific." He paused. "And just sitting here I think I should remember more than I do, but I don't. It's like part of me is missing."

"You left it behind," asked Garrett, "in 2020? Is that what you're saying?"

"Garrett, you are not helping," barked Hector, who moved to stand next to Bobby.

Bobby lifted his eyes from the floor. Wade and Brian sat fixed in their chairs. Gregory drummed his nails on the desk, as did Garrett. Uncle and nephew. Same annoying habit.

"Not surprising. Been trying to catch Pittsburgh for years," said Gregory. "But for a, what, twenty-year-old, you've got a decent grasp of the, uh, history of the game."

"I got that from my older brother. He is a student of the game," said Bobby. "Just doesn't play it well enough."

"How much older?"

"Eight years."

"What's he doing now?" asked Hector. "I mean, what's he doing . . . where you come from . . . uh, you know, in 2020, I mean, now? Ah, I don't know what I mean. Tell us about him."

"He's a dancer. In New York City."

"A dancer?" taunted Brian, Hector, and Wade at the same time. Bobby, used to tolerance in 2020, had forgotten about the stigma of the male dancer a generation or two ago. He laughed. The sound of it lowered the temperature in the room.

"Yep. Might be the only straight dancer in New York City."

"Not much of an athlete?" chided Simmons.

"Solid athlete. Got into dance when he broke his foot playing on the freshman basketball team. Doctor told him to skip the physical therapy and take some ballet lessons. Lotta cute girls in ballet class."

"OK. ..."

"No, really," said Bobby. "There are. If you're a straight guy, and you have any interest in dance, well, it's a dating service. Better than Tinder."

"Better than Tinder? What's Tinder?"

"Are you—"

Bobby stopped and grinned.

"Don't let your kids and grandkids use it," he said and let out another laugh.

"Wade, Hector, get this, whoever he is, down to the field and put him in right, or at second base! I don't care." He turned to Bobby. "Right now, I don't give a rat's ass who you say you are, because we will figure that out. In the meantime, let's find out if that tape-measure shot you hit off Vernon Santiago was a fluke or not."

"I—"

"*What!?*" shot back Garrett.

"I-I really just want to find out what's going on," said Bobby, whose trembling now matched Garrett's. He squeezed his eyes shut to stop the oncoming tears, but several leaked out and covered his cheekbones. "It can't be 1975. It just can't. I woke up today in 2020. My brother took me to the stadium. I—"

Again, Enriquez held up his hand in Garrett's direction to stop any escalation. He walked over to the young player and placed a hand on Bobby's left shoulder.

"I promise you. We will figure this out. We just wanna see you play. That's all. Think you can do that?"

"I don't know." Bobby steadied his hands.

"You don't play, you're in breach of contract," mentioned Garrett.

"Garrett," said Gregory to his nephew. "That's enough."

Bobby lifted his head to look at Hector.

"What do you say?" asked Hector, moving closer to Bobby. He looked the young man in the eye. "It's coming up to the third inning. We'll come back up here in a few hours to sort this all out. Is your glove in the dugout?"

Bobby got to his feet.

"Yep. Got my name and address stitched on the inside. Mom did that."

****

The Lions finished their at-bat at the bottom of the second inning and the Quakers trotted into the dugout. Bobby and Hector joined them from the clubhouse. Jack Slavik walked up to Bobby and shook his hand.

"Helluva shot," said the third baseman. "Jack Slavik."

"I, uh … thank you, Mister Slavik."

Slavik smiled and scraped his cleats on the cement floor of the dugout as he took a seat on the bench. Bobby sat down and looked on as Ricky Davis, Omar Clarke, and Ike Jackson jogged into the dugout. Davis and Clarke barely glanced at him, but Jackson looked him up and down.

"Where are you from?" asked Ike.

"New Jersey."

"Damn. That kinda power you either find in the South or in Harlem, not in Jersey."

Hector worked his way over to Brian Murtaugh and whispered something. Murtaugh turned and looked at the bench.

"Anybody want an early night?"

Before anyone could open their mouths, Omar Clarke, glove in hand, stood and left a vapor trail down the dugout steps and into the clubhouse. Murtaugh turned toward Bobby.

"OK, Flash in the pan," said Murtaugh, pointing at Bobby. "Next inning. You're in at second. Introduce yourself to Ricky Davis, the shortstop."

****

Murtaugh cleared putting Bobby back into the game with Ben Fergis, the Lion's manager. Since it was an exhibition game for charity, the umpires accepted the change. Fergis told Murtaugh he looked forward to it.

And Bobby's glove was in the dugout . . . in 2020.

"Didn't think so," said Murtaugh. "Nice touch about his mother stitching his name into it. We'll never know, will we . . . "

"Brian," interrupted Hector.

Murtaugh grunted and opened a personal-sized locker in the dugout and pulled out a glove stashed by the coaching staff, but Hector Enriquez had other ideas.

"Hang on, Brian," said Hector, and disappeared inside the clubhouse. When he returned, he had a glove in his hand, which he tossed to Bobby.

"I use it to pitch at batting practice."

Bobby smiled for the first time that day and slipped the glove over his left hand. It slid on as if he owned it. He grinned and shook

Hector's hand. Bobby trotted out to second base. Brian Murtaugh and Hector watched as the young man covered the diamond.

"2020?" asked Murtaugh.

"That's what the lad believes," replied Hector.

"How about you? What do you believe?"

"I believe I'd like to see another at-bat or two," he said to Murtaugh, who nodded as Hector continued. "But come on, Brian. 2020? Who is this kid? He's from somewhere and I'm going to find out where, but I'm also going to play along because if I don't, he's going to vapor lock on us."

"And why is that, Hector?"

"He's a kid, Brian, and I know kids. Not much holding him together right now. Let's find out why." Hector took off his hat and ran a hand through his white hair. "And, if he really is from 2020 . . ."

Hector forced out a laugh.

Bobby stood straight up in the area between the first base and second base bags. He'd taken a grounder or two from Ike Jackson. His throws back toward first looked like something from a T-ball game. Jackson wrote something in the infield dirt with his left foot waiting for the second toss, it took so long to get to him.

Jackson fired the ball into the dugout after Grantland Garvey finished his warmup pitches. He turned his attention toward the batter, Herky Cutler, the Lion's center fielder. Cutler stepped into the batter's box on the left side of the plate.

Bobby remained frozen in his upright position. Garvey glanced at Bobby, who still didn't move.

Jackson motioned for a time-out.

The first base field umpire waved off the pitch. Jackson walked over to Bobby and barked at him from two inches away. Bobby smelled stale cigarettes.

"This guy, Herky Cutler, is a first-ball hitter," he said. "You don't get ready, you're going to wake up in the infirmary." Jackson placed his glove on Bobby's chest and then slapped it. Hard. He pushed the second baseman back with enough force to move him off his cleats and set him on his rear end. The Richmond Field crowd applauded the move.

Bobby shook his head like a bloodhound after a reprimand. He returned to his position prior to the Jackson assault, and crouched. Jackson trotted back to first base. Garvey delivered a slider.

Which didn't slide enough.

Cutler scalded the offering, which headed toward the gap between Bobby and Ike Jackson's recent infield artwork.

Jackson didn't budge. Out of his right eye he spotted a blur.

The ball short-hopped on the infield dirt as it headed for the outfield grass. Bobby's glove snatched it on the bounce. He spun 360 degrees on his right knee, and delivered a fastball to Ike Jackson, who stepped on first for the out.

Herky Cutler slowed three-quarters of the way up the line when he realized he was out by the proverbial mile. In the dugout, Paul Skountzos, the Quakers' 6'6" future Hall of Fame lefthander, shoved his frame off the bench, as did a few of the other players.

"Who is this guy?" asked Skountzos. "Roy Hobbs?"

"Hobbs was pushing forty in the book," said Javier Slocumbe, Skountzos' teammate from their St. Louis Knights days together. "This kid might not be able to drink legally."

Richmond Field, which had been boisterous just a moment before, sat in silence. Cutler applauded. The stadium crowd followed suit. Bobby took off his Quakers' cap and waved to the crowd. He mouthed, "Thank you."

"He sure acts like he's pushing forty," said Skountzos to Slocumbe. Both stood at the top of the dugout steps, while Murtaugh dashed to the phone and called upstairs to the owner's box.

"Greek," said Slocumbe to Skountzos. "I started playing for Saint Louis when I was eighteen. Scared the hell out of me. Jeph Tudor and The Chief were on that team. Bert Chope was the fulltime catcher. Man, could that guy play that position. I never thought I'd get behind the plate with him there. Best fielding catcher I ever saw."

"And?"

"That's a lot of presence of mind out there for someone about that old."

"Who is this kid?" asked Skountzos again. "And don't tell me Roy Hobbs."

"Don't know, but I have a feeling we're going to have to find room for him, and Omar Clarke ain't going anywhere," replied Slocumbe. "Hobbs, by the way, was a loser."

"Yeah, I know that, Javy," said Skountzos. "Maybe Hollywood should make a movie, you know, with a happy ending and all that."

"A happy ending? Of *The Natural?*" asked Slocumbe. "That would be sacrilege."

Skountzos mumbled something. Slocumbe winked at his teammate and they watched the completion of the inning, hoping for another spectacular play from the unknown rookie.

The Quakers filed back into the dugout at the conclusion of the inning, and after the bottom of the fourth, the players shifted their body language because Bobby, or "Flash" as he was already known, was about to lead off the top of the fifth.

On the mound stood Doyle "Gemini" McGirr, a major contributor to Oakland's run of three consecutive World Series victories. His arm had been bothering him during spring training, but he kept it to himself and managed to hang on to his roster position. His time on a major league mound, though, neared an end.

"One more season in the sun," he muttered to himself. McGirr had pitched the previous inning and managed to escape with a quick three outs, though all three batters hit the ball well—just right at the Lions' defense.

He finished his warmup pitches and held the stitches on the ball knowing a fastball no longer existed in his arsenal. The first batter stepped into the left-side batter's box. McGirr thought he would be facing the rookie who had slammed an enormous home run off Vernon Santiago, McGirr's best friend on the team. But that round-tripper had come from the right side of the plate.

"A switch hitter?" asked Skountzos of Slocumbe. "What else can this guy do?"

"Better hope he can't pitch," joked Slocumbe.

"Or catch," returned Skountzos. "You and Randolph—"

An explosive crack of the bat interrupted Skountzos. Every head in the stadium looked up into the darkening sky and watched the flight of an aspirin tablet as it ascended and then plummeted, like Apollo 11, into the ocean of seats in center field. It clattered around like a ping-pong ball in a typhoon, and another crush of souvenir hunters descended on the area.

"Not as far as the first one," said Slocumbe, which drew a laugh from Skountzos.

"Yes, looks like he's lost some of his bat speed." Slocumbe buried his head in his uniform sleeve, and joined his teammate in the humor of the moment.

Out on the diamond, Bobby circled the bases. This time he drew some handshakes from a few of the Lions. He sprinted down the third base line and crossed home plate.

****

After the home run, Hector hustled back up to the owner's box. He walked in on Garrett and Simmons.

"Don't overreact, Garrett," said Hector Enriquez, as he watched the aftermath of the group wrestling match that had just subsided in the stands. Rabid fans fought over the souvenir of a home run of someone nobody knew. "This is an exhibition game."

"I'm trading Brancatelli," replied Garrett. "Some of the bloom is off his phenom rose, but Saint Louis was very interested last year. They're in the market for a right fielder, and there is no way I'm shipping Omar Clarke out of town. We just signed him."

Hector blew a long breath and slumped into one of the understuffed chairs in the box.

"Brancatelli's a good guy, and he's great off the bench and can run," said Enriquez. "The only thing we've seen this guy do today is pluck a ball off the turf and trot around the bases."

"You must be joking," snapped Garrett. "If you saw a player do this in an American Legion game or Division I college, you'd grab him, and don't say you wouldn't."

"I would," admitted Hector. "But he'd be in Triple-A for a while."

"Oh, like Jefferson Carter?"

"Come on."

"Or maybe we should have sent Butch Reynoso down after his first season. I mean, he didn't play well after we traded him, did he? He was only an all-star with Kansas City four times."

"Hey, I had nothing to do with that trade."

"Are you serious? You were the one touting Lonigan as the second basemen of the future."

"Yes, and Lonigan had a few good seasons over there in the American League, didn't he?" asked Hector. "This ain't an exact science, Garrett. Sometimes we give up on players too soon."

"And sometimes not soon enough," continued Garrett. "I'm not sitting on my hands with this team. It's on the rise and —"

"And what? This time-traveling goofball is the difference-maker? Still need more pitching." Hector had gotten out of the under-stuffed chair and began pacing the owner's box.

"Yep, and I like that rookie righthander, Greg Stroemel. *You* like Greg Stroemel," said Garrett. "I'm going to ask Saint Louis to trade him for Brancatelli. Might have to throw in some cash, but I'm willing to do that, too."

"I like Stroemel as well, but he's green."

"Like Jefferson?"

"Just let me know," said Hector, who moved toward the door. "Will you tell Ostrowski if we get Greg Stroemel? He'll want to know, and, of course, we're going to have to strip someone from the roster, which I thought was set."

"It was." Garrett picked up the phone.

CHAPTER THREE

Back to Philadelphia

The balance of the exhibition game featured plenty of additional drama. Bobby ignored the shocking events of the day and blasted a triple in his final at-bat in the eighth inning. He hit it into the gap between right and center field. Most players would have been satisfied with a stand-up double, but Bobby cut off the bag at second and kept going, taking advantage of a disinterested Satch Remington. The ball landed closer to Satch's right field position, but he decided to let the speedy Herky Cutler retrieve it. Cutler made a brilliant throw to third base, Bobby barely beating it to the bag.

Bobby raised his hand, his signature move since Little League. He never called for a time-out. If the umpire didn't spot the signal, Bobby would make the sign of a "T" and not leave the safety of the base until the ump called it out loud.

He stood up to the cheers of the appreciative Richmond Field crowd and waved.

In the field he was flawless, handling six chances including two double plays with Ricky Davis. One of them he tossed to the Quakers' shortstop from his knees on the center field grass, stealing a hit from Pat Houston.

****

The game ended. The players lined up along the area between home plate and the pitcher's mound and shook hands. Several from both teams surrounded Bobby, including Vernon Santiago and Foster Tillis, who Bobby had victimized for the triple.

"Hope to see you in the Series," said Vernon Santiago. "I owe you one."

"Got lucky," replied Bobby, who was looking for a way out of the crowd. Foster cut off his exit and extended his hand.

"I think I got *lucky* keeping you in the park," said the relief pitcher.

Bobby smiled and shook the great reliever's hand, but started to back away from Foster, who stood stunned at Bobby's distracted behavior. The rookie fixed a thousand-mile stare into the emptying stands as his voice lowered to a whisper.

"George?" Bobby asked so softly that his voice didn't rise above the noise of the other players speaking with each other. His vacant stare looked over Foster Tillis' shoulder.

"What's that?" asked Foster.

"Thanks, it was an honor," said Bobby to Foster, as the young man cleared his throat and turned away. He bulldogged his way out of the crowd. Then he sprinted toward the dugout, down the steps and through the clubhouse. He found himself in a concrete-enclosed hallway outside the locker-room door. Fans clogged the walkway trying to exit the stadium, ignoring the wet-eyed player as he pushed past. Once in the locker room, Bobby wiped his eyes again on his uniform undershirt.

"1975?" he asked himself. "Mom would have been five years old. Dad, six. This is not happening. Not to me."

He walked to an empty corner of the locker room. The other players were changing into street clothes and packing their bags for the flight home to Philadelphia. Bobby broke down again, and headed out the exit door. Two men in work clothes grabbed him.

"Hey!" The single word exploded from his throat, and he shook himself free.

"Mister Revenell needs to have another word with you."

They advanced on Bobby, who backed away.

"I hope it's the word, 'Surprise!'"

Neither of the men smiled.

"How about we do this the easy way?" asked one of them.

They closed in on Bobby, who slumped forward and allowed himself to be led away and back to the elevators.

"Of course, it's not my birthday for another couple of months, so it won't be a surprise party."

Still no reaction. However, at the far end of the hallway just before the entrance to the locker room, stood Chip Dunkirk, the

Quakers' reserve outfielder. Chip waited until the elevator doors closed. He hustled up the stairwell toward the owner's floor.

****

Bobby looked from side to side at the thuggish bookends and hit the emergency stop button as he had on his previous elevator ride.

"I'm a college junior. That's all."

"We're going to the owner's box."

One of them released the emergency button and the elevator ascended. Bobby hit the button once more and the elevator slammed to a halt again. He turned to the thug on his right.

"Just tell me what year it is."

The man on Bobby's right, the larger of the two, sported a decent amount of facial hair. He reached into the side pocket of his work jacket. Bobby literally swallowed hard. The man laughed.

"Mister Revenell thought you would ask that question."

He pulled out a folded up "A" section of the local newspaper, the *Oakland Tribune*. He handed it to Bobby.

"Mister Revenell says the date is under the name of the newspaper. Says you might not have seen a newspaper where you come from."

Bobby unfolded the section. The headline read,

"Chiang Kai-shek, leader of the Republic of China, dead at 87" with the date, April 5, 1975. He took a step back and had to be steadied by the two men, one of whom then released the emergency button. The car arrived and they led Bobby out into the hallway and down the ramp to the owner's box.

Gregory Revenell sat in a chair in front of his nephew, who had taken up a position again behind the desk. Bobby walked into the middle of a conversation.

"You trying to fix 1964 more than ten years later?" Gregory asked Garrett. "This isn't the way to do it. I am not ready to give up on RJ Brancatelli. We give up too easily. Reynoso, Lonigan, Dumanski, Cavenaugh, and, Jesus H. Christ, Carter. Jefferson is tearing it up for the Senators."

"What if I am trying to erase 1964, Greg? How would you like to do it? Keep bringing mediocre players in with the hopes of them maximizing their potential? We've been doing that since 1965 and it has yielded us nothing but a losing record."

Gregory looked Garrett straight in the eye. His nephew returned the glare.

"Just who is this kid?" asked Gregory.

"We don't know."

On that, one of the security guards coughed. The Revenells ceased their quarrel and turned their attention to Bobby.

"Come on in, son," Gregory said.

The scion of the team gestured to Bobby, who moved away from the security guards and to the desk. He sat in a chair next to Gregory when it was apparent the Revenells were waiting for him to do so.

Gregory turned toward Bobby. The older man's face took on a softer aspect. His mouth went from a straight line into a wan smile. He opened his eyes wider.

"I understand you have quite a story, Bobby. Why don't you tell it to me, and don't leave anything out."

Bobby looked at his hands and took a deep breath. Gregory turned to Garrett, whose right leg had started doing the Anxiety Shake. Garrett ground his teeth so hard, the sound could be heard throughout the room.

"Not a peep out of you," said Gregory, and then turned his attention back to Bobby. "But I would like to wait for Brian, Wade, and Hector, if you don't mind."

"Don't think I'm going anywhere," said Bobby, looking over at the two security guards standing in front of the door.

Gregory Revenell pointed at the guards, who exited the box, the door shutting behind them. The two marched up the hallway toward the elevator. Neither of them spotted Chip Dunkirk, who watched as they passed through the door.

Chip, who looked like a handsome version of the Scarecrow from *The Wizard of Oz* waited for the elevator doors to shut.

He walked closer to the owner's box and pressed his ear against a door hinge, which had some light leaking through it.

"I can't keep you here, Bobby," Chip heard Gregory Revenell say. "Where do you want to go?"

"I'd like to go home."

"Like Dorothy?" Garrett scoffed.

"Garrett," snapped Gregory. "I am not going to tell you again. One more sound and you are outta this meeting! You want that?"

Bobby and Garrett shifted in their chairs, their movements choreographed.

"Yes, like Dorothy," said Bobby, who fixed his gaze on Gregory.

"You did blow in here like a tornado," said Garrett.

"Not my choice."

Hector Enriquez and Wade Simmons arrived with Brian Murtaugh in tow. Garrett pointed them to nearby chairs. He stood to address them, taking a break from his discussion with Bobby.

The phone rang. Garrett and Gregory hesitated to pick it up, but Wade Simmons, showing a pulse, dashed over and grabbed it.

"Simmons!" he barked into the handset. His eyes moved from left to right. At one point he fixed on Garrett.

"Got it. We'll have him on the next flight out. I'll work out the details on the other player, and I'll call you right back." Simmons nodded then hung up.

"Saint Louis will take Brancatelli," he said to the Revenells. "And they want someone we signed, but haven't designated yet."

"And who would that be?" asked Gregory.

"Rod Amarel, catcher."

Everyone looked over at Bobby, who made a tilting motion with his hands that meant, "not bad, not great."

Gregory Revenell made a twirling motion with his right index finger. Simmons picked up the phone again and dialed. A voice greeted him after one ring.

"Send the paperwork to our offices at Bicentennial Park," said Simmons. "Have Stroemel report to me first and I'll get him squared away through one of my assistants." Simmons stopped and covered the mouthpiece. "I'll let Brancatelli know he's to report to Saint Louis." He returned to speaking into the phone. "Anyone new there since the Skountzos trade that RJ should see?"

Simmons wrote down a couple of lines on a notepad on the desk and thanked the caller. He hung up.

Simmons turned back to the room. Bobby shifted in the chair and sat back into its uncomfortable recess. The Revenells looked over the paper with Simmons' notes regarding the Brancatelli-and-Amarel-for-Stroemel trade. Hector Enriquez moved to the geographic middle of the luxury box and held court.

"We are finished with the preseason of 1975," he announced to everyone. "I'm not telling anyone anything they don't know. But where do we go from here?" He hesitated. "Other than back to Philadelphia, of course."

That drew a few laughs.

"We've traded away RJ Brancatelli, someone we have given a lot of time and energy to in order to build a solid outfield," he continued while looking at his watch, a Seiko digital, new on the American consumer scene in 1975. "And according to my Japanese watch, we have about an hour to figure out what to do with this young man who might be taking his place."

"An hour?" asked Garrett, who had spent most of the last ten minutes taking paper clips apart and putting them back together, rendering them useless.

"The one-day contract Bobby signed expires at midnight," offered Murtaugh. Brian rose from his chair. "I'm heading down to the locker room. Let me know how to fill out my lineup card in a day or two."

Murtaugh spat out the last few words and trotted out the door. Hector turned his attention to the Revenells.

"You two have *got* to get better at informing your manager regarding personnel." He stared at Garrett, who looked away first. "You can go ahead and do whatever you like, but Brian should be informed before you ship anyone out of town. You're lucky that RJ

Brancatelli wasn't one of his favorites. You do that with Mariano Alvarez, and I guarantee you a mutiny."

"We own the team, Hector, don't forget that," said Garrett, pulling another unlucky paper clip out of an organizer.

"He's your manager, and a good one," replied Hector, voice rising. "Don't forget *that*. Almost finished at .500 last year. Ain't seen that number since the middle of 1967."

"You've got a job to do, too," Gregory Revenell said coming to his nephew's defense, and rising to his feet.

"Is that right?" Hector shouted. "I've been offered this same job with the Colonials *and* with the Senators. And that doesn't take the Cosmopolitans into consideration, who called yesterday while I was getting on a plane to come out here!"

Hector marched over to the desk where Gregory stood and Garrett sat. He put both fists down on it and pressed forward, his pronounced handsome features stretched into a grimace.

"And I *know* I could get more money out of any of the three of them!" He paused and closed his eyes. Took a deep breath. "I don't want it because I'm a Philadelphia Quaker. I'm not a Red Sock, or a Titan, or a Whatever-the-heck-a-Cosmopolitan-is. I want to stay here, but you two aren't making it easy."

Gregory and Garrett dared not move. Hector had more to say to them.

"Ownership has plowed this franchise into the second division for most of the past quarter century!" shouted Hector. "Let's not continue with *that!* Will do all I can to turn things around, but I need the help of whoever owns this ballclub. And this year that's the two of you."

He stepped back.

Gregory placed his hand on his nephew's arm. He got out of his chair and spoke directly to Hector.

"All right, Hector," he said. "What should we do?"

Hector turned to Bobby.

"Don't know if this is fair or not, sport," he said. "Let's do right by this kid, whatever his story might be."

"I've told you my story."

"Yes," said Hector, giving Bobby a fatherly look. "But let's make it easier for you to be here."

Hector addressed the Revenells.

"Look, I know what we're paying Chet Gilbert, and I think that's a good number for Bobby."

"*What?*" Garrett Revenell got to his feet and yelled at Hector. "Chet's established himself as a darned good center fielder, and—"

"Sit down, Garrett," ordered Hector. "This ain't up for debate. Draw up the contract. One year, a thousand *less* than Chet, so *he* doesn't get his nose out of joint, and let's all pack for Philadelphia."

Hector spun on his heel and faced Bobby.

"This is my suggestion for you, Bobby," he said. "I want you to stay with me and my wife when we get back to Philly. We'll help you find someplace of your own soon, but it would be a good way to start your first season. A little stability before we work on 2020."

"But I want to go home." Bobby's words sputtered out of his mouth, his composure gone.

"Well, Bobby," said Hector. "If you can tell us where that is, we will gladly take you there and discuss the terms of the contract with your parents, but unless this whole escapade is some big prank, I'm not sure the McGlaughlins would take to you crashing on their couch at number nine Hillcrest Road in Stratford."

"But that's where I live—"

Hector, a father of four teenaged children, exhaled, put a hand on Bobby's shoulder, and squeezed. In spite of arthritis, he bent at the knees and looked the young man in the eye.

"It's the best I can do for now."

Bobby looked away from Hector. An attempt at a smile gave way to a trembling lower lip. His eyes clouded over from the mist of the tears that overwhelmed his last stab at courage. His efforts failed, and he broke down in front of the room of older men.

CHAPTER FOUR

Chip Dunkirk:
The Clown Prince of the Quakers

Hector walked Bobby out of the office. He escorted him to the elevator and rode to the players' level of Richmond Field. They exited. Hector led Bobby to the locker room, where the older man held out his right arm and stopped the young man's progress.

"Before we go into the locker room, did you tell anyone on the team what you told ownership, Wade Simmons, Coach Murtaugh, and me?" asked Hector.

"Nobody seemed much interested in talking to me." Hector snickered.

"Yeah, it's a team with the cork in a little too tight. Doesn't surprise me, but have you talked to anyone else about how you arrived?"

"No. Just told them I was from South Jersey. Like I said, no one talked to me, didn't even ask where I was during spring training, which is strange, don't you think?"

Hector laughed again, and lowered his arm.

"I'm going to formally announce to the team that you're on the final roster," said Enriquez. "But until we come up with a backstory on you, you will confide in no one except Chip Dunkirk. Got it?"

"Dunkirk? Why him?"

"Because he's just crazy enough to believe you without taking anyone else into his confidence. But make sure you tell him that your story is just between the two of you."

"And he'll do that?"

"I think you'll be able to answer that after you meet Chip. Come on. Inside."

Bobby held back, but Hector ushered him into the noisy scene. A few of the players took a longer-than-expected look at Bobby, but most paid no attention to the mystery man who had taken Vernon Santiago and Doyle McGirr "downtown."

Hector spotted Chip Dunkirk, the team's stand-up comedian, right away. The reserve outfielder stood on one of the benches and held court.

"And there, sports fans," he shouted above the noise, "are Monsieurs Slavik and Skountzos, currently working on their latest boys' night out to track down the UFOs they're sure have landed several times in their respective backyards."

Chip paused to enjoy the weak applause. He put his right hand above his eyebrows in a salute, looking for his next victim or two.

"Ricky Davis!" yelled Dunkirk, gesturing with his right arm. "The best shortstop in the National League, but no one knows it but him! Hey, Ricky! How about calling in a few favors from the mob? You're Italian, right? With a little help from your paisanos, you too could become as famous as Al Capone."

At this Davis glared at Dunkirk, but Chip continued.

"Look over there," he continued. "Davey 'Viejo' Gonzales and Ike Jackson, still discussing the 1964 season. I'm surprised you two—"

Ike Jackson, not known for his sense of humor, spun on his cleats and picked up one of his 40-ounce bats. He pointed it at Chip.

"You might want to stop right there, Goofy, les' you wanna be walkin' funny." Ike Jackson handled the war club as though it had the weight of a pipe cleaner. Dunkirk stepped down from the bench.

"Dunkirk," barked Hector, "if you're done asking for trouble, get your bench-riding self over here."

Chip, halfway to a sitting position, got back to his feet and walked over to Hector and Bobby. He grabbed Bobby's right hand where it hung at his side, and shook it with all his abundant personality.

"Chip Dunkirk," he said, announcing himself. "Glad you're in this locker room. Got a lively bat, rookie. Where you from?"

"I—"

"Chip, could you not talk for more than five seconds?" asked Hector. "I gotta get back upstairs. Now pay attention, Goofy. Bobby here is your new roommate on the road. Help him get packed. I don't think he has much, so you'll be able to assist him without a whole lotta effort. Think you can handle that?"

"Whoa," said Chip. "What about Brancatelli?"

"You messing with me, Dunkirk?" asked Hector.

"No."

"We traded him."

"For who?"

"Just help Bobby. OK?"

Enriquez walked out of the locker room.

Chip waited until he left, then turned his attention to Bobby.

"What a jack—" said Chip, stopping before finishing the pejorative. "Good thing I like him. Hector, I mean. By the way, where were we? Yeah, right. Where did you say you were from?"

"South Jersey."

"Liar."

"What?"

"No one is from South Jersey, you rube. You're from outside New York City, or, at worst, you are from Philadelphia, City of Brotherly Love."

Many of the players had showered and dressed during Chip's stand-up routine, so the locker room slowly emptied. There were a few stragglers, but even they neared the end of their post-game routine, which consisted of shoving the last of their personal equipment into carry-on bags.

Chip surveyed the area, and save for his locker, all the others sat empty, doors open. He gestured around the room.

"Now, I'm supposed to help you pack for Philadelphia. Why don't you show me where your street clothes are stowed in this garbage-scow-of-a-stadium locker room, and we'll get you squared away for the flight back."

Bobby stepped toward Chip and clamped his hand on Chip's shoulder. He led him to the part of the room furthest from the door. Bobby sat down and motioned for Chip to do the same.

"Mister Enriquez, uh, Hector, told me I could give you a lot of information about how I ended up playing in only one exhibition game. He said you'd believe just about anything."

"Is that right?" questioned Chip, his voice rising at the end.

"I gotta know that's true."

Chip noticed Bobby's eyes had taken on a shine.

"OK," said Chip, and leaned back on the bench, grasping his left knee with both hands. "If someone walked into this locker room and announced that a baseball player, a twenty-year-old rookie who no one had heard of or seen before tonight, would waltz in and hit two majestic home runs off the starting pitchers from the most recent World Series champs, I can guarantee you there would only be one person in the room who would believe it. And that would be me. So, let's get rolling on your hopes, dreams, and aspirations before they turn the lights out."

****

Murtaugh vacated the visiting manager's office. He joined the Revenells, Enriquez, and Simmons in the owner's box.

"You don't want to wait to find out where this kid is really from?" asked Hector, his fatherly aspect changing to pragmatic talent scout. "It's 1975, not 2020, so he's got to be from somewhere."

"I want to get ahead of this," said Garrett. "We just need to agree on what *this* is, and what we can do about it."

"You're talking about fraud," said Simmons. "We fabricate this player's background and we could be held liable. You want to take that chance?"

"I want to get in front of this," Gregory Revenell said, echoing his nephew's statement. "But, Wade, I certainly understand your point of view on this. Brian?"

"Bobby goes into the lineup on Day One," said Murtaugh, still standing by the doorway. "We traded Brancatelli, remember?"

"OK, Brian," snapped Garrett, who started twiddling his thumbs like he'd been hooked up to a car battery. "We've apologized for that move."

Murtaugh exhaled.

Before Brian could finish exhaling the breath, though, Gregory Revenell jumped in.

"Let's do this in parallel," he suggested. "Hector will work his scouting assets and see if Bobby has been playing anywhere." He reached across his desk and stilled his nephew's annoying thumb-twiddling. "Garrett builds the identification for Bobby."

Gregory squeezed Garrett's hands.

"Keep this as legit as possible, OK?"

"What's that supposed to mean?"

"You know what it's supposed to mean," said Gregory. "Let's give it a week, and then reconvene after Hector finishes a thorough investigation and Garrett has secured documents that we hope we do not have to use."

Simmons nodded.

"I'm fine with that," said Hector. "Also, the kid is going to be staying with me initially so I'll be able to keep him close by, at least until he gets his own apartment or maybe shares a place with that goofball, Dunkirk, which would be my guess." Hector laughed, something unexpected. "Rooming with Chip? Now, that should introduce him to the majors quick."

Gregory turned to Murtaugh.

"Brian?"

Murtaugh reached for the doorknob.

"Just keep me updated."

"Charter has most likely left the parking lot by now. Drive to the airport with us."

Murtaugh grunted, and slammed the door behind him. His cleats clattered down the hallway. Gregory waited a few seconds and addressed the remaining staff.

"Let's go, gentlemen," he said, getting up. "We've got a plane to catch."

****

Chip Dunkirk stood after Bobby finished relating the events of the past five hours. He walked to his locker and undressed to take a shower.

"Young?" A sleepy voice belonging to one of the clubhouse attendants got their attention.

"Over here," replied a towel-wrapped Dunkirk.

The attendant, an ex-hippie still recovering from the hangover of the 1967 Summer of Love, shuffled over to Chip and Bobby. He dropped a plastic bag in front of them.

"Hope you like the threads." The effort it took for the attendant to form a complete sentence signaled he had recently inhaled something other than tobacco.

Dunkirk opened the bag and pulled out a change of clothes for Bobby. A concert T-shirt from Emerson, Lake, and Palmer's *Brain Salad Surgery* tour, a cotton sweater, Army/Navy store fatigues, white socks, and a pair of Converse All Stars. Dunkirk's laugh echoed through the empty locker room.

Bobby examined the clothes.

"No underwear?"

Dunkirk displayed two socks and a pair of boxers that hadn't seen bleach in months.

"The socks are safe, but I definitely wouldn't trust Wavy Gravy's underwear, whether he vouches for them or not."

Wavy Gravy returned a few minutes later.

"Sorry," he said, pulling back his long hair and tying it into a ponytail, which exposed Wavy's receding hairline. "Forgot this. Best we could do, but it's new. Still in the box."

He handed Bobby a jockstrap and a pair of new athletic socks.

"The socks are from Vernon Santiago. Says he'll see you in the Series."

Chip gave Bobby some soap and shampoo. They showered and changed. The Quakers' road trainer, Eddie, came in and collected their uniforms. He looked at Bobby's jersey.

"Seventeen? What gives?" asked the 65-year-old stooped, South Philadelphia Italian. "Ain't that Phillips' number?"

Chip scanned the room for signs of any stragglers.

"Phillips got released today," whispered Dunkirk.

"News to me."

"Yeah," said Dunkirk. "Ron was a good guy. Never quite had the kind of year that would put him over the top."

"Good tipper," said Eddie, with a wink at Chip.

"Yeah, we get it, Ed. Why don't you have a real Italian name, by the way?"

"I do, but you're never going to know it."

Eddie left, carrying two canvas bags with the balance of the team's uniforms and towels stuffed inside.

"Let's go," said Chip. "Don't forget your glove and shoes. Actually, hand 'em over. I'll stow them in my travel bag. We have to get you one of those when we get to Philadelphia. By the way, we're playing the Cosmopolitans in less than three days at Doubleday."

Bobby didn't move from his seat. Chip picked up the glove and spikes and turned to go, but saw that his new teammate was fixed to the bench, his head lowered, eyes following a crack in the locker room floor.

"This isn't happening, is it," said Bobby to the concrete. "I mean, I'm walking out of the on-deck circle in Oakland in 2020, and get to the plate and it's 1975? How does that work? Do you know?"

"Uh, no, I don't. Listen to me, rookie."

Bobby's eyes misted over again. His broad shoulders lifted and fell a couple of times while he inhaled and exhaled. Chip stood over him.

"This has been a crazy day, and you're at the center of it. You've shaken up the team, and it needed it. Let me be the first to say I'm glad you're here."

"What?"

"I'm glad you're here."

Bobby's head dropped and he wept, loud and long. The cold concrete floors and walls carried the sound out into the corridor. Chip could only watch. And he did, not moving from the spot. Bobby finished. Chip passed him a hand towel, which only sent Bobby back into a crying jag. This one interrupted by Wavy Gravy.

"Hey, man, I gotta close up."

Chip lifted up Bobby by the right armpit and helped him stand. He walked Bobby out the door and toward the player's entrance to Richmond Field. The charter bus idled just outside, still waiting for the two and for Brian Murtaugh. Chip dragged Bobby on board after covering the young man's head in the towel to help hide his tears.

"It's only human," said Chip. He looked to the back of the bus.

"Sorry, Antonio," said Chip to the driver, whose classic good looks earned him the nickname "Zorro." "Dragging a little bit. Must be jet lag."

"Don't sweat it, Goofy," said Antonio. "I was still waiting for Brian, but just got a message that he'd meet us at the airport. He's driving over with the Revenells. You know how much he hates to do that."

"Really?" asked Chip. "An hour alone with Garrett and Greg? What fun!"

"Yep. That's where I'd wanna be right before a long flight."

The driver closed the charter bus door and engaged the gear. The vehicle chugged away from Richmond Field.

CHAPTER FIVE

Opening Day: Doubleday Park

On April 8, 1975, Bobby Young played his first professional baseball game. He faced the legendary pitcher, Marty Eliot. The future Hall-of-Famer was coming off a mediocre 11-11 season, but was in the prime of his career, and healthy for the first time since the 1973 World Series, which the Cosmopolitans lost in a memorable seven-game, network-satisfying, soul-crushing contest.

The Quakers, as the away team, batted first. Eliot made short work of Omar Clarke, who swung at the second pitch, a sinker that dropped about a foot, and grounded out to Oswald Aaronson at first.

Bobby Young walked to the plate. He stepped in batting righthanded. Eliot stepped off the rubber and waited. Bobby accidentally dropped his bat, which drew a laugh from the Doubleday Park fans. Bobby blushed and picked up the bat. He stepped out of the box.

"Righthander!" someone shouted from the crowd.

He switched to the left side.

Eliot had seen replays of Bobby's home run against Vernon Santiago. The Quakers televised the charity game every year, and as a student of preparation, Eliot watched all of Bobby's at-bats multiple times.

The day before the opening game, in the film study room with battery mate, Red Devine, Eliot blew a long breath toward the screen.

"Haven't seen reflexes like that since Henry," said Eliot, referring to Hank Aaron.

"Yep," said Devine. "Seems to be content to wait on off-speed stuff, too. That triple was on a curveball."

"Let's start him inside," said Eliot. "Then I'll throw him something outside of the strike zone to see if I can get him to chase."

"Got it. How about Slavik?"

Eliot turned back to the projector and they worked their way through the Quakers' lineup.

****

Bobby stepped in. The PA announced him.

"Batting second for the Philadelphia Quakers, right fielder, number seventeen on your lineup card, Bobby Young."

Eliot blazed an inside fastball. Bobby stepped forward with his right lead foot and crushed the pitch, *off the bat handle*, into the seats in right field, but foul. Red Devine, the catcher, stood and watched the flight of the ball as it landed in the upper deck. It missed being a home run by about a yard.

Devine took a new ball from the umpire and tossed it to Eliot. The Cosmopolitans' catcher called for a curveball off the plate. Eliot obliged.

"Ball," said the ump.

Devine called for the same pitch. This one was closer, but still off the plate.

"Ball two."

"It's early, but that kid's got a good eye," said Eliot to his glove, before he received the ball back from Devine.

Devine once again called for a curveball off the plate. Eliot shook him off and the catcher gave the sign for a fastball off the plate.

Eliot wound up and delivered. Bobby watched the pitch. The seams weren't spinning for a curve. *Fastball* clicked through his brain. *Off the plate, same as the last two curveballs.* He shifted his lead foot toward the pitch and connected, pulling the ball toward the right side of the Cosmopolitans' infield.

The ball found the seam between first baseman, Oswald Aaronson—not known for his glove—and the bag. The ball skidded past the bag and into right field. Chi-Chi Yarhi chased it down, but the former Houston Wildcat had lost more than a step.

Bobby raced around first and saw Yarhi lumbering into the right field corner. Bobby streaked toward second with one eye on third base.

Yarhi picked up the ball after it pinballed around the corner. He fired it to the cut-off man, second baseman Clint Woodson, who made the rookie mistake of allowing the throw to turn him clockwise, away from third base.

Bobby kicked up some infield dirt and slid under Felipe Lopez's clumsy tag.

Triple.

"Three bases for the rookie, Young," said Skeeter Thompson, the former Quaker. "The fans at home wanted to see one of those impressive home runs, but Bobby Young showed some Olympic speed there, getting from second to third."

Clyde Wilhelm, Thompson's broadcast booth mate, added, "Really great bat control."

Eliot grumbled when he got the ball back from Devine. It would be a rough start for the future Hall-of-Famer.

****

The game ended mercifully for Cosmopolitans fans, in the minimum nine innings. The Quakers had thumped a team picked by some to win the National League East, along with their best pitcher, 10 to 2. Paul Skountzos pitched a five-hitter, and Declan "Deke" Reilly tossed a scoreless ninth.

The big story was, as expected, unknown rookie Bobby Young. He went four for five with two home runs, three runs scored, and four batted in. The only time the Cosmopolitans' pitchers retired him was on a great play by long-time original Cosmo, Billy Pierce, a defensive fill-in for Oswald Aaronson at first.

Batting from the right side of the plate against seldom-used southpaw, Alan Joy, Bobby had scalded an opposite-field connection meant for extra bases. If it had turned into a double, the Quakers' rookie would have hit for the cycle in his first major league game.

The underrated Pierce dove for the ball, knocked it down, and delivered a laser to the hustling Joy, who beat Bobby to the bag by less than a step. The 50,000-person sigh from the stands showed that even Cosmopolitans fans were disappointed.

****

The Philadelphia and New York press descended on Bobby after the game, catching him at his locker. But Chip Dunkirk abruptly cut them off after the first, "So, where do you hail from, Bobby?" question.

"I almost got to play tonight," said Dunkirk. "Don't you all want to ask me about that? I mean, I was in the batter's box and everything!"

"Get outta the way, Pine," said one of the reporters, an obvious dig at Dunkirk's bench-player status. The comment only motivated Dunkirk.

Chip Dunkirk took over the Q&A.

"I had a bead on Eliot," said Dunkirk. "By the way, that's Dunkirk with two 'k's." Chip had to dodge several inquiries into how the team landed such a talent. No one in the press corps had been able to find out a thing about Bobby, which only added to their enthusiasm for "The Unnatural," a nickname earned through the combination of his talent and mysterious appearance in the Major League Baseball season. "Flash," as far as sports media was concerned, disappeared as a moniker. Bobby would be "The Unnatural," at least to them.

"It's one game," said the taciturn Skountzos. "I'm happy we have him, but let's see how these post-game charades are playing out during the dog days of summer. OK?"

Skountzos turned his back to the reporters. The Quakers' enigmatic lefthander had nothing to add. After a few more entreaties, the press departed the locker room.

****

The next evening, the Quakers trounced the Cosmopolitans again, and their number two starter, Skip Masterson, by a score of 9 to 0. Grantland Garvey pitched a complete game shutout. Bobby hit another home run and added a single. During his second plate appearance, the Cosmopolitans intentionally walked him for the first time in his short career. Jack Slavik, insulted by the move, jacked a home run into the middle deck in center field.

"I have never seen Jack show emotion like that," said Rick Nayle to Ike Jackson at the top of the Quakers' half of the sixth, which had them out in front, 7 to 0. "He's usually such a sourpuss, ain'tcha, Slavik?"

"Intentional walk to the guy in front of *me?*" Slavik's voice bounced out to the field, where the forlorn Cosmos limped out of the dugout. "Do that again! I'll hit you so hard your whole family will hurt!"

The team boarded the charter bus for the ride back to Philadelphia and their home opener against the cross-state rival, the Pittsburgh Miners. Sportswriters across the board had picked the Miners to run away with the division. As had Bobby in the owner's box at Richmond Field.

"Maybe not, eh, Un-Nat?" asked Dunkirk during the ride home. "Hey, what's wrong?"

"Headache, Chip," answered Bobby. "The future is fading for me. Memories are leaving, including my family."

He rubbed his temple.

"It hurts physically to remember my parents," he continued. "What they look like and where my sister is."

"Bobby —"

"I've been here less than a week."

"Uh."

"My life is evaporating, Chip. Evaporating."

****

"That was BB," said Garrett, behind the confines of his desk in the owner's offices at Bicentennial Park.

"What's that supposed to mean?" asked Wade Simmons. Today, Ichabod dressed in a pair of casual green pants, an off-white work shirt, brown boots, and a knit sweater. Gregory Revenell looked him up and down.

"You know, Wade," said Gregory. "You may want to dress up a little more. You do know your nickname?"

"Yes. Yes. Yes. Ichabod Crane from 'The Legend of Sleepy Hollow'."

"Just a suggestion," said Gregory, turning back to Garrett. "BB?"

"Before Bobby," replied Garrett, depositing a copy of *The Sporting News* on the desk. "Pittsburgh was supposed to run away with this division, but that was before whoever this guy is dropped in our laps."

Garrett delivered the last line with an edge. Hector Enriquez, who also sat in the owner's office, folded his arms across his chest. He glared at Garrett.

"Are we going over this again, Garrett? Thought we'd resolved our plan? *You* get the identification and *I* look into Bobby Young's background."

"Hey, I'm the one says the Miners were the favorites BB. Before Bobby." Garrett smiled, which could have been more forced, but no one in the room could imagine how.

"I get the feeling you're not totally on board with this."

"Hector, we don't need to go over this again. Garrett has agreed," snapped Gregory.

"Fine, but I don't want any of his personal or, ahem, professional, connections venturing over into my territory. I'll figure out where Bobby came from."

"What's that supposed to mean?"

A knock at the door interrupted the escalating discussion.

Bobby stuck his head in.

"You asked for me?"

Gregory Revenell waved him in.

"Come in, slugger," said Gregory. "Helluva Series. We're just waiting for Brian."

"Thank you," said Bobby. He shut the door behind him. It creaked before the top hinge lost a stripped screw. The door slipped from the hinge and the lower corner hit the floor with a thud.

"What the—" Startled, Bobby struck a boxer's pose back at the door. He exhaled a ragged breath. "Sorry. I don't know how that happened."

Hector Enriquez looked at the Quakers' young star. Bobby's demeanor changed from professional athlete to 20-year-old kid whenever the youngster left the playing field. Hector held back a laugh.

"Hector?" asked Garrett, still spoiling for a fight.

"No," said Hector, but he turned to Bobby. "You really are just, well, not a teenager, but close. What are you going to be in five years?"

"Twenty-five?"

The room laughed as one, except for Garrett.

Brian Murtaugh entered the office and stood next to Simmons. The two of them could have stepped out of a J.R.R. Tolkien novel — Simmons as previously described, and Murtaugh, still in his street clothes, which weren't much of an upgrade from Simmons' farmer wear. Their facial features more cartoonish than realistic. Both had pronounced noses and ears, their graying hair uncombed and presenting itself in runaway tufts.

"We need to ask you about 1975," said Gregory, getting right to it. He glanced at the clock, an old industrial type used in public schools.

Batting practice in less than an hour.

"What about it?" asked Bobby.

"Do you recall anything? How did we do? Do the Miners win the division?"

"Uh, Mister Simmons, all that has changed now that I'm here."

"We know that," said Enriquez.

"I'm not supposed to be here," said Bobby. "I was not on the roster in 1975 . . . well, the 1975 that I know about."

"But what do you remember about what happened before you left 2020?" asked Garrett, and then he spoke a little too loud. "We're going to have a serious discussion about this."

"Garrett, shut up and listen or get out." Gregory walked over to his nephew. Garrett's nails had dug a few scratches into the surface of his desk. He faced off against his uncle, the younger Revenell taller and looming, but Gregory did not shrink from the challenge.

Garrett sat.

"Bobby?"

Bobby scratched the back of his neck. He looked down at the carpet.

"Yes, the Miners won the division, but lost to the Bucks in the playoffs. It was an incredible World Series between Cincinnati and

Boston, but I can't remember who won because that event has changed. If it hadn't, I'd have remembered."

"So, we don't win the National League East."

Bobby concentrated on the floor.

"The Quakers finished second, but that team didn't have Greg Stroemel. It hadn't unloaded, uh, RJ Brancatelli or Ron Phillips. And you didn't trade Chet Gilbert soon enough."

Bobby's last words disappeared under a blanket of crosstalk. Brian Murtaugh scurried around the room like a wind-up toy bumping into anyone who would engage him in conversation about who owned the lineup card. Simmons and Brian shouted at each other about personnel responsibilities. If there were just a few other animated characters in the room, the subject matter would have been centered on who would carry the One Ring to Mordor.

"Chet 'The Jet' Gilbert?" Gregory Revenell's voice rose above the noise. "We *trade* him this season? He's a very good player. Just missed Rookie of the Year a few seasons ago."

"I know. To that catcher from Atlanta, who never played anywhere near as well again. Now, I can't remember his name."

"Moose Huggins."

"Oh, right. He didn't have much of a career after that, did he?"

"Not so far."

"Chet Gilbert's not turned into the next Roberto Clemente, either."

Garrett shot out of his seat and shook his finger at Bobby.

"Gilbert hit .300 last year, and you say we trade him? Are you joking?" Garrett laughed much too loud, and Gregory ran over and wrapped his arms around him.

Garrett shoved his uncle away.

"To who? For who?"

"The Rockers. For Moses Pendleton."

"No!" Garrett shouted. Before he could continue with his protest, one of the stadium security guards ran into the room. Garrett ignored him and pushed his uncle even further away. He raised his voice to a level worthy of Bedlam. "Chet Gilbert isn't going anywhere! Who the *hell* is this guy?!"

Outside the owner's office, the Revenells' bodyguard, Woody, hustled in, and reached for his sidearm. He held his hand on the outside of the holster. Garrett kept pointing a finger at Bobby.

"We're fine, Woody," said Gregory, who motioned Woody out of the room. "Appreciate your concern."

"I heard some yelling," said Woody, his hand remaining over the handle of his service revolver. He stared at Garrett, Woody's athletic 225-pound body tense and leaning forward.

"Won't be the last time," said Simmons. He walked over to Woody and placed a hand on the guard's shoulder. "Woody, thanks for responding so quickly. Just a disagreement between management as we like to say . . . and will be saying a lot more."

"OK," said Woody, as he walked out the door and into the hallway, motioning the stadium guard to join him. "But try to keep it down. Don't like what I was hearing."

Before Garrett could react, or overreact, Hector squeezed the young man's forearm and sat him down.

"OK, Bobby," said Hector. "What other moves did we make? Sounds like it still didn't put us over the top."

"I can't remember anything, except that you didn't trade Ron Phillips."

"We actually sent Ron down to the minors to coach," said Hector. "I'm thinking of asking him to join me in scouting. He's got an eye for talent."

"Yeah," said Garrett. "He just doesn't have any."

"OK, Garrett."

"Never worked out for us."

"He's a good guy, Garrett," said Simmons. "And he was a great asset in the locker room. I'm going to miss him. Let's not get sidetracked. Anything else, Bobby?"

"I can't believe we're seriously thinking about trading Chet 'The Jet' Gilbert!" Garrett shouted just loud enough to bring Woody back into the room. The bodyguard stepped aside just as Garrett flew through the door, then stomped toward the elevators.

"Don't bother," said Garrett, over his shoulder. "I'm outta there."

CHAPTER SIX

The Pittsburgh Miners, Defending National League East Champs

At the Philadelphia home opener for the 1975 season at Bicentennial Park, the Quakers took on the Pittsburgh Miners. Andy Escott, the Miners' muscular All-Star catcher, took warmup tosses from Matias Munoz, the opening day starter for the Miners. He did it under a deluge of boos from the Philly fans. Andy received another pitch, stood up, and waved at the crowd, an electric smile splitting his features. It brought another chorus of proverbial Bronx cheers.

"Always liked Andy," said Dunkirk, who watched the Miners' catcher play to the crowd. "Good sense of humor."

"There's a surprise," said Murtaugh. "And let's not talk up the opposing catcher while Randolph's on the injured list. Mariano! You're calling the game today. Don't forget. You looked a little lost out there during warmups."

Mariano Alvarez, the reserve catcher, lifted his hand.

"I'm good, coach."

"You better be. This ain't Reading, Pennsylvania," he said, referencing the Quakers' Double-A minor league team.

Murtaugh pressed forward on the dugout rail. Omar Clarke took his first few whacks against the Miners' starter.

Nine innings later, the Quakers had beaten the Miners 8 to 1. Their third win in a row.

The 1975 Philadelphia Quakers were off and running.

****

Chip Dunkirk, who got into the game as a pinch-hitter and played two innings in left field as a defensive replacement for Rick Nayle, collected two hits in his two at-bats. He decided to let everyone know about it. Chip occupied his familiar position on top of the training table in the locker room, normally reserved for the pitching staff.

"And who, might I ask, is the leading hitter for the 1975 Philadelphia Quakers? Batting a cool *one thousand!* Who? I'll tell ya who! It's Chip Dunkirk. That's who!"

He laughed at himself.

"All right, Goofy, let's put a cork in the bottle," said Brian Murtaugh. He walked into the middle of the noise. Behind him, Phil Ostrowski, the pitching coach, banged a bat against the metal lockers that rimmed the clubhouse. The team snapped to attention, most half-dressed, still sweaty from the game. Chip Dunkirk dropped to the floor in his Spiderman crouch and crab-walked to the beach chair he kept for post-game rituals.

"Good game, gentlemen," said Murtaugh. "One hundred fifty-nine more just like this, and we might actually make every sportswriter, including the local Philly boys, look like the dunces they are." He paused. "But we do have one hundred fifty-nine more, and remember, another one against the Miners tomorrow, who will be out for payback. Don't get ahead of yourselves."

Many of the players muttered some appreciation for Brian's words.

"Great start, Tony," said Gilbert, who shoved his signature blue glove into his locker. "Made them Miners look Triple-A."

"Scary lineup," said Tony Edwards, up for his first full season with the club.

"We're ready for tomorrow," Ricky Davis added.

Ostrowski banged the bat again, and the team quieted once more.

"I wanna give out a couple game balls. I know it's early, like I said, but let's acknowledge a few performances that I hope continue."

He handed a scuffed ball to Edwards, the starter.

"Great game, rookie," said Murtaugh. "Study the pitching books. The League is going to figure you out. Stay ahead of them."

Another one to Nayle.

"Nobody likes pitching to you, Rusty."

Murtaugh put his hands on his hips.

"Now, Flash in the Pan, or The Unnatural. Geez, two nicknames inside of a week," he said to Bobby. "Good hitting. Great fielding, but I can't give you a game ball until you start to shave."

That broke up the locker room, and the team resumed getting ready to head home or out for the night.

"Hey!" shouted Ostrowski. "BP tomorrow, one o'clock, and I know what a hangover looks like."

"Lotta good ballplayers on the bench," said Murtaugh. "Don't make me put someone in because you overdid it."

Murtaugh and Ostrowski departed.

Dunkirk sidled over to Bobby.

"He was talking about me there at the end!" Dunkirk announced, after cupping his hands to increase his already considerable volume.

The roster, to a man, unloaded abuse on Dunkirk, who stood and took a bow.

"Wanna get a beer?" Dunkirk asked Bobby, who laughed at Chip's excellent comic timing coming on the heels of Ostrowski's hangover comment.

"Sure, as long as you don't mind going over the bridge."

"What?"

"Not old enough to drink in Pennsylvania, Goofy."

"See ya in 1976!"

CHAPTER SEVEN

Garrett Revenell and the New Documents

The man on the other end of the phone said, "$250,000."

"*What?*" asked Garrett. "It's a driver's license, a social security card, and a birth certificate. I'm not even asking for a passport. And you want $250,000!"

Garrett yanked the handset from his ear and smashed it down on the desk. He thumped it several times on the cushioned borders of the blotter. He blew air out of his lungs, and smacked his palms down to steady himself before retrieving the handset and lifting it to his ear.

"You done? Good." The voice on the line sucked in an audible and asthmatic breath. He wheezed out an exhale. The air around Garrett rattled. "No joke. It's $25,000 for the documents, and $225,000 for us to keep our mouths shut. We know about your boy and his lack of identification. You'd think that would make it easier, but we gotta find some obscure person in the middle of nowhere, who's in a grave and has a social security number. Also, born about the same time—"

"I know all this," said Garrett. "Still doesn't make sense."

There was silence.

Garrett broke the stand-off. He squeezed the handset between his neck and shoulder, and slammed his eyes shut as a migraine appeared imminent.

"There's something else going on here," said Garrett, grinding his words out. He dug his thumbnail into the pressboard desk. "And I wanna know what it is. None of the work you've done for me in the past has ever cost anywhere near a quarter of a million."

"Hang on," said the voice.

Garrett hung the handset down by his side, until he heard the voice again, the asthma heavy.

"Yeah, there is something else."

"OK, what's the deal?"

"Scizzor McQueen has a proposition for you."

"Scizzor McQueen? This is a document request. I don't need some torpedo involved in a payoff for phony papers. Forget it."

"It will get the price down. A lot."

"I see."

Again, the line went quiet.

"What's your answer, Garrett?"

"I guess you can't tell me the proposition?"

"Nah."

Garrett once again dropped the phone down by his side. He ground his teeth, until he heard the voice barking, "Garrett? Garrett?! Garrett!" He lifted the handset back to his ear.

"How does this work then, if you can't tell me?"

"The Library, City Line Avenue, tomorrow. Four p.m. Don't be late. Happy hour starts at five o'clock."

The voice hung up.

CHAPTER EIGHT

Can't Leave Well Enough Alone

The Library Bar, a hip, trendy place catering to Baby Boomers, sat on City Line Avenue, a thoroughfare so named simply because it bordered the City of Philadelphia's western limits. At 4 p.m. the day after the Quakers throttled the Pittsburgh Miners in the home opener, Garrett Revenell entered the establishment.

He smacked into one of the leather-appointed barstools while walking, waiting for his eyes to adjust to the low lighting in the main room.

"Careful there, Garrett," came a voice out of the murk, sounding as if it had swallowed glass shrapnel. "That's a five-hundred-dollar barstool. Some very fine South Philadelphia flesh has perched on it on any given Saturday night."

"I will assume you're talking about young, single women," replied Garrett, who crept toward the voice, careful to avoid another collision with the furniture.

"Single. Married. What's the diff?"

"Hm. You sound like most of my roster."

"Your roster? Isn't Uncle Greg still running that show? And what about Brian?"

"You know what I mean, Scizzor. I *am* talking to Scizzor McQueen, yes?" asked Garrett, who paused. Then he added, "In a couple years, especially if we can take the Series, I'll be in charge."

"Sure, Garrett. Sure."

Garrett, right eye twitching as though he'd licked an electrical socket, finally found Edward "Scizzor" McQueen in the shadows. Attired in his signature houndstooth suit and a pair of black leather ballroom dance shoes encasing two flat feet. Garrett examined the nattily attired "contractor." His eyes landed on the shoes.

"Can you actually dance, Scizzor?"

"Not a step, but they do make running a lot easier."

"That's not surprising," deadpanned Garrett.

Scizzor McQueen, built like a chorus boy, landed on the expensive barstool next to Garrett. He twisted his slender frame away from the younger Revenell, and back again.

"Why am I here, Scizzor?"

Scizzor smiled and displayed his bright white teeth, a particular point of pride for him.

"In addition to cranking out some outstanding fake documents, we've been following your boy without him knowing," he said, pulling out a brown cigarette and offering one to Garrett, who waved it off. "Unless Bobby Young is the greatest poker player in the world, he has no idea he's being tailed. And he is one interesting budding superstar."

"How's that?" asked Garrett. "You're already following him? No one asked you to do that. What gives? You do know that Hector Enriquez has been tasked with doing that for the Quakers?"

"Yep. Actually, seen a couple of guys working the hamlet in South Jersey where your White Roberto Clemente lives."

"Roberto played center field. Bobby's in right."

"Got it. Yeah, Hector's boys are on it, but they aren't as good as we are. You know what they found?" At this, Scizzor drew a circle in the air. "A great big zero. Nothing. I can promise you more than that. I've already got more than that."

Scizzor lit the cigarette with a match from the Library-logoed matchbook. He waved the flame out and drew deep on the tobacco. No filter. He blew the smoke away from Garrett and toward the empty dance floor. It drifted along the floor and passed the dust illuminated by a single work light. The white vapor looked like a wave coming ashore.

"Your boy, Garrett," said Scizzor, "is a ghost so far. Hector ain't going to see nothing like him. We haven't. He leaves the stadium after a game. Goes straight to Hector's place and hangs with him and his family. Hasn't got a clue that it's so Hector can keep an eye on him. The kid's twenty and he's spending his nights with Ozzie and Harriet."

"I'm intrigued, but why would you want to follow Bobby Young? I only agreed to pay your ridiculous sum for phony documents, which you still owe me, by the way."

"Yeah, and you still owe me $225,000, unless you're interested in the discount."

"Like I said, I'm intrigued. Hector hasn't found anything at all. So, I'm just supposed to turn over a lot of cash for a great, big, fat zero? Is that what the extra $225,000 is for? Hah!"

"The surveillance is for free. Well, not exactly. We've been tailing a lot of your boys. Bobby's just another one, but I've got a particular interest in him because of the fake ID request, and the proposition, which will be offered soon." Scizzor paused. "And it won't be a big, fat zero coming *your* way. 'Cuz I like you, I'm gonna give you some information, and then we'll get down to it."

Scizzor blew another smoke wave across the dance floor. He reached into the outside jacket pocket of the suit and pulled out a series of photographs, standard size 3" x 5". Generated by a high-end camera and lens, they revealed a skinny man in his 50s walking toward, and then getting into, a 1965 Mustang Fastback. Blue.

"So?"

"So, one of my locker room touts overheard your boy talking about his grandfather's car and that's why Bobby bought his very own Mustang Fastback. 1965, powder blue. A bit of a reclamation project, but your boy's got it running after only a couple of days. Bobby also let it slip that the old geezer lived in Audubon, New Jersey, another fine and exciting South Jersey community."

"OK, you've found some guy with a Ford. I don't see how this helps."

Scizzor finished the cigarette, smashing it into an ashtray the size of Rhode Island.

"The old geezer's daughter matches the name of some family member Bobby mentioned in the locker room. My guy didn't catch the relationship. But the exact same name, Elizabeth Kathryn Leonard."

Garrett sucked in the stale air of the club, but stopped himself from mentioning that Elizabeth Leonard was Bobby's mother's name, as Bobby had told Quakers' management. Garrett reached across and removed one of the brown cigarettes from the hammered-aluminum case Scizzor had set on the bar. He lit it and inhaled.

"Rather breathe this than the air in here," Garrett said and exhaled.

"You know how stupid that sounds."

Garrett blew his smoke at Scizzor, who waved it off.

"Jesus, Garrett. Don't you know what this means? We found someone that your superstar might be related to. Always nice to have some leverage. Maybe the old guy is Bobby's illegitimate father. Ever think of that? Given your boy's mysterious past and all that."

Garrett leaned back.

"What? You found a little girl with the name Elizabeth Leonard? How many girls in the '50s and '60s were named Elizabeth by their parents? And Leonard? Yeah, that's an uncommon family moniker. I think it means Smith in German, or maybe it means Leonard. Again, how does this help me?"

Scizzor removed another cigarette, but left this one unlit and shoved it between his first two fingers.

Garrett smoked and looked out onto the empty dance floor. He checked his watch. 4:30.

Don't have much more time before the horny happy hour bunch will crowd into The Library.

"Garrett, you have got to be the dumbest silver-spooner ever. You're looking for this kid's family? Or at least some sort of connection that removes the mystery around this guy?"

"Yeah? So?"

"You know," said Scizzor. "I gotta ask. What do you care? He's a fantastic player. It's early days, but this is the best start the Quakers have had in a decade, and you're worried that he's invented his past? What do you care? Maybe he was slapped around as a child and wants to forget."

"OK, Scizzor," said Garrett, drawing on the cigarette. "The kid is a fraud, an imposter. The League could threaten us with litigation if we've done something outside the rules, and they can take the team from present ownership if they prove anything. That's why I have to find out who he is."

"Maybe Hector will figure it out," offered Scizzor.

Garrett drew on the cigarette and fired a plume of smoke away from Scizzor. He started trembling, and Scizzor, aware of Garrett's lack of control, shot upright on the barstool and stared until Garrett received the message to calm down.

Garrett ceased trembling and jammed the cigarette into the ashtray.

"You understand? They can remove the Revenells as owners, Scizzor," he spat out. "They can't do that to me! It's my team. *MINE!*"

He shouted the last word so loud, it echoed through the empty room and two men brandishing handguns crashed through the double doors from the kitchen. They stood with their feet apart, guns pointing at Garrett and Scizzor when they reached the dance floor.

Scizzor jumped off the barstool and held up both hands. He put his arms around Garrett, who kept shouting.

"*MINE!* They want to take it away and it's all because of this nobody from Nowhere, U.S.A.! Who the *hell* is this kid!?"

"OK, Garrett, calm down. You're talkin' crazy now."

Scizzor tightened his grip around Garrett.

"I got this!" Scizzor shouted to the gunmen, who put their guns away and found chairs.

"No, I'm *not* overreacting" Garrett shouted. "They'll cite Major League Baseball rules about the hiring of players, and . . . and . . . well, he isn't who he says he is, and that's a problem. The League is searching for his past like Hector is. I know it! I'll bet they've even sent reps down to the Texas-Mexico border to find the team that he supposedly played for before our scouts discovered him. Guess what? That team doesn't exist!"

"He'll get excellent documentation. We'll make sure of that," said Scizzor, who now held Garrett by the shoulders. "Birth certificate. Driver's license. Social Security card. We're throwing in a passport." Scizzor paused and took a Bette Davis drag on the cigarette. "And the person we borrowed it from is not only deceased, but let's just add, not identifiable. Bobby Young's numbers are from a stiff whose record is a, well, a dead end."

Scizzor squeezed out a laugh at his joke, but held his composure. Garrett's trembling went up another notch on the Richter scale.

"And how many Mexican League teams go belly up inside of a season?" asked Scizzor. "All of them."

Another forced laugh from Scizzor. Garrett broke free.

"Does not matter! He has no school records. No hospital record of his birth, despite the birth certificate. No one remembers playing a single frame with him."

Garrett dropped onto his barstool, and relit a cigarette from the ashtray. He took a steady pull. Scizzor hopped over the bar and grabbed a bottle of tequila. He poured a couple of ounces into a rock glass, which Garrett downed in one gulp. Another pull on the cigarette, and Garrett had the trembling under control.

"They're on the trail as much as, no, more than, Hector has been. If the media gets hold of Bobby and he blabs about his background—"

Scizzor cut Garrett off.

"And just what is his background? You've never really explained the problem to me, to us."

"Better you not know."

The two goons remained in the chairs near the dance floor until the doors to the club's kitchen opened. A woman bearing a strong resemblance to Jaqueline Bisset strutted into the main room. She had been poured into a three-piece suit, tailored to her athletic frame. Her cupid-like mouth held a black filter-less cigarette.

Ignoring Scizzor, she continued strutting to the bar and shook Garrett's hand. His cigarette dropped to the floor. She crushed it with the pointed heel of her stiletto.

"Mister Revenell," she said in a formal tone.

"Max," replied Garrett. His voice broke as he continued. "Good to see you, but I did not know you would be here."

"Probably for the best," said Maxine Hughes, known as Mad Max to some. Mad Max cocked her head at Scizzor, who took the cue to leave the bar. Garrett watched the man depart. Scizzor passed the goons and slid into the kitchen.

Mad Max did not take Scizzor's seat, but instead leaned against the mahogany bar top. She shoved a full ashtray onto the floor of the bartender's area, where it hit the perforated rubber floor mat and spilled its contents.

Maxine, pushing fifty, had a delicate nose, but an otherwise masculine, model-sculpted face. Her black hair, streaked with white, accented her Black Irish attractiveness, but her lethal nature and notorious place in the Philadelphia crime world made her asexual to anyone who knew her.

"Now, Garrett," she rasped out, her voice masculine in pitch. "Perhaps you can explain to me how *your* efforts to uncover Bobby Young's humble beginnings have failed you?"

Garrett refused to meet Mad Max's eyes.

"There hasn't been any information at all from Hector," said Garrett. "But I didn't hire you to follow him around. I, well, it's just not a good move on your part."

"Yes," responded Mad Max, ignoring Garrett's last comment. "That is strange that nothing can be found on such a remarkable ballplayer. Mister Robert Young does appear to be a phantom. Born wholly formed. A power-hitting Frankenstein, if you will."

"Not helping your situation, or mine for that matter."

"No? I believe Scizzor shared the photograph of the Mustang's owner with you?"

"Yes. So what?"

At that, Mad Max grabbed Garrett by his right ear and forced his head down on the bar. She held it there for a minute.

"Are you forgetting our appointment called for putting forth a proposition to you?"

"No. I did not," said Garrett, gasping out the words. "N-now let me up."

Mad Max pressed Garrett's head further into the soft mahogany. Both heard a very gentle crack, which is usually the sound a hairline fracture makes when enough pressure is applied to a bone, but only the bar's wood surface was damaged.

"Didn't quite hear you," said Max, the secondhand smoke from her black cigarette filling Garrett's lungs.

"No. No," Garrett choked out. "I haven't forgotten."

"Good," said Max as she released Garrett.

Mad Max stood and moved away from the bar. She spun to face Garrett, and lit another cigarette, though her first one continued to burn on the mahogany bar.

"Damn it!" shouted Max, flicking the burning cigarette onto the rubber mat behind the bar. "Oh well, easy fix. When you own a bar and there's a lot of smoking, repairs are a fact of life."

Garrett coughed once more.

"Uh, it's almost five, Max."

"Yes, it is."

She inhaled from the freshly lit cigarette.

"I don't know why I'm thinking the World Series is in the Quakers' future this year. Even with Bobby Young," said Max, "I'm not sure you can beat the Bucks."

"Or the Miners. I read the sports page. What's your point?"

"We need to start speaking with some of the players—Clarke, Davis, Nayle, Echevarrian, and Garvey, to be specific. Well, maybe not Clarke and Nayle. We've got intel on all your boys. If the Quakers do beat the Miners and then the Bucks, there will be a lot of money on the American League Champs, and we need to make sure it stays with the American League Champs. Do you know what I mean? Are you understanding this proposition?"

The blood drained out of Garrett's face. He rubbed his left temple.

"The Quakers get to their first World Series in team history and you want to fix it?"

Max had already walked away from the bar and over the dance floor. She stopped just before pushing her way into the kitchen.

"That's an unfortunate choice of words, but our feeling is that Echevarrian's arm problems will force him into early retirement. Garvey about the same. Davis never felt appreciated in Philadelphia. I'd say that's a perfect storm, wouldn't you, Garrett?"

"Nayle and Clarke?"

"On second thought, don't think so. Clarke is too much of a Boy Scout and Nayle is too temperamental. He'd never hold up."

"You've got this all figured out?"

"Baseball players ain't complex, Garrett." She laughed her whiskey-and-cigarettes laugh.

Garrett straightened up.

Max's silhouette, illuminated by the work light but softened by an abundance of cigarette smoke and poor ventilation, still appeared recognizable on the dance floor.

"I can't do this. Not for $225,000."

At that Max charged back to the bar and held Garrett by the throat, her sharp, manicured nails digging into his flesh. Garrett offered no resistance and sagged back against the bar.

"OK, you better, ahem, play ball and at least make the inquiries with your overpaid players. I'd start with Ricky Davis. If you don't, we'll send some anonymous tips to the League office about Bobby Young and his phony identification. I don't know what sort of trouble that would cause the franchise, but I can't imagine that anything good would come out of it. Can you?"

"I'll, uh, I'll pay the $225,000. There is no way I can even entertain throwing the World Series."

Mad Max backhanded Garrett onto the floor. She stood over him. The two thugs joined Max as she hovered over Garrett.

"I don't think that's an option anymore. Associating with a known criminal? Not good, Garrett. You might prove it wrong at trial, but you'll never be allowed near a baseball team again. Listen to me one last time—I just want you to check with a few ballplayers. Be discreet. I guarantee you they're open to it, particularly the ones I mentioned. That's all I want you to do. You do that, and you not only save $225,000, but if Davis and the two pitchers won't go for it, you're off the hook. I guarantee you that as well. Deal?"

Garrett pulled himself to his feet. Neither Max, nor Scizzor, who had raced out of the kitchen after hearing the commotion, nor the thugs, offered to help.

"Is there anything else?" Garrett asked when he had steadied himself.

"Yes," said Max. "Get me one of the relief pitchers. They're good insurance."

"Which one?"

"Since you're part of this now, I'll let you pick," said Max. She motioned the entourage toward the kitchen doors.

The group crossed the dance floor. Garrett staggered out to the parking lot, passing a number of early happy hour attendees, who barely noticed the disheveled owner of the hometown Quakers.

CHAPTER NINE

118 East Pine Street

Kathryn Leonard, nee Hillner, pushed her substantial frame through the front door of 118 East Pine Street, the modest home she shared with her husband of more than twenty years. She dropped her handbag and cloth grocery sack on the Victorian rug, and waddled over to the green velvet couch from the same period, collapsing into a corner of its overstuffed cushions.

Her workday at the Campbell's Soup Company cafeteria in Camden, New Jersey had taken another toll on her middle-aged body. She'd gotten heavy since the birth of her now five-year-old daughter, Elizabeth, who she called Betty. Several minutes—and a short nap—later, Kathryn grunted and wiped the drool from the corner of her mouth with the back of her hand. The grocery sack containing the food for that night's dinner sat on the floor. She bent with effort to pick up the sack and pushed her bulk off the couch.

"One kitchen to the next," she said aloud to herself.

****

A couple of hours later, her husband, Wendell, scampered through the door. He snuck by his wife, who had her considerable back to him. He made his way to the one bathroom in the two-bedroom, single-story home.

Wendell looked into the mirror. An eggplant-purple bruise had formed on his left cheekbone; his lower lip remained cut from a different blow. He smiled, because taken as a whole, he had fared far better than his opponents, the neighborhood Puerto Rican gang kids who'd come to rob his produce stand on Delaware Avenue in the City of Philadelphia.

He raised his fists in front of his bruised image.

"And they kept coming back for more," he said and smiled, much as it hurt.

"Wendell! That you?" Kathryn's ever-so-German accent filled the phone booth confines of the house.

Wendell washed his face, wiping away the dried blood, inhaled, and prepared for the daily interrogation.

"Wendell! Answer me! I'm heading for the frying pan if it's not you!"

"Christ's sake, Kathryn, I just got home. Let me get washed up," said Wendell. He glanced in the mirror. His face broke into a scowl. He spat into the sink.

He shuffled out of the bathroom, untying his green work apron as he exited. Wendell sat down at the dining room table opposite from Kathryn.

The two of them formed a modern-day version of the children's nursery rhyme, "Jack Sprat." Wendell, lean to the point of scrawny, styled his black hair slicked back in an homage to a classic widow's peak, and Kathryn wore a floral print dress several years out of style and four sizes too small for the rolls of flesh that assaulted it.

Breaking up the illusion, in a chair between the two of them, sat Betty, home after the morning session of kindergarten. The child, blessed with the flawless angular bone structure of her father and the porcelain skin of her mother, stiffened as she braced herself for the usual dinner conversation.

"You been fighting with the customers again?" asked Kathryn.

"Gangs ain't customers, Kathryn."

"Really, Wendell," she went on. "You're not a kid anymore. You could get hurt."

"Hah! You should see those 'Rikkens. None of 'em came out of the brawl looking anywhere near as good as me."

"That's not saying much."

"As I," whispered Betty.

Both turned to her.

"What was that?" Wendell asked, pulling his arm into a backhand position. Kathryn reached under her chair. He saw the move and abandoned any thoughts of corporal punishment . . . for now.

"As I," said Betty. "You should use the right words, Daddy."

Wendell placed his hands on the table and pushed his chair back. Betty shrank in the oversized confines of her seat. Kathryn, her gaze never leaving her husband, reached under her chair and pulled out a frying pan. She showed it to Wendell.

"You want some more of this? If you do, just get a little closer to Betty."

Wendell's hand went to the back of his head. A bump and a scab, neither of which had fully healed, met his touch. He did not stand, just moved the chair closer to his food.

"Good," she said, and turned her attention to Betty. A smile appeared on the little girl's face. "Now, munchkin, how was school today?" She looked over at Wendell, who had returned to busy himself with the pork chop and scalloped potatoes. "Did you play nice with the other children?"

Betty giggled as she nattered on about the day. Her mother listened attentively. Her father worked at his meal.

****

A garish red Lincoln Town Car turned a corner and slowed to drift by the Leonard's home.

"That's the place," said Scizzor from the back seat. He patted the driver's right shoulder to get his attention and pointed.

"We goin' in now, chief?" asked the driver, pulling over in front of the house next door to the Leonard abode.

Pine Street, a ragtag assortment of architectural afterthoughts — modest two-story Colonials, and pre-World War I bungalows — stretched to the White Horse Pike at its eastern end, and to Atlantic Avenue at its western end. The railroad tracks cut off any further extension.

"What? No. We're just supposed to check this out and report back to Max," replied Scizzor. He reached over the front seat, pushed in the electric cigarette lighter, and ignited yet another brown coffin nail. "From what I know, we're months away from taking a look inside that dump."

Scizzor pointed the thumb and forefinger holding the cigarette like a gun barrel in the direction of the home.

"Gotcha," said Hammer, one of Max's arsenal of bodyguards. Scizzor took a pull on the cigarette and held it as he rolled down the window.

"Let's find some place around here where we can watch the game," he said as he exhaled. "I don't feel like bucking traffic to sit with Max while she screams at the bay window in the luxury box."

"I hear dat," said the driver. "Max does love baseball. How about Someplace Else over in Cherry Hill? It's only ten minutes from here."

"They got TVs? Thought they just had a lotta tail looking for free drinks."

"Dey got bote."

"Hammer," said Scizzor, "that's downright funny."

"T'anks, chief."

Part Two:

The Season from the Halfway Point

CHAPTER TEN

Bobby's Happy Birthday on July 1, 1975

"To the soon-to-be Rookie of the Year, Happy Birthday!" Chip Dunkirk yelled above the noise in the locker room.

The Quakers had just staged another late-inning rally to pull out a victory against the Knights. Bob Randolph hit a two-run homer in the bottom of the eighth and Bobby Young did the same in the bottom of the ninth to win the contest 7 to 6. The hometown crowd cheered all the way to the parking lot exits.

The dinger was Bobby's 20th of the season. He was on pace to eclipse the Major League rookie mark of 38. The Quakers also sat in first place, alone, for the first time all season, and for the first time in July since the infamous year of 1964.

"Did you have to let everyone know, Chip? I was trying to keep it quiet."

"Ah, come on, game-winning home run, and who, might I ask, was on base to allow you the opportunity to win the game?" Chip laughed while saying the last few words. His pinch-hit single with one out put the tying run aboard in the ninth.

"You were, Chip."

"Yep. Chip Dunkirk has done it again." He shoved his thumbs under his armpits and strutted along the bench like a chorus boy from *Oklahoma*.

"Yes, you have," said Bobby. "Now sit down."

Dunkirk hopped down from the bench. Several of the players walked over to wish Bobby a happy birthday, and to congratulate him on his late-inning heroics. He thanked them all and returned to talking at Chip, or rather, listening to Chip. No one actually talked *to* Chip Dunkirk.

"Are you finally gonna break your no-drinking-in-Pennsylvania rule?" Chip asked, the proverbial Cheshire Cat grin never vacating his face. "Now that you're legal?"

Bobby dropped a dress shoe onto the floor. He looked at it. A penny loafer, something his mother insisted he and his brother, George, wear to church. He leaned forward against the uninviting steel of his locker cage, and shut his eyes hard enough to force out a couple of tears.

"Well?" Dunkirk asked, which startled Bobby out of another episode of remembering, or *not* remembering, the latter becoming more frequent.

"Nope. Not a chance. That's all I need. Busted for drinking and driving."

"Never gonna happen," said Dunkirk. "Look. Let's go to The Library. There's a VIP room. Very private. No one will bother us. They know who I am and who you are. Please don't make me drive across a bridge."

"Private entrance?"

"Yep."

"Private parking?"

"Valet disappears the cars like a magic trick. And they reappear when you're ready to leave."

"One drink."

"One."

"If you order a second round, you're on your own, and you're taking a cab back to your apartment. I am not driving drunk."

"Lightweight."

"Yes, I am. A smart one at that."

"Come on. You're twenty-one now. Legal!"

"It's not the years, Goofy," said Bobby, looking at Dunkirk.

"Yep, it's the mileage."

Bobby's voice dropped.

"And I've got an extra forty-five years of mileage on everybody in here, including you."

"So you say."

Bobby put the other loafer on the floor. Before he faded back into another memory lapse, he slipped his feet into the shoes.

"Yes, so I say."

****

They arrived, as Chip promised, at the back door of The Library. The valet, an overhyped Philly fan, practically threw his skinny body on the ground in front of Bobby when the kid recognized the rookie superstar.

"Great game tonight," he gushed. "Every night!"

"Thanks," said Bobby, handing the keys to the Mustang over to the kid. "Treat the car with the respect you'd give a, uh, Lincoln?"

Bobby spoke the last line after surveying the parking lot. Several dozen Town Cars of various gunmetal colors filled it. There were just as many Cadillacs in just as many bright shades of green, silver, light blue, and red.

"Uh, Chip, you do know who owns and frequents places like this?"

"Sure do. The Philly mob. Actually, I've been told some of the New York and Atlantic City mob stop in once in a while."

"Great. Just how I wanted to go out of this world."

"What? Oh, that's just stupid. They're not going to shoot you. Unless they had money on the Knights."

"Funny, Chip. Funny."

At the VIP entrance, an older version of the valet parking attendant met them and had the same reaction to meeting the two Quakers, Bobby the star and Chip the clown.

"Great game tonight," he gushed. "Every night!"

"How you doing, Bennie. Is that your son?" asked Chip, laughing at the verbatim repeat by the two men.

"Yes," said Bennie, the middle-aged clone. "Dennie is working here for the summer. Starts at Ursinus College this year. Going into his freshman year."

Bobby felt the blood rush out of his head. He wobbled and bumped Chip.

"Where?" asked Chip, forgetting his usual warmed-over quip about dad and the kid's name rhyming. Bobby pushed himself away and rubbed his temples.

Bennie laughed, and stepped even closer to Chip and Bobby. Both players looked for a way to slip past the ardent fan and through the narrow doorway. Bennie continued to gush.

"Yeah, we get that all the time. U-R-S-I-N-U-S. It's a real small liberal arts college out past Valley Forge. I think the student body is smaller than Dennie's high school."

"Really?" Bobby asked. "I used to —"

Chip clamped his hand over Bobby's mouth and twisted his body back toward Bennie.

"Uh, that's great, Bennie. Can we —"

"Hey, isn't that Ricky Davis? It *is* Quakers' Night here at The Library!" Bennie looked out past Bobby and Chip to the parking lot, where one of the green Lincolns discharged a passenger.

Davis scanned the lot and walked with purpose to his car, a refurbished gray BMW. He got in and exited the lot onto City Line Avenue. The whole event took less than a minute.

"Guess he changed his mind?" surmised Bennie. "About coming inside, I mean."

Chip took advantage of Bennie's distraction, and shoved Bobby inside the VIP entrance.

The interior of The Library consisted of a reddish-flocked wallpaper straight out of *The Godfather,* and worked-over shag carpeting. A plastic statue of a wood nymph occupied the center of the room. The representative of Roman mythology held a goosenecked jug. Water poured out of it and into a faux marble fountain tub.

Spotlights of varying colors accented the nymph's figure, which bordered on Dolly Parton proportions. The players' feet walked through soft carpet, which appeared golden at night. During the day, the cleaning crews worked for hours repairing cigarette burns, scrubbing out drink spills, and vacuuming up all manner of hair and dirt.

A young woman, shaped a little too much like the wood nymph, escorted Chip and Bobby to a corner of the room. As they walked toward it, they passed a man and a woman wrestling each other. Nearby stood a bodyguard squeezed into a suit a couple of sizes too small. He nodded at the two ballplayers.

They sat.

Dolly Parton's ginger-haired doppelganger leaned over to hand them cocktail menus. Her significant cleavage got close enough to Chip for him to inhale the perfume that lined her bosom. She straightened and smiled.

"Please don't ask if I see anything I like," Chip gibed as his voice rose an octave.

"See anything you like?" she asked.

"Chip," cautioned Bobby. "Don't."

"Yes, two things," said Chip. "Both Michelobs."

She laughed loud, throwing her significant hair back and putting a stress test on her outfit's top.

"Good one, Chuck Dankirk," said Dolly's twin.

"Guess you're not a baseball fan."

"I am now."

She departed, her tight microskirt losing its fight with a shapely derriere.

Chip exhaled. Bobby, though, paid no attention to the cocktail waitress. He stared at the red exit sign over the door.

"Hey!" Chip said, surprising the bodyguard, who turned his attention to the two ballplayers. Chip's shout had disturbed the gyrating clench of the couple next to them. He stuck a goofy grin onto his face, then he lifted his hand and spun it in the air and shouted, "Sorry about that! Please continue to dry hump each other!"

Chip slapped Bobby on the bicep and broke his teammate's reverie.

"What was Davis doing here? Who was in the car with him?" asked Bobby, still staring at the exit sign.

"Geez, would you throttle back on the controls? How about some champagne? Maybe you can loosen *your* cork while I pop the one on the bottle."

"You're not curious, Goofy? He didn't even come inside."

"Nah. Maybe he was, uh, *blowing* off a little steam?"

"He got out of the passenger side of a car that obviously doesn't belong to him, and walked over to his vehicle. And then left in a big hurry."

Another waitress, every bit as stacked as her colleague, stopped at their table. She leaned in as her workmate had, and put two glasses on the table along with the Michelobs.

"Can I get you boys anything else?"

"You're kidding, right?" quipped Chip.

"Nope," she replied, and batted her eyelashes.

"Uh, no thank you. I think we're fine for now."

If anything, she leaned in a little closer. The same perfume filled the tight space between the ballplayers and her bosom.

"OK, if you change your mind, my sister and I will be right by the bar."

Chip swallowed and forced his eyes past her cleavage. He spotted the first cocktail waitress. She leaned against something, not illuminated well enough by the dim lighting in the room to identify its shape, though hers was easy to discern.

"Sister?"

"Yes," she said. "You hadn't noticed the family resemblance? We're both 5'5" with auburn-colored hair."

She laughed at her nightly joke, tugged her skirt down to prepare it for battle, and returned to the bar.

Chip pushed the glasses aside and chugged down half the bottle.

"That is some serious flesh."

Bobby said nothing.

"OK, Flash," said Chip, resigned to addressing Bobby's curiosity about Ricky Davis' appearance at The Library's parking lot. "Yes, it's weird, but Davis ain't the first ballplayer to get into someone else's car in a nightclub parking lot. I gotta remember you're just old enough to drink."

Before Bobby could answer, Chip stuck the other bottle of beer into Bobby's hand and raised his half-finished one.

"To the Quakers." He clinked Bobby's bottle, then a second time. "And to your twenty-first birthday."

"To the Quakers," said Bobby, returning the toast, but looking back at the exit.

"That's the spirit! Come on! Tomorrow, we can talk about the mysterious Ricky Davis, but let's at least have one beer and enjoy a great victory."

"OK, Chip, but I'm going to hold you to that. I got a bad feeling watching Ricky get out of that car."

"Yeah, I know," said Dunkirk, who settled the beer bottle into a ring of condensation on the lacquered table. "Me too."

CHAPTER ELEVEN

The Steel Cage Death Match:
Enriquez versus Maberry

A week passed. Bobby forgot about Ricky Davis' odd appearance at The Library, and Chip Dunkirk did not bring it up. The Quakers moved on to Atlanta for their next road series.

With two outs in the seventh inning in the first game against the Blues, Tony Edwards, the rookie southpaw, ran out of gas. It was a shame, because the Quakers had staked him to a 3 to 1 lead.

Edwards gave up a double to Nazzareno Bernardi, the Blues' catcher, "named after a Latin pig in Pig Latin," Chip Dunkirk would say. Pinch-hitter Zeb Burwell drew a four-pitch walk. Murtaugh slogged to the mound to buy some time for his relievers.

Murtaugh signaled for Slade Maberry by waving his right arm *over* his head. Maberry stood more than six-and-a-half feet tall and Brian's sign language told the bullpen coach to get the towering righthander up and throwing.

Murtaugh took the ball from Edwards, but then handed it back. He chatted with the southpaw for another thirty seconds. He saw the impatient umpire move from behind the plate. The Philly manager turned to walk back to the dugout.

"Maberry?" asked Phil Ostrowski, after Murtaugh trotted down the steps to the bench.

"Deke Reilly needs a rest. Can't use him this game. It's only the seventh inning, and I gotta get Tony outta there. He's tired. I can tell. This humidity ain't helping."

"Are you sure Maberry is the right call, skip?" asked Ostrowski. "I know Nate Watson blew up the last couple times we put him out there, but how about Stroemel? He's been a good spot starter, and he could use the work."

"So could Maberry," said Brian. "And the Blues don't have a lot of lefthanded hitters sittin' on that bench if we go extra innings. We got a couple doubleheaders coming up. Wanna make sure Stroemel is ready to go."

"Got it."

"Tony isn't going to pitch to Rep Durst," said Murtaugh. "He's going to ask for an injury time-out. Get Dominick from the clubhouse. I gotta give Maberry some time to warm up."

"Will do."

Ostrowski headed into the locker room and shouted for Dominick, the longtime Quakers' trainer. The chunky South Philadelphia native waddled up the dugout steps and over to Murtaugh.

"What's up, skipper?"

"Edwards just called for an injury time-out. Make sure you find something wrong with him. Got it?"

"Yep. How much time does—?" The trainer coughed. "Hang on," said Dominick between hacks, as he looked out to the Quakers' bullpen. "How much time do you want me to give Maberry?"

"Another coupla minutes should do it," replied Murtaugh.

Dominick trudged out to the mound and performed the charade of getting Edwards to bend and straighten his left elbow. He looked back into the dugout. Murtaugh nodded in the affirmative. Dominick and Edwards walked off the mound as Slade Maberry made his way in from the bullpen.

Maberry settled in to face Rep Durst, the Blues All-Star lead-off hitter, having an excellent year. Nazzareno Bernardi strayed several feet off second base and Zeb Burwell shuffled his way to a respectable lead off first. The infield played straight away, and Durst laid down an unexpected and beautiful bunt.

Bases loaded. Maberry looked into his glove after getting the sign from Bob Randolph.

He worked from the stretch and checked the runners.

And committed a balk by lifting his leg toward the batter before making a successful pick-off throw to third, where Jack Slavik had snuck in behind Bernardi and would have nailed him easily. No matter. It was now a one-run game.

"Damn it!" Murtaugh shouted, and smacked the palms of his hands against the dugout rail. The hollow metal pipe absorbed the flesh of Brian's middle-aged frustration and bounced the sound of the pudgy thwack off the concrete floor. The bench players jumped at the show of emotion from their coach.

Maberry shook it off. He looked in for a sign and delivered a curveball that didn't curve and plunked Mario Beniquez, the second baseman, on the ribcage.

Two pitches. One hit. One hit batsman. One run. The bases loaded again.

Murtaugh cursed. Maberry swore.

Mitch "Digger" Falwell, the Blues' power-hitting infielder, walked to the plate. Murtaugh hesitated and didn't get his arm up to call time-out before Maberry, angry at himself, threw a ninety-plus mile an hour fastball right down the middle of the plate.

Which Digger Falwell tattooed over the right field wall for a grand slam home run. The Quakers found themselves on the wrong end of a 6 to 3 score.

Murtaugh sagged and dropped down on the bench.

"You want me to go get Maberry, skip?" asked Ostrowski.

"Nah. It'll do him some good to have him finish the inning," said Murtaugh, crossing his arms over his chest, his belly riding over top of the waist of his pants. "As a matter of fact, I'm not making any more pitching changes. We either hit our way out of this or not."

Maberry struck out Moose Huggins to end the seventh. When he got to the dugout, Maberry sat by himself on the end of the bench furthest from the locker-room door.

****

The Quakers struck for two runs in the eighth. In the ninth inning, pinch hitter Davey Gonzales came to the plate with two outs and a runner on second.

"Let's go, Viejo!" shouted Dunkirk. "That hit of Geritol should have your bat speed back to about 1965."

Ricky Davis had singled just before Gonzales came in to take the pitcher's at-bat. The Philly shortstop then stole second on the Blues' rising star, rookie relief pitcher, Ray-Ray Sanfilippo. Davis stood on the base representing the tying run. He took a generous lead off the bag. Gonzales eyed Sanfilippo and waited for the first pitch.

Davis followed Sanfilippo's stretch delivery and leaned toward third. He heard the solid crack of the bat and fired out of his stance. Gonzales jetted for first. The ball took off for the left-center field wall, Rep Durst in pursuit.

Gonzales, head down, caught the sign from the first-base coach to keep running. He cut the bag and closed the distance between himself and second base. Davis did the same around third, and headed for home with the tying run.

In the outfield, Rep Durst chased a drive that appeared destined for home run status. A breath of wind blew in and knocked it down. Now it just looked like extra bases.

At least it did until Durst stretched out and snared the dying baseball in the web of his glove just before it hit the dirt at the warning track.

Ricky Davis crossed home plate as a collective cheer greeted his ears, not the raucous groans from the Atlanta fans he expected. The same for Davey Gonzales as he stomped on second base with what he thought was a stand-up double.

Game over. 6 to 5, Atlanta.

Though Slade Maberry had retired six Blues in a row in the last two frames, it was small consolation for giving up the go-ahead runs. He bolted off the bench bypassing the dugout straight into the locker room, where he sat in front of the cage holding his street clothes. He balled them up and slammed them into his locker. Maberry buried his head in his hands.

He remained on a locker-room bench, his uniform stuck to him with the Southern humidity. Maberry lifted his head a couple of times, but only dropped it as he recounted his lousy performance in the seventh.

"A bunt. A hit batsman. A one-pitch homer," he whispered to himself. "No, that's not right. A one-pitch *grand slam* homer." The last line a lot louder than the first. A few of the Quakers entered the room and spotted the relief pitcher, but even those whose lockers bordered Maberry's didn't approach him.

The balance of the Quakers, shocked by the outcome of the game, filed in. Their cleats made a morose scraping sound across the concrete floor. Murtaugh slogged past and went straight to his office, disappointment creasing a face already filled with a roadmap of wrinkles.

Hector Enriquez, though, entered the room with the emotion of Knute Rockne at halftime and Notre Dame on the short end of the score.

His considerable bulk filled the doorway.

"What the hell was that, Maberry?!" he bellowed. "You just threw the three *worst* pitches in the more than one hundred years of the National League. How did you manage that?"

Maberry got to his feet.

"If you'd moved that fast on the bunt, maybe we wouldn't be—"

His last words were buried under the 220 pounds of Slade Maberry. The relief pitcher, a former NBA player, crossed the locker room and plowed into Hector Enriquez like he was boxing out a power forward for a rebound. He hit Enriquez with his left non-pitching shoulder and drove the formidable team scout into the hallway.

Both men bounced to their feet and squared off.

By the time the first of the Quakers' players rushed to the battle, the heavyweight boxing match between Enriquez and Maberry had reached the middle rounds. Both men had their share of locker room, bar, and street fights. Maberry had scuffled with the likes of Bill Russell and Wilt Chamberlain during his days in the NBA. Enriquez grew up brawling in his Cuban neighborhood.

Blows landed on both of their faces and bodies, but neither showed signs of backing down. It took the combined efforts of Rick Nayle, Chris Escondido, Bob Randolph, Everett Hayes, and reserve catcher Beau Santorino to pull the combatants apart.

"Couldn't stand to watch a pitcher blow up, huh, coach," shouted Maberry through a split lip. "Guess it reminded you of every outing of your great career!"

"Yeah, well, I never gave it away as quick as you did, Maberry! That was one for the ages. National TV, too! I guess the network will trot that one out every time they want to show great all-time choke jobs!"

A few more choice exchanges of expletives followed as players dragged Maberry back into the locker room. Nayle and Chris Escondido pushed Enriquez into Brian Murtaugh's office. Escondido locked the door behind them.

Murtaugh, his head in his hands until the three crashed through the door of his office, shot out of his chair.

"What in *hell* is going on?"

Nayle pushed Enriquez into a chair.

"Do I really have to ask again?!"

Murtaugh stomped over to Enriquez, shoving Nayle and Escondido out of his way.

"I think Slade Maberry took my recent comments about the problems with his pitching mechanics personally," said Enriquez. His voice spit out the statement in spurts as the adrenalin coursed through him. His purpled right cheekbone and his broken nose hadn't quieted him down. He took on the aspect of W.C. Fields' good-looking brother.

"Jesus, Hector," shouted Murtaugh. "What did you say to him? I'm sure Maberry wasn't happy about what happened in the seventh inning. It's part of the game."

Enriquez stood up.

"Where are you going?" asked Murtaugh. "We're not done here."

"I'm going to apologize, and yes, we're done here." He moved toward the door.

Nayle and Escondido hustled over to the front of the door.

"Don't think saying you're sorry is what you have in mind, coach," said Nayle.

As he headed for the door, Garrett and Gregory Revenell walked into the office. Enriquez stopped. Nayle and Escondido hustled out and back to the locker room to give some privacy to the club owners.

"What the hell, Hector? Slade Maberry?" shouted Gregory. "You do know he's been our best righthanded reliever for the past month?"

"Not tonight he wasn't," said Enriquez. "Credit to Brian for keeping him in the game to get his confidence back, but he imploded big time when it counted."

"All right, Hector," said Garrett. "You've had your say. I'd suggest you get back into the locker room and apologize to Maberry."

"Not a chance."

"Hector?" asked Murtaugh. "Weren't you just on your way to do that?"

"I was, but now that the suits have chimed in, I've decided that I'm not babying a ten-year pro. Either he figures out how to come through in the clutch, or he can go back to Detroit and sit on the bench."

Garrett walked out the door.

"Garrett? Where are you going?" asked Gregory.

"I'll go talk to Maberry if Hector doesn't want to. We need all twenty-six players, and Maberry is going to help us. Already has."

"Again, not tonight he didn't. I wouldn't play to it, Garrett!"

Hector shouted the last sentence as Garrett made his way down the hallway.

"Really, Hector," said Murtaugh. "That'll do."

****

Garrett walked through the locker room door. Most of the players had dressed and gone. Slade Maberry sat on the bench in conversation with Ricky Davis, who had managed to avoid getting trampled during the fight.

"One bad inning, Slade," said Davis. "We've all had them. Hell, I've had bad weeks."

"Yeah, I know, but Hector just rubs me the wrong way. If not for you and some of the other guys, I'd ask for a ticket back to Atlanta."

"Or Detroit."

Maberry laughed at the reference to his brief NBA career with Detroit.

"Too hard on the body. Pro basketball is like playing football with only a jockstrap and sneakers."

Now Davis laughed.

"Come on. Get showered. We'll go grab a beer. I got something I need to talk to you about. You may find it interesting."

Garrett backed away from the locker room careful not to be discovered and headed for the elevator. He took it to the business floor of the stadium. Garrett found an open office and made his way to a phone in the middle of the room. He lifted the handset but held it in both hands.

Come on, Garrett. Davis is obviously working Maberry. I can check with him privately.

He dialed.

Scizzor answered.

"Yeah?"

"It's Garrett."

"Man, Garrett, you are one brave SOB. Calling a known mobster on the company line? Hang up and call me from a pay phone."

"We're in Atlanta, but I think we've found the reliever."

"Good. Goodbye."

Scizzor clattered his handset into the cradle. Garrett hung up. He made a mental note to call Davis into his office to discuss his "contract."

CHAPTER TWELVE

July 25, 1975:
The Dog Days are Coming

"And it's my brother's birthday today, Saint Louis," yelled Bobby at the pitching machine, repeating his spirited performance from earlier in the month of July. "Thanks for the doubleheader!"

The fans applauded. A few "Happy Birthdays!" filled the stadium.

Bobby, fresh off an all-star appearance for the National League just over a week ago, stood in the cage for batting practice. He turned and waved to the crowd as a fastball from the pitching machine buzzed into the netting behind him.

"Ball one!" he shouted at the pitching machine.

The crowd laughed, and Bobby waved his bat in the air, a lá Ted Williams.

Brian Murtaugh and Hector Enriquez watched from behind the cage. Murtaugh spat next to nothing onto the artificial turf. Hector kept an eye on Bobby and glanced sideways at Murtaugh.

"I'm Ted Williams, the greatest hitter in baseball!" Bobby shouted at the pitching machine. He stared at the mound as the machine released another white pellet in the direction of the batter's box. Bobby swung and delivered a metal-rattling bullet straight at the machine. It conked off the front. Bobby spun around to the left side of the box.

"Here comes Clete Morelli and that overrated slider of his!"

Another fastball by the machine.

A clean, smooth connection, and another baseball headed for the right field stands in St. Louis' Memorial Field. Bobby waited for another offering.

"Opposite field!"

He shifted his left foot a few inches away from home plate and met the aspirin tablet, as he called it, with another solid stroke that sent the ball soaring into the left field stands.

"Hey, Flash in the Pan!" Brian Murtaugh snapped from behind the netting. "Pipe down and take a couple more whacks. Then get outta the cage."

"Yes, sir," said Bobby, who deflated and took a halfhearted swing at a few more pitches, then skulked his way back to the dugout.

"Geez, Brian," said Hector, who stood next to Murtaugh. "You heard the kid. Today is his brother's birthday. Cut him a little slack. This ain't easy and he's adjusted better'n I thought he would. Better'n anybody could."

"His brother?" asked Murtaugh. "And where is the mysterious George Young? Older brother, dancer, baseball historian?"

"Yes, Brian, his brother," said Hector. "The one in 2020. The one he misses, along with his parents and his sister."

"I'm still not buying the story," said Murtaugh.

Hector turned and looked Murtaugh in the eye.

"You got a better one?" asked Hector. "Look, Brian, I'm hanging on here with the kid, and trying to convince myself about where he came from and why we can't find any records of him. He's moved out of my house into his own place, and that change of address is not helping us solve this mystery. Right now, we should be concentrating on winning the East. The Miners won today, which means it would be good if we swept this doubleheader."

"You wanna manage the club too, Hector?"

Hector took a step forward. Brian squared up to his scout.

"The Miners are not taking their foot off the gas. They'll be with us for the entire 1975 season, and we still have half of it to go. Ease up on the kid. You've done a great job keeping everyone else loose, but he's only twenty-one. It's different with Skountzos and Slavik. They're veterans. Remember, no matter what his story is, Bobby Young is a rookie. And yes, I know, he certainly doesn't act like one. I get that, but he is. He's barely out of his teens. Don't forget that."

Hector pushed himself away from the batting cage netting just as Chip Dunkirk juked his way to the plate. Dunkirk spun the bat like a ninja working out with nunchucks, and stood in to hit. Dunkirk laid down a few bunts. Hector sidled up to watch batting practice again.

"Chip!" shouted Murtaugh. "Cut it out. Take some swings and quit screwing around!"

Dunkirk winked at Murtaugh, which drew a laugh from Hector.

"Game's also supposed to be fun, Brian," said Hector. "Fun. Remember?"

Murtaugh pressed his belly against Enriquez's.

"Doesn't feel like it."

Dunkirk swung away and drove a pitch deep into the right-center field gap. New center fielder Moses Pendleton, acquired from the Rockers for Chet Gilbert despite Garrett Revenell's adamant protests, gave chase and grabbed the ball on the warning track.

"OK, Hector, I'll remind you of all this fun the next time you and Slade Maberry decide you're going to figure out who gets to face Ali at the Garden for the title. That sure looked like fun. Was it fun?"

"Maberry earned it."

"So did you," said Murtaugh. "So don't lecture me about fun, because it looks like your idea of it includes beating the tar out of one of my best relief pitchers."

"*Our* best relief pitchers," corrected Enriquez.

Murtaugh turned back to the cage as the crack of the bat told him another baseball would be picked up by the grounds crew somewhere in the stands.

"Well, will you look at that," said a grinning Chip Dunkirk, as he trotted out of the batting cage. "Who the heck needs Bobby 'The Flash' Young when you've got Joltin' Chip Dunkirk!"

Murtaugh stopped himself from saying something to Dunkirk.

"That's the spirit, Brian," shouted Hector, slapping Murtaugh on the back. "Let the boys have some laughs and we just might stay ahead of the Miners."

****

The Quakers led the Knights 3 to 2 after the seventh inning. Slade Maberry, still recovering from a couple of facial bruises incurred during his fistfight with Hector Enriquez two weeks before, surrendered two runs to St. Louis in the eighth inning. Now the Quakers trailed 4 to 3 as the game entered the top of the ninth.

A Maberry versus Enriquez rematch seemed imminent.

The team held its collective breath as the Knights took the field. The Quakers, down to their last three outs, braced themselves for Maberry's arrival into the dugout. Some looked around for Hector Enriquez. Few hoped for a rematch.

Maberry stomped into the dugout. He hurled his glove against the wall. The force of it chipped the paint and creased the sheet rock underneath. No one on the bench, including the usually effusive Chip Dunkirk, said a word. The memory of the brutal street slugfest between Slade and Hector a few weeks prior filled the dugout. For several days after, Maberry and Enriquez had looked like a road map of an Eastern European outpost after the Soviet troops marched through.

"God, don't let Hector show up here," whispered Beau Santorino.

"Get in the clubhouse, Slade," said Murtaugh, whose voice lowered the dugout temperature. "We'll win this one for you. You've done more than your share for us this year."

Maberry, who hadn't exhaled since exiting the mound, raged down the ramp to the visiting team's clubhouse. Murtaugh turned to the bench.

"Joltin' Chip Dunkirk," he said. "You're in for Maberry there. No screwin' around like it's batting practice. Let's see what you can do in a real game."

"Stand by and watch this, skipper," boasted Dunkirk, who grabbed a bat and sprinted from the dugout to home plate, evil-mad-scientist laugh trailing him the whole way.

Dunkirk, who had the confidence of a Hall-of-Famer but the resume of a good, solid, bench player, dug in for so long the umpire had to stop him from kicking up dirt.

"Let's go, Dunkirk, or you're not gonna see the first pitch."

On the mound, the hilarious Knights reliever, Janos "The Romanian Rifle" Constanou, went through his pre-pitch ritual, which included the trademark visit to the area just shy of the second base bag, where he would slam the ball into his mitt and turn to face his opponent.

Dunkirk, never at a loss for histrionics, started dancing at the plate while he waited for Constanou to toe the rubber. Both players screwed their respective corks in and got down to the business of pitcher versus batter. Constanou blazed in a slider. Dunkirk took a vicious home-run-worthy cut and dribbled a swinging bunt down the first base line.

The Knights' first baseman, Jerry Steinmetz, had been playing Dunkirk to pull the ball. By the time he got to it, Chip stood on the first-base bag congratulating himself on, as he would tell it in the locker room, another scalding cannon shot.

Steinmetz checked Dunkirk and tossed the ball back to Constanou, who snapped the throw into his glove.

"You looked like Willie Mays on that one, Dunkirk!" Constanou shouted at Dunkirk, who still wore his teenage-boy grin, covering the area between both ears.

"Surprised it stayed in the park?" cracked Chip. "Me too!"

Constanou went through his ritual and struck out Omar Clarke, the Quakers' lead-off man, on three pitches. He stomped to the back of the mound and prepared to face the number two hitter, Bobby, who asked for a time-out the same way he had all season long—he made a "T" with his hands and waited until the umpire acknowledged it.

Bobby twisted the handle of the bat while Constanou, the human equivalent of a triple espresso, fumed at him from the mound. After Bobby stepped back into the batter's box, Constanou wound up and fired a fastball that sailed a foot off the plate. A great play by the Knights catcher saved an advancement by Dunkirk.

Constanou's next pitch went to Bobby, who hit it out of Memorial Field so quickly that the Quakers' exuberant play-by-play announcer, Oscar Markley, could only spit out, "Long drive. Gone!"

The home run turned the momentum of the game back to the Quakers and by the time the third out registered, Constanou was relegated to carrying on his histrionics in the shower. The Philadelphia Quakers had tacked on six more runs. The Knights went down in order in their half of the ninth. Game over.

The press crowded Bobby's section of the locker room. The rookie, not great with sportswriters, ignored their textbook entreaties.

"How'd that dinger feel, Bobby?"

"Where would this team be without you?"

"Is the nickname 'The Unnatural' a good one for you?"

"Where are you from, Bobby?"

The last question flipped a switch. Bobby made the "T" sign and unrolled some surgical tape and sealed his lips shut.

Press conference over.

Bobby joined Chip Dunkirk on a bench. He tore off the tape, but as he opened his mouth to say something, his jaw slackened. No sound came out. Chip laughed at first thinking it was a joke, but Bobby had vapor-locked. He stared at the floor. Dunkirk grabbed Bobby's shoulder and shook him. Some of the players, still enjoying the win, turned. What few press members were still in the clubhouse noticed the two seated players.

"Hey!" Chip shouted. "You OK? What the hell is—"

Bobby slapped himself on the top of his head, and closed his mouth. The press closed in.

"I gotta talk to you," he said. "Private."

Dunkirk shoved the press out of the way and walked Bobby into the unoccupied shower area of the locker room. He folded his arms over his chest.

"Tell me you're not sick," said Dunkirk.

"I don't think I am, but—"

"But what? We got a second game to play you know. My uniform is still clean, but you need to change and get ready to go. We ain't got a lotta time," said Dunkirk, speeding up his delivery on the last couple of words.

"We weren't supposed to win that game."

Dunkirk blew air out his nostrils and waited while a couple of the Quakers players used the adjoining bathroom.

"Not this again. You've got to stop this obsession with how we're changing so many things. It's because you're here, right, and you're not supposed to be?"

"Yes," said Bobby. "We're messing with the past. My memory is getting worse, but every so often it comes in loud and clear. We dropped both games of this doubleheader. Didn't even achieve a split. The *Quakers* were in second place after today, not the Miners."

"I suppose you're going to invoke that Brad Cadbury book again."

"Ray Bradbury, and it's a short story, 'A Sound of Thunder.' Messing with the past is not a good idea."

"It's a *book!*" shouted Chip.

At that, Phil Ostrowski stomped into the shower.

"Let's go, ladies. Doubleheader. Remember?"

The Quakers beat St. Louis in the nightcap 8 to 0, and now led the Miners by two-and-a-half games.

****

Up in a private box at Memorial Field, Garrett Revenell, Hector Enriquez, and Wade Simmons remained in their chairs after the last out of the second game. Simmons pressed his lips together, and Garrett rubbed the area between his eyebrows for a full minute.

"The League's equivalent of internal affairs," said Garrett, who leaned forward and placed his head between his knees. On the desk next to him lay a binder of information on Robert Wendell Young, the Quakers' brilliant right fielder. A young man with no past.

"And how in the world are they going to track anything down, or—"

"What are you two worried about?" demanded Hector. "Bobby has documentation. His life's a set of instructions for a Rube Goldberg invention, which nobody, including Major League Baseball's flunkies, can follow."

"Rube Goldberg?" asked Garrett, his question ignored by Hector and Wade.

"That's the problem. It's becoming a distraction," said Simmons. "They're sending reporters to Bobby's house every day and to Bicentennial Park. Hector, you know that."

"So what?"

"Sooner or later," said Simmons, "all of this commotion is going to affect his performance, and when that happens, it's going to affect the team's performance. I just don't want—"

"A repeat of 1964?" asked Hector.

"Yes, if I could just weigh in here," said Garrett as he looked up. He raised his hand. Hector, along with Simmons, ignored him again.

"If you two girls are going to act like Joe Carroll did in September of that year, you just might have a repeat. If you'll calm the hell down and let me deal with the media that seems to be living on Bobby's sidewalk, this will all turn into a load of white noise," insisted Hector.

"And that's the problem. We don't need the noise."

"Yes," parroted Simmons. "We don't need the noise."

"*White* noise, for God's sake. Oh, forget it."

"We have yet to explain to the League's satisfaction how Bobby Young appeared in our charity game without showing up at all during the preseason!" Garrett shouted at Hector.

Hector, who had been stalking around the private box like a bullpen pitcher who had taken too many warmup throws, stopped and put his hands on his hips. He pulled himself up to his full height.

"All right, enough. If Bobby and the Quakers can't deal with a nosy reporter or three who can't seem to figure out why one of the best players in the game doesn't seem to have a clear history, then our team will certainly fold up before September thirtieth."

Before Simmons or Garrett could reply, Hector continued.

"Because the Miners ain't going away. And, in case you've forgotten, Cincinnati has a better record than we do and is absolutely loaded."

Hector paused.

"What's your point?" asked Garrett.

"Are you messing with me?"

"No."

"It's a long season, Garrett, Wade," said Hector, lowering his voice. "There is going to be a ton of pressure on the team, especially with you two hysterics continuing to bring up 1964."

Simmons and Garrett leaned forward.

"Believe me, if we're still in first place in September, the fans and the newspapers will be running it as a headline 24/7," said Hector.

He turned to walk out of the box. Just as he got to the door, he spun around.

"And the last thing the Quakers are going to need, starting on Labor Day, is ownership and management piling on. Get your act together. I won't say it again. Bobby Young is a ghost. Got it? A ghost. Anything they 'find out' about him was developed by us and planted by us. They'll come up with nothing we don't already know about."

Hector's heavy footsteps echoed in the hallway. Simmons and Garrett didn't say anything to each other until they were certain he was gone.

"Let's get to Chicago," said Simmons.

CHAPTER THIRTEEN

You're Single and a Sports Hero

The Quakers had a rare day off. They held a two-game lead over the Miners with Labor Day but a week away.

Bobby hated being idle, even for 24 hours. He invited Chip Dunkirk over to his house to get in a light workout. Bobby had rented the house on Summit Road, a mere block from where he spent his childhood.

"You're nuts," said Chip Dunkirk.

"Whose nickname is 'Goofy?'"

Chip reclined on one of the two couches in Bobby's living room. He took a moment to marvel at the Early Men's Dormitory design scheme. In addition to the couches, the room contained a recliner, a twenty-inch, console-style television, and a set of floor-to-ceiling bookshelves, which did not contain books. Bobby used the bookshelves to display his collection of hundreds of Hot Wheels cars, his talent for layout evident.

"And," continued Bobby, "I'm not the guy running the bases backward after a home run, so I'd lay off the 'nuts' comments."

Bobby moved to the bookshelves, where he repositioned a piece of track an inch closer to the edge. He rolled a Pontiac Firebird, replete with phoenix emblem on the hood, down the length of it.

"Is this what you do all day? Play with toy cars?"

"What do you think?"

"I think you need to move into the city, closer to the ballpark," said Chip. "Living where you supposedly grew up ain't a great idea."

"Trying to figure out how this happened."

"Can't you do that from an apartment in South Philadelphia? There's some nice property to be had and *closer* to the ballpark."

Bobby spun another sports car model down the track hard enough to watch it fly off the end of the shelf and drop onto the cushions where Chip sat. It bounced up and landed next to Dunkirk.

"Come on," said Bobby. "Let's go work out. Kids should be outta school by now. We can use the open space near that elementary school down the block."

"Another torture session?"

"Yep, and you'll thank me when you're able to play into your forties."

"If I don't hurt myself first doing your, what do you call them? Boot camp moves."

"Try not running the bases backward after a home run, or flipping baseball bats around like circus props. Might keep you from a serious injury."

"Are we walking by number nine Hillcrest by chance?"

"It *is* on our way."

"Only if you have no sense of direction, or you're blind."

"So that explains your strikeout-to-walk ratio?"

"Probably," replied Chip.

The two picked up some hand weights and ankle bands. Bobby had crafted them out of materials he'd found at Kmart.

"You do know you could make a fortune with these things," said Chip.

"Not going to happen, Chip. You know my feelings on taking advantage of my knowledge. I am not giving in to the easy way out. Got it?"

"Yeah. Yeah. Yeah. You're no fun sometimes."

"Most times."

CHAPTER FOURTEEN

Hall of Fame Nut Jobs

Prior to a late summer game against the Los Angeles Stars, Paul Skountzos and Jack Slavik sat across from each other in the clubhouse, a card table between them.

"If you travel along the space/time continuum, which we all do, it is possible to deviate from the path."

"It's not. It's a constant."

"If that's how you feel, then there's no reason to have this conversation."

Chip Dunkirk stood in front of his locker, listening to Jack Slavik and Paul Skountzos discuss the likelihood that the team's rookie sensation, Bobby Young, might really be a time traveler.

"Can't you just accept the premise?" asked Slavik. He pulled on his number 20 jersey and scratched his *Magnum P.I.* mustache. "Is it that outrageous?"

"Yes," said Skountzos, squeezing a rubber ball in his pitching hand.

Slavik laughed his dry laugh and yanked his baseball cap onto his head. He leaned down to tie his shoelace.

"Greek," said Slavik. "For a guy I think of as like-minded to me, you're a bit of a Luddite."

Dunkirk slammed his locker shut. It brought Slavik and Skountzos out of their theoretical physics chat.

"I'm almost sorry I brought you two dopes into my confidence. Can you not stick a rectal thermometer up everything you discuss?"

"Why's that, Pine Rider?" Slavik asked.

"Ah, kiss my —"

Brian Murtaugh and the balance of the coaching staff walked in and interrupted Chip's request.

"Just a few things before we hit the field, gents," said Murtaugh, as he looked over the players, all of whom were fully dressed and ready to play. His eyes traveled to Slavik, Skountzos, and Dunkirk.

"What's going on over there, Goofy?" Murtaugh asked.

"Nothing, chief," replied Dunkirk.

"Let that serve as a warning to all of you," said Murtaugh. "When Dunkirk says nothing is going on, something is going on. And that's what we need to talk about."

Murtaugh stood behind a folding table. A water dispenser and some plastic cups perched on top. He leaned forward and his considerable belly bumped against it, knocking some of the cups over. He pulled a slip of paper from his pocket. He glanced at it.

"It's been a great season so far, gentlemen," said Murtaugh, his eyes darting from player to player. "The League though, never happy with the success of any team save for the Titans and the Stars, is trying to figure out where our right fielder came from."

Slavik, Skountzos, and Dunkirk exchanged a few glances after Murtaugh's last statement, but the rest of the team kept their attention on the coach.

"What does that mean, skip?" asked Greg Stroemel, standing by the water cooler.

Murtaugh sat on one of the more substantial folding tables generally used for training purposes and rubdowns. He looked down at his hands and moved his eyes back up to the team. He continued.

"For some reason, Greg, being a player that comes from anywhere but the League-approved pattern of minors to majors draws scrutiny," said Murtaugh. "Especially one having a spectacular season. … So, as a twenty-year-old pitcher with less than a season in Triple-A, you may want to be careful about which reporter is asking you questions about your popular teammate. You could be next, given you're on your way to a pretty darned good 1975 yourself."

"OK, coach," said Stroemel. "But we've all been good about not talking to reporters. I think I can speak for the team, we're all curious ourselves."

Murtaugh put his hands across his belly and dropped his head.

"Yes, of course, Greg, but we're going to concentrate on baseball, which includes today's game, *then* on winning the National League East. And we are *not* going to get caught up in a lot of old-lady gossip by the vultures in the press. That's a sure way to lose."

Stroemel took a seat.

"Now," Murtaugh said turning to the players. "This is our last meeting on this issue. Don't want to discuss this anymore within the organization or outside it. Too much bad information out there. It's only August, boys. Saint Louis and Pittsburgh are right behind us. The challenge I put to you is, are we going to finish this? *Are we?*"

"Don't want to hear about 1964 anymore," said Moses Pendleton. He ran a pick through his modest Afro.

Bobby stood up. Murtaugh pointed to him.

"Just want to say that it's been great playing with all of you," Bobby said. "Followed this team since I was a kid."

"*Was?*" quipped Chip, his 100-tooth smile taking over his face, and the room.

The laughter broke the tension in the clubhouse.

"All right, then," shouted Murtaugh. "Let's hit the field!"

CHAPTER FIFTEEN

First Place, the Pittsburgh Miners, and the Last Game of 1975

Bobby sat in the visitor's dugout at Doubleday Park. He stared at a few article headlines in the sports section of the *Philadelphia Inquirer.*

"1964 redux looms as Quakers fall to Cosmos. Miners win."
"Lead now ONE GAME"
"Season finale today—can the Quakers hold on?"

"What is this?" Bobby asked Greg Stroemel, who shared the dugout bench with him. The two rookies sat at the end closest to the clubhouse doorway.

"Guess you don't remember 1964?" asked Stroemel, only half joking.

"I did. I mean I thought so. Yes, of course. I was eleven at the time."

"Maybe ten?" asked Stroemel. Curiosity rose in his voice.

"Uh, yes, you're right."

"What's going on there, Flash? You getting senile?"

"Could be."

Bobby trotted into the locker room before Stroemel could probe any deeper.

Bobby's recollection of the past continued to fade during the season. He swore the Colonials would be in the Series, but the Titans clinched the American League East a week ago. Since then, more and more baseball history disappeared from the catalogue in his brain.

He returned to the dugout. Stroemel hadn't moved off the bench.

"Not pretty, that 1964 season. Losing ten in a row at the end of the year and blowing the National League pennant," said Bobby. "A constant reminder of it ain't a motivator, is it."

"I don't know," said Stroemel. "The last thing I want to see is a picture of someone like me with Skountzos on the front of the sports page alongside Frank Vail and Walter Hutchinson. *If* we don't win this. Besides, you think Philly *fans* are bad? The sportswriters are worse."

"I know all about the sportswriters, Greg. I don't see Coach Murtaugh pitching you on two days' rest down the stretch, do you? He kept the rotation intact, and Echevarrian and Garvey have come up big a few times."

"Yes, but like Caspar Collins in 1964, I'm the number four or five guy, so I know I am safe, sort of. Caspar was on the mound when—"

"—Nestle Gancio stole home. Yeah. Got that."

Stroemel reached to his right and picked up his glove.

"But I agree with you. There is no way Murtaugh is going to a rotation of Skountzos and Echevarrian, though it has a nice ring to it."

Bobby pointed his right index finger at Stroemel and jabbed the air with it.

"We're not talking about this anymore," he said to Stroemel. Chip Dunkirk entered the dugout from the clubhouse.

"Whoa," Chip jumped in when he saw Bobby's face and heard his teammate's tone. "Who took the jam out of your doughnut?"

"No more Philly wallowing in the past," Bobby spat and turned his attention to Chip. "That habit is why Philadelphia is always going to be a second-tier sports city. Our pro football team went from champs to chumps in less than a decade. Our pro hoops team losing to Boston constantly. Our pro hockey team and the Stanley Cup Finals."

Dunkirk, still wearing his signature grin, dropped his glove on the bench.

"OK, what about them? Our hockey bullies won two Cups in a row and only dropped the finals to Montreal because Childe and Glennon couldn't go."

"BS!" shouted Bobby. "There's always excuses in Philadelphia, isn't there?" He paused and looked at Chip and Stroemel. "Chamberlain didn't have the surrounding cast that Russell did. Our football team makes too many bad trades. Don't get me started on those hockey goons. They've only been around for what, eight or nine years? But the first chance they get, the backpedaling starts. And the

Quakers? We're coming up on one hundred years in this League and the team has never played a game in October. Players get on the Quakers and can never close the deal."

"What's that supposed to mean?" growled Stroemel, the politeness gone from his voice. His face twisted into a scowl.

Bobby shot an admonishing look at Dunkirk, before stomping out of the dugout. He hustled out to right field with Dunkirk close behind. Chip eventually caught up to him, but just as he did Bobby took off, sprinting. Chip gave chase and soon the two were laughing as they circled Bicentennial Park's outfield artificial surface. Both collapsed to the turf when they ran out of gas.

"Stroemel doesn't know, does he?" Chip asked, between gasps. "Are you going to tell him? You two are good friends."

"No, I'm not. He's a serious person. You're a goof, and Skountzos and Slavik are tin-foil-hat types. I can tell you three that I'm from 2020, but not Greg Stroemel."

"And why is that?"

"Because he'd go out and get shelled in his next start," said Bobby. "Couldn't handle it."

Chip stood up.

"How do *you* handle it?"

Before Bobby could answer there was a shout from the batter's box.

"Fly ball!"

Chip spotted it first and tracked down the fungo near the center field warning track. The number "410" stood out on the green fence. Dunkirk treated it like a bulls-eye, and went into a slow-motion, highlight-reel carom off it before crumpling to the ground. He got to his feet and dusted himself off.

"Hey!" yelled Chip back to home plate. "Give us a heads up when BP starts!"

"Sorry," shouted the batter, fellow jokester and retired player, Luke Demarest. "Maybe you two should cut the small talk."

Chip flipped Demarest off.

"Well?" he pressed Bobby.

"What? How do I do it?"

"Yep."

The crack of the bat brought another fly ball and Chip chased it down again. He grabbed Bobby by the shoulder and pushed him into foul territory.

"Two more minutes, coach," shouted Chip back to Demarest.

Demarest slumped his shoulders and waved the bat in Dunkirk's direction.

"One minute, and then you're in the cage, Bobby," said Demarest.

Bobby dropped his glove on the ground and folded his arms over his chest.

"Every day I wake up, Chip," said Bobby. "I look out the window of my bedroom and expect to see a Chinese elm. Dad planted it when we moved in, two years after I was born. The tree grew fast, and it was the first thing I'd see in the morning."

"OK," said Chip. He squeaked out the word when he saw Bobby's eyes welling up with tears.

"Yes," said Bobby between short, shallow breaths. "So, one day, I'm going to wake up and that tree is going to be out my window and this incredible dream is going to be over."

"Dream?"

"Yep. You got a better explanation?" challenged Bobby, and he trotted off toward the cage to take batting practice. Chip followed his friend and teammate. "Now 2020 feels like a George Lucas—I think that's the name—futuristic movie. Doesn't even feel like I was there. Was I? Or was it someone else?"

He stopped running. Chip bumped into him.

"You say so," offered Chip.

"I can't even say so anymore, Chip." Bobby's voice broke. "How does this work? Do I just give up and start my life as a twenty-one-year-old in 1975? The parents I know are forty-five years younger than when I think I left."

"And?"

Bobby slapped his gloved hand on Chip's right shoulder, and drew his lips into a straight line.

"Let's go hit. Sick of shagging fly balls."

****

The Quakers finished batting and infield practice, the pitchers warmed up on the sidelines, and the Cosmopolitans looked to crush a Philadelphia World Series dream.

The Cosmopolitans, two seasons removed from their own World Series appearance in 1973, had fallen to a .500 ballclub in 1975. The Quakers, though, had to beat them to win the division outright from the Miners. Pittsburgh won earlier that day, setting up the crucial importance of the game.

The Cosmopolitans trotted out onto the field to start the game. The crowd, a representative 12,000 of New York City's reputation for fair-weather fandom, exhaled a pathetic cheer along with a smattering of applause, and settled in to complain about the end of a dismal season.

Cloudy skies and high humidity cast an oppressive pall over the final game of 1975 for the Cosmopolitans. Both clubs fell into a stupor from the outset, and played as though it were a late February Grapefruit League contest.

On the mound however, lefthander Skip Masterson, one of the heroes of the Cosmopolitans' run to the World Series title in 1969, looked five years younger than he had all season and today of all days, threw like it. No longer a dominant southpaw the last few years, Masterson was turning in a gutsy performance. He'd given up some runs, but kept big innings from the Quakers, who sat at the short end of a 5 to 4 score as the game entered the ninth inning.

"Let's go, boys," said Murtaugh, as the Quakers came off the field at the end of the Cosmopolitans' half of the eighth inning. "Unless y'all feel like packing your bags for Pittsburgh. It'll be forty-three degrees there tonight. The Miners would love a one-game playoff at their home stadium and that's where we 'd have to go."

And by the last inning, the temperature in New York had dropped as well. Autumn's chill added to the Quakers' malaise.

Several of the players donned warmup jackets. They huddled next to each other, closer and closer, and watched as Bob Randolph popped out and Ricky Davis had a sure double stolen in left-center field on a tremendous play by Desi Mineola, the Cosmopolitans' slow-footed center fielder.

"Couldn't make that play again if he wanted," said a dejected Omar Clarke. "Desi ain't known for his glove."

Davis, true to his temper, smashed his bat against the top of the dugout steps. It shattered, shards flying in all directions. One of them pierced the shortstop's left cheek, and blood gushed from it. Murtaugh swore at the cold night air and Ricky hustled off with the team's trainer to receive several stitches. The shortstop stumbled down the hallway to the training room.

"Goofy!" shouted Murtaugh, his voice breaking as he spun on his heels, and spotted Chip Dunkirk balancing a baseball on his nose like a trained seal. "Grab a bat. You're hitting for Deke."

Dunkirk shot off the bench, pulling his jacket off and throwing it behind him. He headed to the on-deck circle, kicking up dust on his way.

Chip spun around.

"Hey! Viejo!" shouted Chip. "Get warmed up. We're going extra innings, and our starting shortstop barely missed with his hari-kari effort."

Chip's remarks, directed at Davey Gonzales, the Quakers' 40-year-old veteran infielder, echoed around the dank dugout and threw about 10,000 volts into the moribund bench-bound team. Jamie Wright, the reserve outfielder, stood up, joined by Moses Pendleton. The two pressed to the edge of the dugout and watched as Chip dug in against Bob Gomez, the Cosmopolitans' relief pitcher.

Dunkirk kissed the barrel of his bat and spat out some imaginary dirt.

"Mmmmm," said Chip to Red Devine, the Cosmos' catcher. "Bourbon flavored."

"Dunkirk, you are such a jack—"

"Let's go, gentlemen," interjected the umpire, in no mood for Dunkirk's antics.

"Ready when you are," Chip snapped and waited for Gomez's first offering.

" —ass."

Devine's last word prompted Chip to swing at the pitch that Gomez tried to sneak by in a quick delivery.

The rest of the Philadelphia bench leaped to their feet and pressed forward as Dunkirk's unintentional cut at the pitch drove it to the exact same place as Ricky Davis' near-double snatched by Desi Mineola.

Mineola, surprised by Chip's first-pitch swing, lost a half-step on the ball, and this time, the plodding outfielder couldn't get there. The ball shot by him, but to his credit, he hustled after it as it caromed off the fence. Mineola came up throwing.

Chip was having none of second base. He rounded the bag, despite entreaties from the Quakers' third-base coach. He blazed past Austin Becker at shortstop.

Mineola fired a laser to Clint Woodson, the Cosmopolitans' second baseman, who spotted Dunkirk going for three bases. He yanked the ball out of his glove and shot a bullet to Travis Norman at third, in time to get Dunkirk, who slid headfirst into the bag just *after* the baseball arrived. Norman went to apply the tag for the sure out, and the end of the game.

Norman dropped the ball.

Dunkirk was safe.

Chip lay on the ground for ten seconds, hugging the third base bag, panting like a dog after a long run in the summer heat. Dunkirk raised his left hand and signaled for a time-out, a habit he acquired from Bobby.

Oscar Hyschka, the only manager in Major League Baseball who made Brian Murtaugh look attractive, emerged from the Cosmopolitans' dugout and dragged his 50-year-old injured body across the diamond to argue the call.

"He had the ball long enough, Duke," he shouted at the field judge.

"Not a chance, Oscar," shouted Duke back at Hyschka. "Not even close."

"Ah, you're blind."

"Now that's original."

"OK, you're deaf, too."

"Oscar."

"And mute."

"Oscar."

"You cost me this game, you're gonna hear about it."

"Thought I was deaf?"

"You know what I mean."

"You done?"

"Yep."

Dunkirk brushed his uniform pants and stood with both feet on the third base bag and both arms folded across his chest. Norman, upset at his error, took up his position just to the left of the foul line and readied himself for Omar Clarke, the Quakers' lead-off hitter. Bobby stood in the on-deck circle and prayed that Clarke got on base.

****

Clarke stepped in and Gomez checked on Dunkirk, who seemed content to stand on the bag. When Gomez gave Chip a glance, the Quakers' outfielder waved at the Cosmopolitans' relief pitcher. Unnerved by the encounter, Gomez threw two feet over Clarke's head, and only a great play by Devine kept the ball from becoming a wild pitch.

The Cosmopolitans' catcher jogged out to the mound.

"Roberto, you're going to have to ignore the clown at third base," said Devine, jamming the ball back into Gomez's glove. "Ignore him or you'll make yourself crazy, and skip will pull ya. Dunkirk's a buffoon."

Gomez looked over at Dunkirk, who smiled and waved again.

Devine walked back to the plate, glaring at Chip the whole time.

Gomez turned his attention to the batter. He decided not to go from the stretch so he wouldn't get distracted by Dunkirk and the third base side of the field. He wound up and delivered a curveball that Clarke fouled off. Gomez wound up again and threw a fastball that hit the radar guns at 94 mph.

"Strike two!" shouted the umpire. Clarke thought it low, but the count now stood at one and two. Omar had one more strike to go before the Quakers would be booking a charter to Pittsburgh.

Clarke slumped his shoulders and ground his teeth.

Gomez received the ball from Devine and immediately went into his windup. He missed Chip Dunkirk dancing down the line.

Who broke for home.

Gomez finally saw Dunkirk in his peripheral view and released a blazing fastball that took off and required Devine to make another leaping grab, as Dunkirk slid under the tag.

"Safe!" shouted the umpire. "And that's ball two."

The players streamed off the bench to greet Dunkirk. It was the first steal of home in a Quakers' game since Nestle Gancio had done so in 1964, triggering the infamous ten-game losing streak that cost Philadelphia the pennant.

"Hey!" yelled Murtaugh. "We're only tied right now. Everyone back into the dugout!"

Under his breath, Murtaugh muttered, "RIP Nestle Gancio."

Oscar Hyschka took the opportunity to walk to the mound and remove Gomez. He called for Gary Fenner, a lefthanded relief pitcher to counter Clarke, who hit from the left side of the plate. Fenner shut the bullpen's gate-style door behind him and walked to the mound, still squeezing the baseball he'd used for warmup tosses. The crowd buzzed about Chip Dunkirk's steal of home. Fenner flipped the warmup ball into the stands as a souvenir. The Cosmopolitans fans settled down.

Fenner turned his back to the catcher after taking a new ball from Hyschka.

"Gary," said Oscar. "How about getting us outta this inning on one pitch?"

Fenner rubbed the bridge of his nose and took a few warmup tosses to Red Devine. Satisfied, the reliever signaled ready to the umpire. Clarke stepped in.

"PLAY BALL!"

Fenner delivered and Omar Clarke jacked a 400-foot home run over the right field wall. As he circled the bases, Hyschka put his hands on his hips and shouted out to Fenner.

"Not the *one* pitch I was talkin' about, Gary!" He leaned over, and felt a spasm go through his chest.

Sometimes I just hate this game.

This one failed pitch propelled the Quakers to their first post-season trip in their ninety-two-year history. Dunkirk led the Quakers out to home plate after hugging Brian Murtaugh. The team poured out of the dugout and mobbed Clarke.

And Bobby Young, in the on-deck circle during the chaos at the plate collapsed and lay there for several minutes, ignored by his raucous, celebrating teammates. Chip spotted him, and helped him into the dugout.

Bobby sat up on a training table.

"We aren't supposed to be here, Chip." He paused, the words catching in his throat. Bobby buried his head in his hands. "I'm not supposed to be *here*."

"Don't start with this again. Not today. Not now."

Dunkirk pulled him to his feet and ushered Bobby to the locker room just before the players and the press arrived to uncork the champagne.

"You'd better get ready to celebrate, Flash. Clear your head. Cincinnati?"

Bobby forced a smile.

"We're not supposed to be playing them. Pittsburgh is. Look, Chip, I meant what I said to the Revenells. My memory comes in, well, uh, flashes. I, uh, I—"

"What?"

"There's something wrong with the 1975 World Series. I can't remember what it is, but the Quakers are not supposed to be in it."

Dunkirk playfully swatted Bobby across the face with his glove.

"You keep talking that way, we ain't gonna be. Let's go."

****

The next day, the Quakers were front-page news in *Philadelphia Inquirer*:

"GANCIO NO MO'!
Quakers in playoffs for first time in team history!"

"Sparked (spooked?) by the actions of one Charles Everly 'Chip' Dunkirk, Jr., the Quakers finally blew away the specter of 1964 and the ghost of Nestle Gancio. Gancio, a phantom fixture in the dugout and clubhouse for eleven lousy seasons, finally cleaned out his locker.

"Ironically, our Quakers will face Gancio's former team, the Cincinnati Bucks, in the playoffs for the National League pennant. The winner will face either the Titans or the World Series champs three seasons running, the Oakland Lions."

CHAPTER SIXTEEN

The Red Juggernaut

Ferris Humaris watched the flight of the baseball until it disappeared into a mist that surrounded the lights illuminating the stadium. He sat on the bullpen bench. The emptiness of a thrashing by the Philadelphia Quakers on his home field came to rest on the Bucks' relief pitcher.

Next to him sat Cal Krumper, who, along with Humaris, was one of the "Twins," the Cincinnati Bucks' self-proclaimed nickname for their two exceptional relievers. Krumper's head settled squarely between his knees since giving up five runs in the eighth inning.

When the latest home run off the bat of Ike Jackson landed in the middle deck of left-center field, the Bucks trailed the Quakers 18 to 5, heading into the bottom of the ninth. The National League Championship Series would soon be tied at two games apiece in the five-game set. The next day's contest would decide the senior circuit's representative to the 1975 World Series.

****

Emanuel Emerson, in addition to being the Bucks' manager and the best reason to not smoke cigarettes since Nat King Cole, didn't move away from the dugout steps for several minutes after the last out at the bottom of the ninth inning, his back to the players on the bench.

The mist, which had covered the upper deck and light stanchions during the top half of the final inning, drifted down to field level. The thin vapor spread across the infield and found its way into the dugout.

"What the hell?" Emerson asked his favorite question to the mist and stared down at his spikes. He faced the players. "Gentlemen, that, as you know by now, was just about the worst effort you have all *ever* made. If you *don't* want to go to Philadelphia, let me know. You're welcome to stay in Cincinnati. Most of you didn't show up tonight, so I am not sure you'll be in Philly whether you're on the flight or not."

Eric Cibilich, the team's lightning rod, fixed his glare on Emmanuel.

"They kicked our asses, skipper," said Cibilich, who rubbed his hands on his muscular thighs and spat. "Pure and simple. It won't happen again. *Right*, boys?"

There was an undercurrent of "Yeah, Eric," and "No way." Cibilich got to his feet and stood next to Emmanuel.

"That's it? That's all we got?"

He paced along the dugout bench. The newly arrived bullpen pitchers crunched their cleats down the dugout steps and joined their teammates. Cibilich waited for them to sit.

"What's the score of tomorrow's game, Cal?" he asked Krumper, fresh in from the bullpen.

"What?"

"Are you deaf?" Cibilich yelled, charging over and standing an inch from Krumper. "Are you?!"

"No."

"What?"

"I said—"

"Yeah, I barely heard you . . . like your slider barely slid tonight! The score of tomorrow's game is nothing to nothing. Clean slate. We get a chance to hang eighteen on them, and ya better start thinking we will."

"Eric." A voice from the bench, Morris Stearns.

"I ain't done with the pitchers, Morris. I'll get to the defense in a second."

Morris, a half-head taller than Cibilich, stood. He headed for the clubhouse. Emmanuel interrupted the first baseman before he got to the dugout door.

"Sit down, Stearns," demanded Emmanuel. "Or you will sit down tomorrow. Don't care what's on the line right now."

Morris returned to his place on the bench. Cibilich sat down.

"Flight leaves at nine tomorrow morning," said Emmanuel. "If you ain't on it, I guess you're OK with what happened tonight."

CHAPTER SEVENTEEN

Game Five – Quakers/Bucks, and Hedging Your Bets

Scizzor and Mad Max sat side by side in a Bicentennial Park luxury box on the home team side of the field. Both puffed away on their respective brown cigarettes.

"How is Eric?" asked Scizzor.

"He's good," replied Max. "Gave the Bucks the old rah-rah-Coach-Herb-Brooks speech at the end of the game yesterday."

"Quinn's in?"

"Like Flint."

"Let's hope the Bucks win this one," said Scizzor. "The Quakers looked like world beaters last night."

"And how did they look the previous three games?" asked Max. "Like they had lost their car keys. The only reason they won the second game is because Skountzos pitched like his side-dish piece of flesh was waiting in his locker."

Max yelled her last sentence louder than the first two. She dropped her cigarette and ground it into the carpet.

"Damn it!" She grunted. "One run from a Bucks sweep!"

"The Red Juggernaut is leaking oil," offered Scizzor.

Max lit another cigarette.

"Don't need to hear that, Eddie. But perhaps you should hike yourself down to the players' level of this cookie-cutter stadium and see if you can catch a quiet moment with one of the players from our fallback team. That's 'phallback' with a 'PH.'"

Scizzor got up and headed for the door.

"Eddie. Eddie. Eddie," admonished Max, shaking her head and handing Scizzor a red-jacketed personal journal along with a ballpoint pen. "Ain't you forgetting something?"

Scizzor looked at the booklet.

"Autographs, dopey. What if someone sees you with a ballplayer? You *are* a well-known, uh, independent contractor."

Scizzor took the booklet and pen and slipped them into the pocket of his signature houndstooth jacket.

"Maybe you can get one from Skountzos," suggested Max, watching Scizzor make his way to the door for the second time. "The guy is such a recluse. Greek's autograph will be very valuable about twenty-five years from now."

"I'll do my level best," Scizzor replied and shut the door behind him.

****

Out on the field, Grantland Garvey, the starting pitcher for this game, threw his last warmup pitch. An October breeze with just the right amount of chill fluttered his shirt sleeves. A brown leaf made its way across the mound, an escapee from one of the ninety-percent-dead trees planted along the perimeter of the stadium.

Garvey stared at it. It flew off the mound and landed on the infield, where it appeared redder because of the contrast to the turf's hospital green.

"Let's go, pitch! Hey! You, out there on the mound! Play ball!" the umpire shouted at Garvey, who broke from his trance.

He served it up to Eric Cibilich, the Bucks' lead-off batter, who graciously crushed it into the right field stands. The Philly crowd, which had been raucous to that point, dropped over dead silent like they had just won an all-expenses paid vacation to Andalusia, Pennsylvania. Fifty-thousand stared as the scoreboard verified what had just happened.

1 to 0, Cincinnati.

While Eric Cibilich circled the bases with his characteristic fist-pumping bravado in a 100-meter dash, Garvey walked over to the leaf, which had not budged since the start of the inning. He ground it into the AstroTurf.

Bob Randolph took a new ball from the ump and fired it in the direction of the mound, where Garvey no longer stood. It skipped into center field. Moses Pendleton, still taking in Cibilich's home run, fumbled with the baseball, which sent the nervous crowd into a symphony of boos.

"Great start," said Bobby aloud in right field. He had watched Cibilich's screeching liner clear the fence and slam into the first row of seats. Randolph's errant throw and Pendleton's mishandling of the toss added to a sense of collapse. Every fan slumped. Every child dropped their foul ball gloves into their laps. The vendors stood in place, as did the Philadelphia Belles, the attractive female ushers. No one stirred. A bag of peanuts spilled to the ground in one of the field-level boxes, the stadium so silent, everyone heard it.

Pendleton got control of the ball and threw it to Garvey. But before the pitcher could face Zach Mueller, the Bucks' second baseman, Bobby ran in from right field, after getting the attention of the field umpire, who waved off any further play.

Bobby arrived at the mound and looked around. His vision traveled from center field, down the Quakers' side of first base, and back to home plate. He lifted his arms.

"Let's go, Quakers!" he shouted to the crowd.

They stood, slowly at first, but building until all 50,000 fans let out a collective roar. Bobby encouraged them. He took the baseball from Garvey.

"You need this out," he said to Garvey, slapping the ball into the pitcher's glove. "We need this out."

Emanuel Emerson made his way up the dugout steps to move the game along, but before he could get to field level, Bobby sprinted back to the outfield. Garvey looked in on Zach Mueller. The Bucks' manager returned to the dugout.

"This ain't high school," he grumbled. "Bobby Young looks like he just graduated."

Mueller, his signature right elbow twitch on full display, stepped in. The cool October breeze returned. The Philly fans pressed themselves closer together. Some pulled on sweatshirts.

Grantland Garvey threw off the cold air. He felt his breath enter and leave his lungs twice, the sound audible to him alone. He relaxed the grip on the baseball and switched to a two-seam fastball, called for by Bob Randolph.

Garvey ignored the catcher's mitt and locked his gaze onto Mueller. Mueller's twitch slowed in rhythm with Garvey's breathing. He wound up, the process taking on the grace of a balletic adagio, and released the ball.

Mueller closed and opened his eyes, thrown off by Garvey's stare. The ball blazed in with the sound of a chainsaw cutting through new timber.

Zach Mueller pushed back from the plate as the pitch headed for his ribcage. He tripped and landed in the dirt. The ball cut just inside and crossed the corner of the strike zone.

"Strike one!" the umpire shouted.

Mueller shot up from the ground and pounded his bat into the turf. Emanuel Emerson covered the ground between the dugout and home plate with the speed of Ali's left jab.

Emmanuel descended on the umpire, who stood from his crouch and removed his face mask.

"How can you call a strike on a brushback pitch!?" Emerson screamed.

"That ball broke over the inside corner, Emmanuel. Don't know how, but that pitch ended up in the strike zone."

"How? How is that possible?"

"Call stands, Emmanuel," said the umpire. "Do you wanna get back to the dugout, or do you want to spend the rest of the game in the clubhouse?"

"Neither. I want you to explain that call to me again."

"Emmanuel, it would take a lot for me to throw a manager out of a playoff game, but I will do it."

"Go ahead!" shouted Emerson. Emmanuel and the home plate ump brushed nose hair follicles as the Bucks' manager continued. "Go ahead. It'll be one more thing I can bring up to the review board!"

Taylor Gunderson, a former big-league slugger with the Bucks and now one of their coaches, ran out of the dugout and wrapped his arms around Emerson from behind, but that didn't slow Emmanuel down. He continued yelling at the umpire, who watched as

Gunderson carried Emanuel Emerson away from the plate and back to the dugout.

Zach Mueller returned to the batter's box. The umpire signaled for a pitch.

And with that, Game Five of the 1975 National League Championship Series had begun.

****

In the bottom of the seventh inning the temperature dropped another ten degrees. The earlier breeze, which reminded everyone of the onset of a typical northeast autumn, turned cold, and winter made its presence known in Philadelphia. The stands resembled those at a football game as fans pressed even closer together. Some cursed their lack of preparation by not throwing on a heavier coat or putting a blanket into the back seat of the car before making for the ballpark.

The game remained 1 to 0 in the Bucks' favor. Darragh Quinn, the Bucks' starter, struck out Grantland Garvey to start the seventh frame, which drew boos from the stands. Murtaugh had decided to stick with his starter and not pinch hit. Philadelphia fans expressed their notorious displeasure. Omar Clarke singled, but Del Carollo, the Bucks' catcher, threw him out attempting to steal second. Quinn ran the count to two and two on Bobby Young. What few Quakers fans stood during Bobby's at-bat, deflated and dropped to their seats.

Bobby stepped out of the batter's box and didn't get back in until warned to do so by the umpire. He took his time. Rubbed the bat. Held up his hand to further delay the pitch. Quinn remained on the rubber and ignored Bobby's antics. Carollo called for a fastball out of the strike zone, hoping Bobby would chase it.

"Batter!" shouted the umpire. Quinn went into his windup.

The fastball tailed away from Bobby but remained belt-high and just off the plate. He shifted his lead foot toward the pitch and ripped it just over the first-base bag. Morris Stearns got a piece of it as it skidded into right field, which kept Bobby to a single. Mickey Rosas got to the ball and fired it to O.J. Arnott at second base.

Jack Slavik stepped in just as the wind picked up from right field. Slavik saw his breath as Quinn fired a curveball that handcuffed

Jack, who fouled it off. Slavik snapped the handle of his bat and grunted at himself for chasing a bad pitch.

"Curveball, Jack," he said quietly to himself. "Curveball. Lefthanded pitcher." He smacked himself on the batting helmet.

Bobby took a lead off first base. Morris Stearns waved his glove at Quinn, who pitched out of the stretch, facing Bobby. Quinn threw to the plate. Fans heard the loud *thwack* as the ball connected with a swinging bat. A crosswind slammed into the baseball as it took flight toward the left field stands. Curving. Curving. Middle deck.

But foul.

Again, the oxygen left the crowd in a collective groan.

Slavik shortened his stance, looking to put the ball in play. Quinn threw and Slavik drove the pitch deep into left-center field. Bobby raced around the bases and caught a glimpse of the ball heading for the fence at the 375-foot mark.

"Go. Go! GO!" Bobby shouted in the direction of the ball. His baseball discipline gone, he ran backward between third and home.

Mike Willits and the ball got to the yellow stripe marking the top of the wall. Just as it headed over the fence, the Bucks' center fielder snatched it out of the air.

Third out.

Slavik, who had run flat out from the time the ball left his bat, pulled up between first and second, took off his batting helmet, and flung it back near the on-deck circle. He looked out into the stands along the first base side. Bobby pulled up between third and home. He stopped for a moment before heading into the dugout to get his glove.

Omar Clarke met him at the top of the steps and offered Bobby's glove to him.

"Two more innings," said Clarke.

"Till what? We lose again? We uphold the Philly tradition of tanking when we can't take the pressure?" Bobby's face loomed inches from Clarke's.

Bobby yanked the glove from the second baseman. Clarke pitched forward.

The second baseman coiled his right arm but before he could strike, Rick Nayle grabbed him by the bicep and held it. Clarke couldn't free his arm, and the balance of the Quakers' bench got between the two players.

From up in the announcer's booth, Oscar Markley watched the melee.

"Something going on in the Quakers' dugout."

"Looks like Bobby Young and Omar Clarke are having a bit of a disagreement over a glove," said Skeeter Thompson.

"I'd say it's a little more than that," remarked Markley, his words tumbling out in a laugh.

"Yep. Here come the umpires, but the dugout is calming down. The Quakers are taking the field for the top of the eighth. They'll have two more chances." Clyde Wilhelm shuffled some papers on his desk and signaled for a commercial break.

Bobby stopped in front of Omar Clarke on his way to right field. Clarke stiffened.

"We are *not* losing this game," said Bobby.

A smile broke out on Omar Clarke's face. The two players shook hands. Bobby trotted out to right field as Clarke took a couple of throws from Ike Jackson.

****

In one of Bicentennial Park's luxury boxes, Mad Max puffed away on what felt like her 1000th cigarette since the game started. The door opened and Scizzor walked in, took a cigarette, and joined his boss in the future cancer ward.

"What did Davis have to say?" Mad Max asked.

Scizzor lit the cigarette, this time an average plain vanilla Marlboro pulled from the signature red box, and sat down next to Max.

"He's in," said Scizzor, drawing on the cigarette. He exhaled. "So are Echevarrian and Garvey."

"How about Nayle?" asked Max.

"Nope," said Scizzor. "Don't even discuss it any further. He threatened to kill Davis for even considering it. Nayle would go right to the cops. Gotta admire that."

Scizzor saw Max stiffen.

"He was just kidding . . . I think."

"Echevarrian? Can he keep his trap shut? He's a wild card."

"We needed starting pitchers. Skountzos would never go for it and the rest of the staff is just too unreliable to be counted on for multiple starts. We needed our own Eddie Cicotte and Lefty Williams if we're going to pull off a Black Sox scandal."

"So that's a yes?"

"Echevarrian is having arm problems. Jose has to put his right hand in his glove during the windup so he can lift it over his head. How he won twenty-one games I'll never know."

"Don't get all sentimental on me, Scizzor. I still need a yes."

"That's a yes."

"Don't think it's going to come to this," said Max. "Quakers can't buy a run."

"If the Bucks win?"

"All in on Cincinnati," said Max. "Titans can't beat them. I don't think anyone can."

"You don't want me to talk to Eric again?"

Mad Max burst into laughter.

"Eric Cibilich?" She continued laughing. "Not a chance. Winning the Series is all he's been about since his rookie season. For all I know, he'd turn us in and agree to give testimony."

Max stopped.

"But even if we could talk someone on Cincinnati into the deal, the Bucks would still win the Series. That's how deep they are.

"The Titans should never have gotten past the Colonials. I'd consider approaching the Titans, but I really don't know how Boston blew it, or Oakland for that matter. The Quakers are it. Let's see what happens."

Max took a drag on the cigarette.

"If the Quakers pull this out, though, my money is on them."

"What?" snapped Scizzor.

"You know, to lose the Series." Maxine laughed through a scratchy throat.

****

On the field, Cincinnati had something going. Garvey's fastball had lost some zip. After retiring center fielder Mike Willits, who lost a footrace to first base with Omar Clarke on a slow grounder Ike Jackson barehanded, Garvey gave up a single to Eric Cibilich and a double to Zach Mueller.

Cibilich held up at third when Moses Pendleton fielded Mueller's hit off one carom, and fired a strike to home, bypassing Ricky Davis, the cutoff man.

Teeth chattered in the stands as Brian Murtaugh slogged out to the mound, his shoulders slumped forward. Garvey handed the ball to the manager. The cold Bicentennial Park air hung on Murtaugh's shoulders. The manager dropped the ball. Both he and Garvey looked down at it.

The bullpen door opened and out rolled the golf cart to deliver reliever Deke Reilly. Bobby spied it over his shoulder and sprinted to the front of it. He outran it to the mound. His breath looked pale white as he landed next to Murtaugh and Garvey.

"Is this the quit?" asked Bobby, snatching the ball off the turf.

"What?" replied Murtaugh.

"You heard me. Have we given up?"

Murtaugh looked Bobby in the eye. Garvey looked down at the rubber. Bobby held the ball out in front of him. He put his empty hand on Garvey's left shoulder.

"You pitched a gem, Grantland. My question is for Brian."

"Get back to right field!" Murtaugh snarled.

"Not yet."

Reilly attempted to snatch the ball out of Bobby's hand.

Keith Tesoro, the 300-pound umpire, famous around the League for his effusive calls and genial personality, thudded out to the mound.

"What in hell are you all doing out here?" barked Tesoro. "Get your boys back into position, coach."

Tesoro turned away and pounded the artificial turf with his size 14 cleats as he trundled back to home plate.

"That guy has to have a serious chafing problem," said Bobby.

"Hee-yeah," laughed Reilly. "That's for darned sure."

"He is generating a lot of friction and a lot of noise with those pants," commented Bobby, as Tesoro finished his journey and stood behind Del Carollo. He glowered at the ongoing conference on the mound.

"We can rally. I know it. We can win this game," said Bobby to the Quakers' charismatic pitcher. He shifted his glance over to Murtaugh. "But it's gotta stay close."

"I'll do my best," replied Reilly and slapped Bobby on the top of his head. "Murt," he said to Brian Murtaugh. "I got this."

Murtaugh shook his head, and for the first time in fifty years, had to laugh. The coach continued chuckling all the way back to the dugout.

Reilly threw a half-dozen warmup pitches. Tesoro signaled for a batter and the lefthanded Mickey Rosas stepped in.

Randolph called for a fastball.

"Fastball?" Reilly asked his glove. "I don't have one of those."

He shook off Randolph, who changed the call to a screwball. The pitch came in. It looked like a changeup. Rosas waited on it, and then teed off.

The ball broke inside at the last instant and Rosas hit it on the thinner part of the barrel, lofting a flyball into mid-left field, where Rick Nayle waited for it, and tucked it away in his glove for the second out.

Eric Cibilich tagged up and headed for home.

Nayle heard "Home!" shouted in unison by both Ricky Davis and Moses Pendleton. He came out of the catch throwing in the general vicinity of the plate.

Reilly hustled in from the mound to back up the usual errant attempt from Nayle.

The throw, to 50,000 shocked fans, and 52 Quakers and Bucks players, arrived on one hop straight into Bob Randolph's glove. Eric Cibilich and the ball arrived at exactly the same time and Eric slammed into Randolph with the force of a linebacker. The ball popped out of

Randolph's glove after tagging Cibilich, and just as Reilly arrived at the site of the collision, passing the human pile in a dead sprint. As he did, the baseball, loosed by Cibilich's jarring impact, appeared in his peripheral field of vision. He reached behind him with his gloved hand, hit the brakes, and skidded through the left side batter's box.

The ball dropped into Reilly's glove just as he, Randolph, and Cibilich hit the ground. All three came to rest just outside the plate, as Cibilich's hand reached for home.

Reilly slapped his glove on Eric's head before the Bucks' star could touch safely.

Keith Tesoro stood over the three-player pileup and delayed before throwing his right arm up with the thumb extended.

"Out!"

The cheers resounded from the stand with the same intensity at which the players collided. Reilly popped up and trotted into the dugout. He hopped down the dugout steps and handed the ball to Brian Murtaugh.

"Had it all the way, Murt!"

Out on the field, Eric Cibilich jumped to his feet and argued the call, but Tesoro explained that the ball never hit the ground and that both Randolph and Reilly had applied the tag to Cibilich before the Buck got to the plate. In either scenario, Eric made the third out.

Cibilich gave up and headed back to the dugout. Randolph, however, hadn't moved. Cibilich's aggressive slide had knocked him out.

****

The crowd watched the medical staff take Randolph off the field, and the excitement from the last play at the top of the eighth inning died when the Quakers went down in order after a lead-off double by Rick Nayle. Ike Jackson lined out to Zach Mueller. Moses Pendleton flied out to right field. The pinch hitter for Bob Randolph, Chip Dunkirk, the hero at the end of September, popped out to short. Inning over.

Reilly set the Bucks down in the top of the ninth inning. The Quakers now stood but three outs away from another disappointing end to a season.

And only two when Ricky Davis struck out. Quinn appeared to have only gotten stronger as the innings wore on. Davis, normally expressive, walked back to the dugout and slid his bat back into the rack. He sat down and entertained himself by picking dirt out of his cleats, shifting from the left shoe to the right. The mood on the bench darkened. A cold wind whipped along the dusty concrete. Numbness took over the hands and feet of the Quakers.

Murtaugh patted his paunch. He had a decision to make. Quinn was a southpaw, and the next batter up after a lineup switch to take Reilly out of an at-bat, was the backup catcher Javier Slocumbe, a lefthanded hitter. Brian asked for a time-out and walked to the on-deck circle. The wind picked up again. Some trash from spent concessions swirled around the field.

Keith Tesoro called time-out and asked the grounds crew to grab some of the errant paper and plastic. Emanuel Emerson grumbled, but kept off the field. The crowd had grown so silent that Murtaugh's first statement could be heard by the entire stadium.

"I need you, Javy," he said to Slocumbe. "We go extra innings, I'm outta catchers if I pull you for a righty. Can't change the lineup now."

Slocumbe's boyishly handsome face took on a grin that could fairly be described as Chip Dunkirk in quality.

"Seen a couple lefties the past sixteen years, skip," said Slocumbe, rubbing the handle of his bat. "Quinn's going to try to sneak that lousy slider of his past me, and that ain't gonna happen. Maybe tomorrow, but not tonight. *Not tonight.*"

Murtaugh walked away. Slocumbe stood in against Quinn, who missed inside with a fastball. Ball one.

"Slider," mouthed Slocumbe. "Stay in the box."

Quinn loaded up the pitch and threw *at* Slocumbe, who stood his ground. The ball broke away from him and into the strike zone. Slocumbe made the kind of contact that meant nothing but extra bases.

In center field, Willits took off at the sound of pine connecting with horsehide and just missed an acrobatic catch. The ball squirted away, and Javier Slocumbe stood on second base with a stand-up double.

The Quakers' crowd, as faithful as a trophy wife and as quiet as a George McGovern rally, exploded with noise. Omar Clarke stepped in. Emanuel Emerson called time and signaled for Ferris Humaris. Murtaugh did not take the chance of putting in a pinch runner for Slocumbe. The bench had no more reserve catchers on it, Santorino and Alvarez having been traded before the deadline.

After Humaris' warmup tosses, Clarke greeted the Bucks' reliever with a seeing-eye single between second and third base that moved Slocumbe to third base. The busy Mike Willits fired a perfect strike to Del Carollo to keep Slocumbe at third. The alert Omar Clarke took second on the throw. Bobby Young stepped up to the plate to a tsunami of cheers.

Humaris, though, intentionally walked Bobby even with Jack Slavik—the team's home run leader with 54 during the regular season—due up next and only one out. The Bicentennial Park crowd deflated as Bobby dropped his bat and trotted to first base.

Slavik stepped into the batter's box. He exhaled through his teeth and stared at Humaris. His grip on the bat handle tightened.

"You'd rather pitch to *me*, Ferris?!" Slavik snarled at Humaris, waving the finger of his right hand at the Bucks' reliever before returning it to the bat handle. "Well, bring it, and it better be good."

Humaris immediately went into his windup and buzzed a fastball at Slavik's Adam's apple. The Philly slugger leaned back, and Del Carollo jumped to his feet and snared the revenge pitch. All the runners held.

Humaris wiped the sweat out of his eyes and looked in for a sign.

Jack Slavik slammed the next pitch into right field. Slocumbe easily crossed the plate.

Tie game.

Bicentennial Park erupted in salvo after salvo of cheers, and then, as only Philadelphians can, the cheers stopped like someone hit the mute button.

Clarke eased up at third base to the collective groans of the Philly "Phaithful." Rosas' throw to Del Carollo would have had Clarke by ten feet had he attempted to score. In the dugout, Murtaugh and Nayle jawed at each other.

Murtaugh, still mad at himself for not pinch-running for Slocumbe, went with his gut and finally made a change with the game on the line. Nayle sat down, and Steve Seacourt walked toward the plate.

Seacourt, a fleet runner and excellent outfielder, had a questionable reputation as a hitter, but if the Quakers and Bucks headed to extra innings, his excellent defensive skills might make the difference.

Seacourt stepped in. Murtaugh looked at his cleats and mumbled something about games like this one and earning his pay.

Emanuel Emerson called time. Just as Murtaugh had done, Emerson moved Eric Cibilich out to left field and inserted Wellington Benson at third, both defensive moves. Roscoe Munsch jogged in from the outfield and took a seat on the Bucks' bench.

Seacourt dug in. Humaris checked the runners and chased Clarke back to third. Murtaugh called time and ran out to talk to Clarke.

"Do not steal home."

"We can end this," said Clarke.

"Ain't gonna happen, Omar. Humaris is looking right at you. You ain't going anywhere."

"Should have left Rusty in to bat."

"Do ya wanna trade positions, Omar?" growled Murtaugh, his voice nearly shot.

"Hey skip, you can kiss my — "

"Yo!" shouted Keith Tesoro, as he moved from behind the plate and "jogged" out to third base. His voice boomed across the field. "Let's play ball!"

Murtaugh and Clarke separated. The Quakers' manager walked away as Clarke eyed home plate like it was the last pork chop on the platter. Humaris went into the stretch and started the sequence of events that would go down in baseball lore as "The Miscommunication Mambo."

Clarke had a huge lead. Humaris switched his concentration to the plate.

And threw to third where Wellington Benson applied what looked to be a textbook tag to nab Clarke and record the second out. But everyone on the third base side—which did not include the field judge who made the call from shallow left field—saw Benson *miss* Clarke's leg when he slapped his glove down to complete the play.

"*OUT!*"

Murtaugh exploded out of the dugout to join Clarke in the argument and found himself trying to restrain the second baseman, who got ejected from the game by Keith Tesoro. The chubby umpire's patient shelf-life finally exceeded its sell-by date.

And for years afterward, replays that clearly showed Benson's miss, tormented Philadelphia fans. Yet another call that didn't go the Quakers' way.

Steve Seacourt, who had yet to see a pitch, returned to the on-deck circle. He sprinted back and forth along the first base line in front of the Quakers dugout to stay warm, while Tesoro struggled back to the plate.

"PLAY BALL!" Tesoro huffed, his voice intended as a mute button. It brought the crowd noise level down. Every fan had been booing non-stop since the pick-off, unhappy with the call or with the Quakers.

Humaris buzzed a fastball just off the plate, which Steve Seacourt took for a ball.

"Strike one!" shouted Tesoro.

"I think that was a ball," announced Clyde Wilhelm in the broadcast booth. "But right now, Tesoro isn't giving the Quakers an inch. This could be a long game with a lot of extra innings."

Humaris looked over his shoulder at Slavik and checked on Bobby at second. He threw another fastball just off the plate, but this time Steve Seacourt reached out and slapped it into right field. Bobby and Slavik took off at the sound of the bat hitting the baseball.

Zach Mueller lunged to his left and knocked the ball down just as Mickey Rosas arrived from right field. Both Mueller and Rosas called for the ball. Both reached for it and grabbed it and ripped it from the other's grasp — as Bobby raced home.

The ball popped up into the air and landed between them, and now both stood stock-still waiting for the other to make the play.

Bobby scored without a throw.

The Quakers were going to the 1975 World Series.

And the 1975 Cincinnati Bucks would be forever marked by "The Miscommunication Mambo" between two future Hall of Famers.

CHAPTER EIGHTEEN

Say It Ain't So, Bo

The jubilant Quakers' clubhouse had the requisite number of ice buckets, champagne bottles, and cases of beer. The floor resembled a hosed-down Manhattan high-rise's sidewalk. Even the subdued duo of Skountzos and Slavik commandeered a dozen magnums of bubbly, which they emptied like circus cannons in the direction of every player on the roster.

One of those salvos smacked Ricky Davis, who held up both hands in surrender. He had enough celebrating. The shortstop slipped out through the clubhouse door. He ran down the corridor, his feet only in athletic socks, and ducked into the parking lot reserved for players, coaches, and Quakers' upper management.

A passenger door to a vintage Aston-Martin opened. The Quakers' shortstop climbed inside. Scizzor McQueen sat behind the wheel on the British side of the car, the right.

"If it ain't Swede Risberg in the flesh," laughed McQueen.

"Shut up McQueen and just give me the numbers."

"Ten million on the Titans," said McQueen. "The odds are only two to one, but if Echevarrian and Garvey come through, along with you and that oddball relief pitcher, you'll get a cool million each."

"Nah. Sorry. I'm making $100,000 this year and next," said Davis, turning to get out of the car. "You gotta give me two million. The other guys can split it three ways. None of them are making any more than $25,000, except Garvey, and he's done after this season."

Scizzor grunted through a few laughs. Davis stared at McQueen, who hadn't shaved in days.

"OK, Ricky. Split it up however you want. It's four million total. You gotta lay down or it ain't gonna be pretty. And make sure those two pitchers, ahem, play ball. Nothing more important."

"That won't be a problem. They're both having arm trouble. It's a huge incentive for a major league pitcher when they see their fastball drop by ten miles an hour."

Davis exited the car and walked to the corridor that led to the clubhouse.

The door opened before Ricky got to it. Out stepped the parking lot attendant and security guard, a long-time and long-suffering Quakers' fan named Cecil.

Cecil, whose family hailed from West Philadelphia for generations, smiled like a kid out on his very first Halloween.

"Congratulations, Mister Davis," said Cecil on the loud side. He stepped forward and shook Ricky's hand. Davis hadn't moved from his spot, and out of the corner of his eye, he saw Scizzor McQueen exit his car and pull something from the breast pocket of his houndstooth suit jacket. Cecil stopped pumping Davis' hand and crumpled to the ground.

"Get out of here," hissed McQueen to Davis as he covered the distance between himself, Davis, and the now-dead Cecil. He slipped the handgun back into his jacket.

"Cecil," croaked Davis, his eyes filling up. The security guard died before he thudded to the ground. The adolescent grin hadn't left Cecil's face. "Why did you — "

"Get out!" growled Scizzor McQueen. He picked up Cecil as if he were a duffel bag filled with baseball bats. He chugged back to his car and stuffed the man into the passenger seat so deftly that Ricky knew Scizzor had done this more than a few times. Scizzor turned back toward Davis.

"Not going to tell you again, Ricky," his voice grating. He spread his arms, which revealed a blood stain that covered most of his jacket, shirt, and tie. "Get back to the clubhouse. This is handled."

Davis staggered through the door and into the corridor. He leaned against the wall, unable to draw a deep breath.

****

Chip Dunkirk, forever the team's nosy neighbor, spotted Davis slipping out the clubhouse door. He'd been watching the shortstop since the celebration began. Something about Davis bothered Dunkirk ever since his night out at The Library with Bobby. The shortstop's play remained at a high level, but his usual locker room confidence and camaraderie had disappeared. The Quakers were headed to the World Series for the first time in the team's 92-year history, and Ricky Davis became more and more distant as they approached the playoffs, and now the championship.

Davis, always looking for a reason to slug down a celebratory drink, sat in front of his locker and looked at his watch every few minutes.

Ten minutes into the champagne dousing, Davis got off the bench and walked out the door of the clubhouse. He looked around and headed for the exit. Dunkirk spotted him and made for the door. Bobby halted his progress.

"Where you going, Goofy?"

"Might be able to get some insight on Davis' visit to The Library the other night," replied Chip. "Don't go anywhere."

Chip exited and caught sight of Ricky walking into the players' parking garage. The door to the garage closed. Chip opened it a crack and peeked out. He caught a glimpse of Davis getting into an old sports car.

Chip stepped back. He slipped into one of the equipment closets and waited. The door swung open. Chip shoved himself as far back as he could into the shadows.

Five minutes later he heard what sounded like a wet firecracker and assumed it had come from the clubhouse. Davis moved back inside and leaned against the wall, hyperventilating. Chip could hear his rapid breathing.

Davis was inches away from Chip, still inside the equipment closet.

Davis stopped hyperventilating, and walked away. Chip, his breath now coming in shallow doses, listened until he was sure Davis was gone. The combination of oxygen deprivation and alcohol made him lightheaded. When he heard the sports car revving and driving away a few minutes later, he dropped to the ground and sucked in the air. His head cleared, Chip returned to the clubhouse.

****

Bobby felt his knees give out, so he sat down on the bench in front of his locker. Greg Stroemel, foam soaking his mustache, joined him.

"Too much of a good thing," he said.

"No, I—"

"What?"

"See if you can grab Goofy for me. I need to tell him something."

Stroemel slapped Bobby on the shoulder.

"What? Something you can't tell your fellow rookie?"

"Inside joke."

"I'm hurt, man. I thought we were friends."

"Just shut up and get Dunkirk over here."

Stroemel laughed and sloshed through an inch of beer, wine, and soda to grab Dunkirk, who had just returned and was entertaining Slade Maberry with a very good imitation of Hector Enriquez.

"Funny, Chip," said Maberry, stepping closer to Dunkirk. "That's such a good imitation, it makes me want to punch you."

Dunkirk smiled like a baby passing gas and backed away from Maberry. He bumped into Greg Stroemel, who steered him toward Bobby. Chip, recovered from the parking garage incident, sat next to his friend and asked Stroemel to give them a little room.

Chip's face showed more frustration than concern. *Bobby's act is wearing thin*, Chip thought.

"I'm guessing that we're going to have the same conversation," said Dunkirk, slapping himself in the face. "Stand by as I prepare myself for another hour of *Bobby Can't Remember*."

"Chip, this is serious," said Bobby. "There is something wrong with this whole season, and now the Series. I can't remember who went in 1975, but I know it wasn't the Quakers and probably not the Titans."

"I remember, though. You told me it was the Boston Colonials and Cincinnati Bucks. Epic Series according to you. And now you don't remember any details at all?"

"No," said Bobby, watching his teammates getting dressed to head out and continue the celebration. Even Slavik and Skountzos looked happy. "I only remember the name, Skountzos, but if what you're saying is true, it had to be the Colonials' catcher, Nick Skountzos, who played in the Series that year. Not us. Not our Greek."

"Get ready to play the Titans, Flash. It's happening, whether you remember it or not."

"You don't get it," said Bobby. "The past is changing, and I'm the reason. What else is going to happen over the next few years? Geez, what's going to happen over the next few *days*?"

"Hey, enough," insisted Dunkirk. "Enough."

"This will not end well," said Bobby, shaking his head.

Dunkirk walked Bobby out of the clubhouse and into the corridor. Bobby, exhausted from the game and the mental gymnastics regarding the past, allowed himself to be led away. Chip stood in front of him and wagged a finger in his face.

"Listen to me. Where's the guy who admonished players for even saying 1964 out loud? Where? That was the past, Flash. Got it? That was the past. And now you're all torqued out about the past again, or some *supposed* future? Take some of your own advice and get in the present, because this is all you've got right now."

Bobby grunted and opened his mouth, but Dunkirk cut him off.

"Shut up," said Chip. "The present is all any of us have now. Let's not be losers and have this opportunity pass us by."

"Chip," whispered Bobby, his face drained of color. "Sometimes I just want to go home, because this ain't it."

Bobby stepped away from Dunkirk, but Chip threw an arm around his friend's shoulder.

"Let's go, loser. You may not get home until late tonight."

CHAPTER NINETEEN

Playing It Straight

"Nope."

"But you were OK with the tip about Rod Amarel."

"What? That it wasn't worth keeping him? How do you know I'm right?"

The afternoon following the Quakers' Division Series win, Bobby joined the Revenells in their office.

Garrett and Gregory sat behind the desk, Bobby opposite. Out of habit he looked over at the owners and the lack of any technology in front of them.

A typical bleak October day let little sunlight enter the office. The threat of snow, but not cold enough to do so. The dark clouds, which initiated seasonal depression, contained no moisture, and cast a blanket of oatmeal-colored light over the artificial turf of Bicentennial Park.

The brisk wind, anything but refreshing, rattled the construction-grade windows of the office. Garrett shifted in his seat.

"You have all this knowledge, or so you say," said Garrett, "but you're not willing to share it with the organization you play for?"

Bobby also shifted in his chair.

"After the start of the season, I noticed that I could not recall certain things," said Bobby. "A Super Bowl champ. A world event. Nothing after April of 1975 is staying in my head. I could tell you things now that won't come true, and yet at one point they were true. I've been to the library to read about time travel. Interesting subject. You should get a copy of 'A Sound of Thunder' by Ray Bradbury. Seems that if time travel were possible, the effects on the future cannot be predicted, and are almost always not good."

"And that means?" asked Gregory.

"That Rod Amarel, because he is no longer a Quaker, could end up as the next Del Carollo. Trading him before he actually left for the Senators in the early '80s might have helped develop him into a Hall of Fame player."

"Ridiculous," said Garrett. "What the hell is wrong with you?"

"Garrett," snapped Gregory. "You can go now."

Garrett took his office chair by the right armrest and flipped it over. It bounced a few times before coming to rest against the wall. He slammed the door on his way out, which caused Gregory to wince and squeeze his eyes shut.

"You sure about this?" asked Gregory.

"No, I'm not, but I've already told you that if history hadn't already been altered, we would be playing the Colonials in the Series and not the Titans. Actually, Cincinnati would be playing Boston, and as I told Goofy, it was the series of the century."

"And you attribute this change to *you*? I should say, to your arrival here in 1975?"

"I opened my mouth and announced my absolute hatred for the Titans and their fat boss, Harris Kentfield. It might have been all they needed to beat the Colonials."

"I see."

"Or just the fact that I'm here might have affected everything," said Bobby.

"You don't know that."

"Mister Revenell," said Bobby. "We're going to win or lose on our own. No help from me, because I might tell you something and it could backfire. I want to play for the Quakers as long as I'm stuck here in 1975 . . . and beyond."

"Stuck?" asked Gregory, leaning back in his chair, eyebrows arched. His lips tightened down against each other. "Stuck? That's how you see it? That's good to know."

Bobby stood.

"But if you get to the ballpark one day and no one can find me, you can assume I've managed to get back home to 2020, because that's where I belong. That's where my life is."

Bobby's colorless lips drew a straight line across his face. He walked out the door of the office.

"That's where I belong," repeated Bobby.

Garrett, just down the hall smoking a cigarette, watched him leave. He walked into his secretary's office and lifted the handset from its cradle. He punched in a number.

"He just left."

****

Bobby exited Bicentennial Park in the early evening, after checking out his uniform and gear for the upcoming trip to New York City. He headed to his car, a blue 1965 Mustang Fastback, an homage to his grandfather.

Bobby had seen it in some old photographs and had an ever-present memory of the car parked in front of his grandparents' house in Audubon, New Jersey.

He opened the driver's side door and sat. Bobby pulled out his wallet and glanced at the driver's license. He smiled at the laminated copy. He stuck the key into the ignition to start the car.

The engine did not turn over. He exhaled, reached into the glove compartment, and pulled out a piece of insulated wire. He left the ignition in the "on" position.

He exited the car and popped the hood. Bobby bypassed the solenoid and the car jumped to life.

"Ford," he laughed. "How the heck did you stay in business?"

"Problem?" asked a voice in the dark. Bobby stood up so fast, he smacked his head on the hood. He dropped to the ground.

"Careful, superstar," said the voice. "Season ain't over yet."

A hand extended and helped Bobby to his feet. He saw a smiling Black man in front of him wearing a security guard uniform, but sporting a Quakers baseball cap from the '50s with the old-style "P."

"Everett Jones," said the man, 50ish, small and lean, his face a dead-on match for his twin brother, the recently deceased Cecil. Being a security guard had not turned him into a chubby chair sitter.

"Robert Young. Everyone calls me Bobby."

Everett laughed, one of those explosive laughs. "Don't I know it."

John Perelli would have called the security guard "jolly," and offered to get him a job as a department store Santa — providing Everett would gain 100 pounds.

Bobby laughed right along with him.

"That's an unusual way of starting a car," said Everett. "Do that often?"

"Only every other time."

Another laugh.

"Replace your solenoid. Of course, down the road, you'll need to replace the alternator and the generator."

Before Bobby got back into the car, he looked at Everett.

"Hope your brother turns up," Bobby said, recalling what he had heard in the locker room about Cecil's disappearance. "Any news?"

"Not even a little," said Everett, and his smile vanished. "Not like him. I'm very, very concerned at this point."

"You saved me some aggravation, Everett," said Bobby. "Anything I can do for you?"

"Yes, there is," replied the security guard, his eyes shining in the fading light. "Beat the Titans."

The grin returned to Everett's face. He shook Bobby's hand.

"We'll do our best, Everett. Thanks for the help."

****

Bobby sat in the driver's seat, closed his eyes, and listened to the uneven rumble of the 289 cubic inch V-8 engine. The four-on-the-floor shifter, a retrofit item, remained in neutral. The driver's license stared back at him after he opened his eyes.

"If you could see what a driver's license looks like in 2020," he said to the brown-and-cream-colored ID. Bobby spoke to the document, but his comments also related to the mechanical and design improvements Ford made to the unreliable 1965 Mustang his grandfather owned so long ago, and today. "Remember when we met? That was an interesting day. Meanest man on the planet, Pop-Pop."

Pop-Pop? He wiped a renegade tear from his right cheek. *Mom?*

He put the car in drive, then returned it to park, as his vision clouded.

Not a good idea, Bobby thought and closed his eyes. As he fell asleep, his mind raced through the rush of the 1975 Major League Baseball season, the Quakers, and his encounters with Garrett Revenell.

Bobby drifted in and out of sleep. He recalled the events that occurred just after the start of the regular season.

Garrett had summoned Bobby to the owner's office. Bobby shut his locker room cage door. He tossed a towel into a bin and walked out of the clubhouse to the elevators.

When Bobby arrived at the owner's box, Garrett handed him a manila packet.

Bobby took the package of fabricated documents—which included a New Jersey driver's license, a birth certificate, and a social security card—and examined the contents. He flipped the license over a few times.

"No picture?" he asked Garrett.

"Picture?" asked Garrett, distracted by something on the desk.

"And it's paper," said Bobby. "How long do you expect this will last?"

"Don't know," replied Garrett. "Get it laminated at Kmart for all I care."

Bobby lifted his eyes from the license, and leaned toward Garrett, who shrunk back behind his desk. They sat alone, distrustful faces eyeballing each other.

"What gives, Garrett?" asked Bobby. "You've been dogging me since I got here."

Garrett coughed.

"I've never been a believer in your cockamamie story, and the success of the ballclub is secondary to the fact that I think you're playing us."

"What?"

"You heard me. You hit a couple exhibition game home runs and slapped around a couple of Cosmopolitans' pitchers. So what? We trade RJ Brancatelli in the hopes that you're some Great White Hope and that Greg Stroemel's right arm will last more than a season? Why is that? Who the *hell* are you?"

"I, uh, I just want to go home, Garrett. That's all." Bobby's tone, choking out his words, put Garrett back on his heels for a moment, but the owner recovered his composure and squared his shoulders.

"Home? Take your phony documents and get out, Wonderboy."

"Oh, so you've read *The Natural*," said Bobby as he headed for the door. He cleared his throat and wiped his eyes with his right wrist.

"The what?"

"That's what I thought."

****

Bobby jerked awake in the Mustang. He rubbed his right eye. The autumn chill, combined with his body heat dissipating in the car, fogged the windows. He reached for his cellphone, which brought a laugh from him.

"Gotta look at your watch, stupid," he said to the rearview mirror. 12:35 a.m.

"Damn," he said. "I've been asleep for ten minutes. I gotta get home."

He engaged the clutch.

In the recesses of the private lot, a gunmetal green sedan turned on its headlights. An automatic garage door opened and the vehicle exited. It drove at a safe distance of several car lengths behind the Mustang, as it made its way to Bobby's home in Stratford, New Jersey.

CHAPTER TWENTY

Garrett and Greg

"Garrett, you're going to have to leave him alone sooner or later and I would suggest that you do it before Christmas, which will be here before you know it," said Gregory to his nephew. His face showed the wear and tear of dealing with the playoffs, a pennant race, the World Series, and his mercurial nephew. Creases had formed that weren't there in April.

"It's not me, Greg," replied Garrett, sitting on a chair in front of his uncle's new plexiglass desk, a replacement for the wooden one trashed during one of Garrett's violent outbursts. "The League is all over us on Mister Robert Young. They are not going away."

"This is not a problem but will become one if you continue surveilling the poor kid, even during the off-season. Is someone parked in his neighborhood now?"

"Yes."

"Are you sure you're my nephew?"

Garrett pressed his lips together. The trembling started again.

"Do not make me call security, and do not toss anything against the wall. I just had this desk delivered and you are not—"

"Not what?" Garrett's temper grabbed hold of him and he pitched backward, ending up on the ground.

"You are such a jackass," said Gregory, but Garrett said nothing and was not moving from his place on the floor.

Gregory yanked the handset out of its cradle and punched in three numbers.

"Jackie? Get the medical team up here, pronto!"

****

A few hours later, Hector Enriquez sat in the chair recently occupied by Garrett Revenell. His posture relaxed. He repeated his nervous habit of running his right hand through his curly white hair.

"Concussion," said Gregory.

"Another one?" asked Hector.

"Yes."

"Gregory, I know that you love your nephew, but grooming him to take over the team might not be in the organization's best interest right now."

"I'll stay on as long as I can, but Garrett Revenell will be the owner of the Quakers if not by the late '70s, certainly by the '80s."

"And Simmons is OK with this?"

"Simmons is OK with it, and before you ask, Brian is good with it, too."

"And your Director of Scouting?"

Gregory dropped both hands on the plexiglass, which filled the office with the crisp slapping sound. He drummed his fingers.

"Don't make me choose, Hector."

"I won't, but if you're grooming him, groom him."

"And what's that supposed to mean?"

Hector glanced out the office's bay window. He grunted at the antiseptic look of the field.

"I miss Connie Mack," said Hector.

"The man or the stadium?"

Hector laughed.

"Didn't have too many winning seasons the last twenty years he coached, but from 1901 through 1931, the Lions went to the World Series nine times and won five. If not for the Lions, the Titans would have won about ten AL titles in a row in the twenties and thirties. So, yeah, maybe I miss Connie Mack, the man. I thought it was the stadium I felt nostalgic about, but let me get sentimental for Cornelius for a moment."

"Oh, shut up."

Hector burst into laughter, as did Gregory.

"OK, smart guy, what should I do?"

Hector inhaled.

"He needs someone to report to without the same last name as him. If he has a direct line to you, his education will be incomplete, and he will never learn the discipline he needs to run a baseball team."

"That won't sit well with him."

"All the more reason, Gregory."

Hector stopped him before Gregory could respond.

"I've suggested it before, and I'll suggest it again. Have Garrett learn the job from the GM side. Simmons is willing to help, but you know that already."

"Garrett will never go for it."

"Again, all the more reason."

"Any other ideas?"

"No. If you don't want to do this, don't, but Garrett is going to continue to do the League's dirty work for them by keeping a tail on Bobby Young. That is going to come to a bad end for Garrett and for the Quakers. Come on, chief, we just won our first pennant. Stroemel and Skountzos are the cornerstones of a great rotation. Slavik is Hall-of-Fame material, and so is Nayle. Are we really going to jeopardize all of this because Garrett doesn't believe *how* a budding superstar dropped in our laps?"

"I don't believe it, either. His story, I mean. And we've uncovered nothing, right?"

"All right, Gregory, then where did he come from? Forget it. Don't answer that. Don't care what you or Garrett believe, and it doesn't matter now, does it?"

Hector got up to leave, but before he did, he warned Gregory once more.

"Believe this, though, Gregory. The Miners and the Bucks and the Stars are going to be back in 1976 with nothing but revenge on their minds. Without Bobby, we're about the *fourth* best team in the National League. And don't get me started on the Titans. That jackass Kentfield is going to reload after this season, despite the surprise win of the American League pennant. He smells blood in the water. I'd hate to be the Colonials right now."

CHAPTER TWENTY-ONE

The Floater

The morning after the Quakers' heart-attack-inducing win over the Bucks, the Brandywine Rowing Club pulled their scull out of the Schuylkill River, and flipped it over to march it back to its staging place inside the clubhouse.

Roddy McPherson felt the back of the scull drop.

"Hey!" he yelled. "Pick up the slack. You're not tired are you, Jinx?"

Roddy lifted the front of the boat and craned his neck toward the eight rowers charged with carrying the scull. David Jinx, number eight, dropped onto his knees in the shoreline mud and vomited.

"Come on!" Roddy yelled again.

Jinx raised his supporting right arm, which caused him to collapse in a heap. He pointed to his left.

On the shore, feet still in the water, lay the body of a Black man, bound and gagged. Cecil Jones' bloated face stared straight up at the morning sky. Roddy dropped his end of the scull and backpedaled in the mud until he slipped and joined David Jinx in the slop. The scull landed with a wet thud.

The police arrived after Coach McPherson called from the clubhouse. They wouldn't get an ID on Cecil for days.

CHAPTER TWENTY-TWO

New York Titans

"Strike three!"

The umpire bellowed the last out of Game One of the 1975 World Series, and added the histrionics of pulling his arm back in a mockery of anyone who had ever picked up a bow and arrow.

Titan Stadium fans blasted the field and the losing team, the Quakers, with a barrage of cheers and recriminations. The hometown Titans had taken the first contest, 7 to 3. Surprise rookie starter Dale Thompson pitched eight masterful innings. Rufus Finn closed it out with a three-pitch K of Bobby Young, who flung his bat behind him in disgust.

He'd gone zero for four with a walk, and made a crucial error in right field that led to three unearned runs in the fifth inning.

The Quakers left the dugout and hid in the visitor's locker room as the cheering from the crowd continued. The Titans had won their first World Series game since 1964, and everyone in the Quakers' locker room realized the significance of that date.

"No pep talk. No criticism, boys," said Murtaugh. "Got another one to play tomorrow."

He looked over at Grantland Garvey, the starter who had to be pulled after giving up four runs in only three innings of work.

Murtaugh addressed Echevarrian.

"Need your best tomorrow, Jose," said Murtaugh.

"You'll have it," replied Echevarrian, who glanced at Ricky Davis, another player who'd had a bad opening game. No hits. A fielding error, too. Very rare for the Gold Glove winner.

But all this was overshadowed by the wretched performance of the anticipated Rookie of the Year, Bobby Young, who didn't change out of his uniform until everyone else left the locker room.

****

The ever-helpful *Philadelphia Inquirer* displayed this headline above the fold the next day, with the first two paragraphs piling on for emphasis:

"Overmatched? Quakers lose first World Series game to Titans."

"The Philadelphia Quakers are in the World Series for the first time in team history. . . or are they? A rookie sensation pitched a great game yesterday, but unfortunately for the Philadelphia Phaithful, it wasn't Grantland Garvey.

"No. It was Dale Thompson, a pitcher with a stellar 4-2 record during the regular season . . ."

****

The next night did not improve the outlook of the Series or the Quakers' team.

"Philadelphia Phortunes do not improve"

"Echevarrian shelled"

"Espinosa goes deep twice"

"Game Two is over, and perhaps the Quakers are as well. Starter Jose Echevarrian, a 21-game winner during the regular season, left by the fourth inning after giving up six runs and two dingers by Danny Espinosa, the Titans' catcher. The final score, 9 to 3 in favor of the home team Titans. The appreciative crowd . . . "

****

After the obligatory travel day, both teams prepared for Games Three, Four, and Five in Philadelphia. Gregory Revenell tossed the *Inquirer* onto the floor of his office. He wheeled his chair to the window and dropped his head into his right hand.

Just a half hour before the start of Game Three, the field crew combed the artificial turf. The stands already held thousands of early arrivals, who booed nearly every practice play by the hated Titans, including shagging lazy fly balls. A few of the groundskeepers hustled out to the infield after the away team finished their drills and batting practice.

Red, white, and blue bunting draped the middle and upper levels in the outfield bleacher seats.

"What the hell is going on?" Gregory mumbled. "Two of our starters don't get into the fifth inning, and Ricky Davis can't buy a hit." He paused. "Our number two and three guys in the rotation looked like what they are, young players with no October experience."

His stare fixed through the bay window of his Bicentennial Park office. The Titans returned to the field after the groundskeepers finished. Quaker batting practice commenced to the delight of the crowd. The defense cursed the artificial turf after two games on grass. Duff Mackie, the All-Star second baseman, dove for a shot off the bat of Lex Slattery. It skipped by Mackie.

"No one hates AstroTurf as much as Duff!" he shouted, referring to himself in the third person.

Buster Hodges, brought in after the always-patient Harris Kentfield fired Manager Ted Lefkowitz at the halfway point of the 1975 season, pulled the trigger on what appeared to be a bad move.

But Hodges' inclusion of Lex Slattery — the reserve outfielder substituted for light-hitting shortstop Ralph Barrett in the lineup for the World Series — proved to be a brilliant move.

At the same time that Barrett found a spot on the bench, Lex Slattery hadn't played the infield since high school. But not only did Lex hit .325 for the duration of the season, he made only one error at the position through the end of the season and the playoffs. It filled a hole and solidified the Titan lineup.

****

Gregory Revenell rubbed his temples and looked down again at a message left on his desk.

"And why the *hell* would someone shoot a security guard?"

****

With only twenty minutes to go before the start of Game Three, and the first World Series contest to be played in Philadelphia since 1931, Bobby stood in front of his locker staring at a stick of deodorant. Chip Dunkirk came up behind him but resisted the urge to scare him.

"Need to tell you something, Flash."

Dunkirk told Bobby about the incident in the parking garage with Ricky Davis, and the wet firecracker sound. He also told him about the discovery of Cecil's body by the rowing team.

"You think that's when Cecil was killed?"

"Yes," said Dunkirk. "I know how much you like his brother, Everett. Mister Revenell wanted me to be the one to tell you."

"Who would shoot Cecil? Why?"

Dunkirk hesitated.

"What is it, Chip?"

"OK, you got the chance to tell me some pretty wild things over this season. You willing to listen to mine?" Dunkirk looked Bobby straight in the eye.

"You bet."

"Come with me to the Room of Silence."

****

"Grant Garvey? Ricky Davis? Jose Echevarrian?"

"Yes, and a reliever, only referred to as the oddball. Four players in total."

Bobby leaned against the workbench used by the Quakers' staff to repair equipment. He picked up a Phillips-head screwdriver and turned it over in his hand.

"You don't know this," said Bobby. "You said yourself you only made it out to the doorway, and by that time Davis was in the car of ... who?"

"A mobster named Scizzor McQueen."

"You didn't actually *hear* anything."

"OK, first of all, both Garvey and Echevarrian got shelled for the first time in over *two months*. You do remember the Black Sox scandal?"

"Yeah. Yeah. Yeah. I know. Two starters were enough to tank the Series."

"And they're up again for Games Five and Six . . . if we get that far with Skountzos and Stroemel."

Bobby put the screwdriver down.

"How do you know about Reilly?" he asked, referring to the Quakers' quirky reliever and purveyor of the screwball.

Now Chip picked up the screwdriver. He flipped it over a couple of times.

"Davis was getting changed after yesterday's loss. He mumbled something to Grantland Garvey about not needing the 'oddball.' He referred to him as their ace-in-the-hole. Since the games were blowouts, no need to tap the bullpen."

Bobby ground his teeth. He pulled his T-shirt off and fired it onto the workbench.

"And Cecil?"

"Taken out by Scizzor. I'm sure of it. I heard something that I thought was a wet firecracker going off in the locker room after the win against Cincy, but now I know it was a gun with a silencer. Not sharp enough to be anything but."

"What can we do?"

"Hope Skountzos and Stroemel bring their 'A' games, and expose Jose and Grantland. If that's the case, we confront Garvey before Game Five."

"Come on. He'll deny it."

"OK, then we go to Murtaugh."

"No way. He'll never buy it."

"He will, if Grantland blows up Game Five."

"Then we're down three games to two heading back to Titan Stadium."

Chip's grin broke his face in half. He slapped Bobby on the back.

"And that, my good friend, is going to be the greatest comeback story in World Series history, don'tcha think?"

"Oh, you are just one weird dude."

"Dude?"

"Forget it. Let's get out of here."

****

The Quakers took the field to the wan cheers of the hometown crowd, anxious to resuscitate their infamous Philly Boo Birds persona, should the, as the *Philadelphia Bulletin* put it,

"Fightin' Philadelphians Phall Phlat"

They didn't have long to wait.

****

Skountzos chatted with Slocumbe at the start of the game after the Star-Spangled Banner. The catcher jogged back to the plate and Skountzos began his pre-pitch nose twitching.

Rafael San Marco, a dangerous lead-off hitter against any pitcher, took Paul Skountzos' third pitch, a hanging curveball, and deposited it neatly over the center field wall. The Titans led 1 to 0, a total of two minutes into the game.

The boos started and continued as the number two hitter, a reborn Lex Slattery, doubled into the gap in right center. Only a brilliant play by Bobby, who snagged the ball just shy of the wall and fired a bullet to Jack Slavik, kept the speedy Slattery to two bases.

The boos escalated.

Skountzos got Gerry Sorrell to ground out into the hole between short and third, but Slattery took advantage of the weak play by Davis to take third base. Davis didn't even look Slattery back to second.

Skountzos recovered and managed to keep Espinosa in the park. The catcher, however, drove Nayle to the warning track in left field, just missing another home run. Slattery tagged up and scored. 2 to 0.

Jorge Ferro worked an eight-pitch walk.

Third baseman Craig Tate stepped into the box and drilled Skountzos' first offering over the first base bag. It disappeared into the right field corner. No one saw it except the fans in that seating area, as Bobby disappeared from the cameras. The only thing they saw was a beautiful throw from out of nowhere.

Ferro took off as soon as the ball was hit. He sprinted, if it could be called that, around third, not slowing down, and headed for the plate. He planned on scoring standing up, so he did not slide.

Unfortunately for Jorge, Bobby's throw landed in Bob Randolph's mitt on the fly, arriving in the vicinity of the plate about an hour before Ferro, who moved like he was rowing a gondola down a canal in Venice with two tourists in tow.

Inning over, but not before the Titans had drawn first blood, and silenced even the boos out of the Bicentennial Park stands.

Omar Clarke walked out to the plate to face Ross Kerwin, the Titans' veteran lefthander, and yet another Kentfield purchase in the off-season. He passed Bobby on the way and stopped.

"We start it," said Clarke, who smiled for the second time since 1973.

He dug in and Kerwin looked for a sign. He wound up. As he did, Clarke cast a glance down at Craig Tate, who played Clarke to pull the ball. The Titans' third baseman stood several feet behind the bag. He also cheated to his right to protect the line.

Clarke locked onto Tate. The ball zipped in. A fastball. Clarke dropped into a drag bunt stance by choking up on the handle and tapping the ball in Tate's direction.

Had this been a game at Titan Stadium, the natural grass would have slowed the ball enough for Danny Espinosa to make a play. But the artificial turf gave the ball the steam to die between Craig Tate and Espinosa. The two players stared at it, and in a scene reminiscent of the ending to the National League Championship Series, neither moved to make a play.

Omar Clarke took advantage of their stupor and continued running. Espinosa made a great throw, but too late.

Clarke slid safely under the tag of Duff Mackie and stood on second base. The near-comatose Quakers' crowd sprang to life and let out a 50,000-person "Yeah!"

Bobby, hitless in the first two games, walked to the righthanded side of the plate for the first time in the Series. He tightened his grip on the bat and shut his eyes, something he hadn't done since mid-September. Bobby listened as Kerwin wound up.

Kerwin, distracted by the strange move by Bobby, unleashed a breaking ball in an attempt to handcuff the batter, but Bobby's eyes snapped open as he heard the hum of the ball, and he moved his left foot away from the plate, taking the handle of his bat out of play.

There was a solid "thock!" and 50,000 people jumped to their feet as the ball rocketed off Bobby's bat and landed in the middle deck of the left field stands in mere seconds.

Tie game.

Kerwin fixed his stare on Bobby as he circled the bases. The "Phickle Philly Phaithless Phans," as one out-of-town sportswriter called them, rose to their feet and let out a Marine-style "Hoorah!" when Bobby crossed the plate. Omar Clarke gave him the obligatory high-five and low-five and the two trotted back to the dugout.

The Quakers hammered Ross Kerwin for five more runs, including a three-run homer by Bob Randolph. Buster Hodges, to a coda of catcalls, walked to the mound like he was attending Sunday morning Mass after a night of carousing with Mickey Mantle.

Paul Skountzos, morose in the dugout since his opening frame, smiled and set about mowing down the hated Titans. Murtaugh pulled him in the eighth inning with the Quakers leading 12 to 2, in the hopes of giving the club's relievers some work.

The Quakers managed to win Game Three, but the performance of Deke Reilly concerned Brian Murtaugh. Reilly gave up four runs in two innings of work. Danny Espinosa absolutely crushed a three-run home run off a pitch that Reilly described as "a screwball that only screwed us."

A somber clubhouse greeted Bobby as he trotted in from right field and shuffled through the dugout. He looked around at his teammates.

"I guess we lost," he announced.

"Hey —"

Ike Jackson started a sentence, but Bobby shut him down.

"Did you think the Titans were going to just pack up and head to the hotel after the seventh inning? Anybody? Uh . . . Bueller?"

No answer from the players.

"You all do know this is a seven-game series?"

Again, no reply.

Bobby skidded over to one of the tables that held the water dispenser. He flipped it over. The dispenser crashed to the floor. Water spouted like Moby Dick's blowhole, spurting from a crack in the top of the plastic. Ike Jackson, the subject of Bobby's scorn, received a jet of the liquid in his face, and Omar Clarke's pants looked like the pants of a child who just had an accident.

Any player who sat down after entering the clubhouse jumped to their feet. Bobby stalked the locker room.

"Best of SEVEN!" he shouted. "BEST OF SEVEN!"

"Yeah, we get it," said Ike Jackson, toweling off his trim Afro.

"Do we?" asked Bobby. "The Titans do. They just hung four on our best reliever and made a statement. They are not giving up, even after one of their starters tanked on them. Now, what are we going to do about it?"

Nothing from the players. Even Brian Murtaugh stood back. The coaches, lining the perimeter, took a full step back. Greg Stroemel stood up.

"I'm the starter tomorrow, and I hear they're coming back with *their* rookie, Thompson," he said. "I'm winning that game, and you're all coming with me."

The tension broke. Bobby walked over to Stroemel and shook his hand.

"Hey!" shouted Stroemel. "Not so hard. That's my pitching hand."

The team headed for the showers, preparing for Game Four.

****

"This ain't good," said Mad Max. She sat on one of the barstools in The Library, smoking, a tumbler of brown liquid in front of her. She downed it in one gulp. "Except for Buddy, the Titans' frontline pitching is just garbage."

"Garvey and Echevarrian."

Max slammed the glass down.

"What about them? The Quakers have one weak spot in the lineup, Davis, and are ready to slug it out with the Titans."

"Yes, I get it."

"We need some insurance, especially if Stroemel pulls one out tomorrow."

"He's gotta beat Thompson."

Max tapped some ash from her cigarette.

"See what you can do about Stroemel."

"We have gone over this," said Scizzor. "Too late."

Max, unused to refusals from her underlings, dropped her cigarette into the ashtray.

Scizzor leaned back, his body language betraying resolve. Max smiled and leaned forward, filling the negative space.

"You saying no?" challenged Max.

Scizzor's mouth twitched. He stuck an unlit cigarette in his mouth, and pulled even further away from Max.

"That's right. I have a better idea, and it involves the superstar."

"Bobby Young?"

"Yeah."

"This better be good, Scizzor, because that kid strikes me as the most, uh, untouchable of all the Quakers. Davis never even had him on any list."

"Got that. This plan takes him out of the equation. However, it's going to require a little imagination on your part, boss."

"Now, Scizzor, give me a little credit." She laughed and hacked up some nicotine.

Scizzor's mouth twitched again.

"OK, you know we think we've found the old man with the 1965 Mustang, if you buy the whole family connection in New Jersey story," said Scizzor.

"Let's say that I do."

"The weird thing is, 'Grandpa' is only old enough to be Bobby's father."

"I thought you said a little imagination."

"Stay with me, because this gets weird."

"Gets?" Another laugh and another cough.

"Trying to give you an option."

"Better be real good at this point, Scizzor. Like I been sayin'."

Scizzor left his seat and walked to the hinged part of the mahogany bar that allowed access into and out of the bartenders' area. He lifted up the gate and moved toward the display rack of the hard stuff. He poured a few ounces of tequila into a glass and threw it down. He moved back along the inside of the bar and squared up to Max.

"Let's go, Scizzor. Feels like you're stalling."

Scizzor put the tequila bottle and a couple of tumblers down on the bar.

"You agree we've found out nothing on Bobby's past. A big blank nothing except for the Mustang Fastback and the Leonards of Audubon, New Jersey. They're Bobby's *supposed* blood relations."

"Yes, I know all that. So what? The kid's a stray."

"Davis got some strange insight from Slavik. Seems Bobby is from the future, 2020 to be exact."

At this, Max slapped her right hand down on the mahogany. It echoed throughout the empty club, but laughter with a layer of broken glass soon followed the echo. She cleared the smoke from her throat and leaned back. Scizzor stole a glance at her figure, just curvy enough to give her latest tailored suit a stress test to hide her cleavage. Scizzor's interest stopped short of leering.

"Oh, man," said Max. "I've heard some good excuses for putting the muscle on someone, but that's the best one so far. Really, Scizzor, the future?"

Scizzor gulped another ounce of tequila.

"Boss, if I was looking at a ten-million-dollar payday, I'd take what I'm about to say seriously, because turning another Quaker ain't in the cards."

Max stopped laughing and stood up straight. She placed her right hand on her hip and leaned in toward Scizzor. The stale cigarette smell put off any further examination of her body.

"Your job is hanging by a hair, Scizzor."

Scizzor poured yet another shot of tequila.

"Well?"

"If this geezer *is* Bobby's grandfather, then the family's five-year-old girl is his mother, and if that's the case —"

"What?" Max laughed. "You going to make Bobby tank the rest of the Series by kidnapping the little girl?"

Scizzor spun the empty tequila glass down the bar.

"That might have been my play, and that's what it's going to look like I'm doing when I get a note to Bobby — if this Series gets any tighter."

"Look like?" asked Max.

Scizzor threw down the tequila bottle.

"I'm going to kill the little girl, Max, and then Bobby is never going to exist."

CHAPTER TWENTY-THREE

The Parking Garage

"I'm sure Scizzor was the man in the garage when Davis was out there talking," said Dunkirk.

"I thought you said the guy was named McQueen."

"Yep, Edward 'Scizzor' McQueen. Local Irish mob."

"You haven't gone to the police?"

"No, Mister Revenell. I wanted to run it by you."

Chip sat in front of Garrett Revenell the morning of Game Four, dressed in his uniform. His long legs ached tucked under the uncomfortable chair that Garrett used to keep meetings with players and visitors to a minimum.

"OK, Chip," said Garrett. "I'll get Philly PD in here, and we'll all sit down and discuss what you saw. I'm sure they'll find it very informative."

"Thank you." Chip got up to leave.

"Wait one moment," said Garrett. Chip hesitated and remained half up and half down. "Why wait until now?"

"Uh, well, geez, Mister Revenell," said Chip. "You just told me about the rowing team and the body and all that. I couldn't be sure."

"Of course. Have a good game."

"Thanks."

Chip exited the office and ran down the hall in his stocking feet. He ducked into the bathroom and hid in a stall where he panted. Sweat beaded above his eyebrows.

"God, I hate that trust-fund baby," Chip said aloud.

Dunkirk remained in the stall for several minutes. He didn't want to go down to the locker room just yet and batting practice was an hour away. He had nothing to tell Bobby.

"Yeah, except Garrett is still a slippery character," he mumbled. "The uncle has got to be so proud of—"

The bathroom door opened. Chip peeked out from the crack in the stall door. A slender man in a houndstooth suit stood over the sink and ran a comb through his hair. He pulled a brown cigarette out of a hammered aluminum case and lit it.

The smoke wafted to the top of the bathroom, and the man appeared in no hurry to leave. Chip covered his mouth and glued himself to the seat, inhaling and exhaling in rhythm with an accelerated heartbeat. The bathroom door opened again.

"What the hell are you doing up here, Scizzor?"

Garrett Revenell.

Scizzor McQueen stubbed out his cigarette on the porcelain sink and spun around from the mirror. He grinned at Garrett.

"Had to stop by and find out what my favorite owner is going to do about his rejuvenated ballclub."

Garrett grabbed McQueen by his jacket lapel and ushered him out of the bathroom. The two walked down the hallway, Garrett on the lookout for anyone else on the floor. The day after a game, there was usually a subdued atmosphere. Staff members sat dutifully at their desks staring out the windows at the field, where batting practice, prior to Game Four, was but 45 minutes away.

They took the stairs down to the garage, hustling by the locker room, and disappeared through the door and into Scizzor's car.

"Drive. And out to the water."

"Easy, Garrett, we got another plan in place but wanted to see if you had any ideas before we proceeded."

"No. Game Five and Game Six are Garvey and Echevarrian, so even if Stroemel pulls this out tonight, it's all over in a few days."

"I'm glad you're confident about that, but you know what happens when the Quakers' bats light up as they did last night. The barrages could go on for the rest of the Series, which means it's over in six games, and *not* in favor of the Titans. Max and I got that feeling yesterday."

Garrett sank back in the bucket seat.

"No argument."

"Good. So if you got no other ideas, I'm putting a safety plan in place and I want you to know about it."

"No!" Garrett shouted. "Nothing. I want to know nothing. Just do it, and don't tell me about it. The less I know—"

"Oh, cut the drama, Garrett."

Scizzor reached over and slapped Garrett with an open hand. The car went silent.

"You're in this. Your take in terms of money will be really good, and your uncle will be outta the ownership chair soon enough. If he doesn't go on his own, a little rumble of a problem will be enough to remove him. He won't be able to handle the pressure."

"Leave my uncle out of this. He's planning on retiring soon."

"Yeah, we know," said Scizzor, jabbing his finger in Garrett's chest. "Just don't want you to get splashed by the blowback, if there is any, provable or not. We need you running the show, Garrett. But we need your uncle to stick around to take the majority of the heat. Leaves you in the clear."

"Oh, no, I'm done with you once the Series is over."

Scizzor howled. His head slammed back into the headrest. He laughed for a full minute before wiping his eyes with a houndstooth handkerchief.

"You're not done with a darned thing, Garrett," he said, reaching into his jacket and showing Garrett the handle of his gun. "There is one way, and one way only that you're ever finished with people like us. Now get out of my car. I've got work to do."

Garrett stumbled out of the passenger side. He stood and brushed himself off.

Chip Dunkirk checked the hallways a few times before he closed the bathroom door behind him, and hustled down the corridor to the locker room.

"What is going on?" Dunkirk asked himself between breaths. "What is Garrett Revenell doing with the mob?"

CHAPTER TWENTY-FOUR

Two Rookies

Stroemel looked in for a sign as Duff Mackie danced off first base. A quick pickoff throw — the Titans' second baseman got caught off the bag. Out. In the visiting owner's box, Harris Kentfield, not known for his reserved manner, picked up an empty beer bottle and looked for someplace to smash it. Before he could, his Director of Scouting, Gus Vallarta, managed to restrain the boss' arm from hurling it across the room. It would have added to the pile of three others the Titans' owner had launched in the first seven innings of Game Four. The brown shards lay in a corner of the room.

"Damn it!" shouted Kentfield. "What the hell are we paying Mackie?"

Gus Vallarta, like a Valium tablet to Harris Kentfield's methamphetamine, sat down in his chair.

"Harris," said Vallarta. "Sit down. Mackie is a big reason we're here."

Kentfield grumbled.

"Picked off first base," said Kentfield. "Rookie mistake. Don't we have anyone in the farm system worth bringing up?"

"Now?" asked Vallarta, hoping the joke would ease the tension. It had the opposite effect.

"Not now, you imbecile. Spring training, so I can get rid of Mackie and his inability to stay on first base long enough to score a run."

"Harris."

"Speaking of runs, how many do we have now?"

"One, Harris."

"One? Really? How did we get that many?"

"I'm not sure," said Vallarta. "Please sit down and hang on. We have two more innings, and Stroemel is running out of steam. He's a rookie."

"Yes, like Thompson," said Kentfield. "Funny, I thought Dale Thompson was a lefty, and it looks like there's a righthander on the mound who is dominating this game, and, well I'll be, he's wearing a Quakers uniform!"

"That's right. We pulled Dale after Young took him deep last inning with that three-run home run. Oh, his second of the game, by the way."

"Gus?" asked Kentfield, sneering. "You doin' this on purpose?"

"Yep. That's a good Quakers ballclub out there, and Buster told everyone in the locker room not to forget that, especially when Skountzos threw for Game Three. We got Greek early, but they hung a lot of runs on us, and even more so than the Quakers' pitching, it's their hitting." He held up a hand to stop Kentfield from interrupting. "They're streak hitters that feed off each other, and these past two games have been a good example. It should be ten to one right now, not five to one, and would be if not for the brilliance of the defense and the grittiness of Thompson."

"Anything else before I fire you?"

"Oh, go ahead. Be the first time today."

Kentfield collapsed back into a chair. He looked for a few empty bottles in the room in preparation for the final two innings.

****

Murtaugh kept Stroemel in the game, and it looked like it would pay off in the eighth as he got two quick outs on Lex Slattery and Rafael San Marco. Stroemel got the ball back from Bob Randolph and wiped his brow.

Randolph saw this and called time. He jogged out to the mound.

"Hey, pitch," said Randolph. "It ain't warm out."

"Yeah, I know," said Stroemel, wiping the back of his sleeve across his forehead. The Quakers fans, in addition to their ambiguous loyalty, also demonstrated a finite amount of patience. They started whistling and chanting. Their boos washed over the field in waves.

"You got this next guy?" Randolph asked about Crash Warren, the Titans' reserve catcher and designated hitter.

"What do you think?"

"You're sweating."

"Give me the damn ball and let's get out of this inning."

Before Randolph could do so, Brian Murtaugh made his way to the mound.

"What's going on?"

"Nothing," said Stroemel. "I'm just trying to get clear on the signs."

Randolph nodded in the direction of the dugout, which spun Murtaugh around. The two walked away from the mound together.

"Get someone up in the bullpen," said Randolph to Murtaugh. "Now."

"Any suggestions?"

"Reilly's gotta get untracked."

"That's what worries me."

"Stroemel will be lucky to get out of this inning," said Randolph.

Murtaugh waved him off, but when he got into the dugout, he reached for the phone and called the bullpen. He had just hung up when Crash Warren launched Greg Stroemel's weakening fastball over the center field wall by a good 25 feet.

5 to 2.

Stroemel walked Gerry Sorrell on four pitches. Sorrell would be the last batter he would face.

In came Deke Reilly to face Danny Espinosa. Bicentennial Park, never a warm and inviting place to play, took on more than the October chill. Reilly warmed up and shook off the familiar feeling that his screwball was not screwing anyone but the Quakers.

Randolph's request for Deke's signature pitch went unheeded twice before Reilly served up an off-speed curveball. Danny Espinosa rattled it into the right field corner for extra bases. Sorrell scored easily, but another great throw by Bobby Young kept Espinosa at second. The tying run, Jorge Ferro, walked to the plate.

5 to 3. Still only two outs.

If Ike Jackson in his prime — with his broad shoulders, narrow hips, and strong legs — was the embodiment of the athletic baseball player, then Jorge Ferro's body defied the odds. Ferro, once called the Billy Kilmer of Major League Baseball because of his lack of off-season conditioning, stepped in.

"Don't let that middle-aged gut fool ya, Deke," said Reilly into his glove. "This guy can hit plenty."

Reilly wound up and released a screwball that actually screwed away from Ferro. Jorge tapped it harmlessly to Omar Clarke, who threw out baseball's version of a "Before" diet picture, by 89 of the 90 feet from home to first. The Titans were done in the eighth, but not before tightening a noose around the Quakers' necks.

****

Not satisfied with the Titans cutting the Quakers' lead, Kentfield bounced a couple of owner's box chairs across the floor and wagged a finger in Vallarta's face.

"Don't give me any of that Pollyanna stuff, Vallarta," he said, his face getting redder and redder.

"Wasn't planning on it."

"Good."

Vallarta watched Rufus Finn take his warmup tosses for the Quakers' half of the eighth inning. Kentfield paced.

"You sure you got nothing to say."

"Nope," said Vallarta.

"I do."

"Nobody is stopping you, Harris."

"Two runs. We just need two runs, and we can tie this up and take it to extra innings, right? That's all we need."

"Exactly right."

"We should be able to get those. I mean we've got Craig Tate and then Smythe and there's two dingers right there."

"Yes. Back-to-back homers would do the trick," said Vallarta.

"That's what I said."

"You're right, Harris."

****

Rufus Finn gave up a lead-off single to Bobby, who now had five hits on the day—two home runs, a double, and two singles. He'd knocked in four of the five Quakers' runs, including the three-run home run. Finn, though, held onto the two-run deficit, even after Bobby stole second and took third on a fielder's choice. Ike Jackson stranded him there with a fly ball that sent Rafael San Marco all the way back to the 410 sign in center field. In any other part of Bicentennial Park it would have meant two more runs for the home team, but all it turned into was a very long out.

The Quakers took the field.

Reilly warmed up before Craig Tate dug in.

"OK, Deke, what's it gonna be?" he asked his glove. Tate abruptly stepped out and asked for time. He walked back over to Buster Hodges, then returned to home plate.

"What a con job," said Reilly to his glove. "Freakin' Titans and their espionage. All Tate just said to Buster Hodges was 'Hey skip, how about a few pops after we come back on these bush leaguers?' What a jack—"

"Hey, Tate!" yelled Reilly, lowering the glove from his face. "How about we play ball?"

Reilly waved at the umpire and finished the last word into his glove.

He wound up and threw another beautiful screwball. Tate swung at the pitch, which made for the middle of the plate, but tailed away at the last moment. He swung so hard he screwed himself into the ground.

Tate found himself staring at the golden-colored dirt in the batter's box. He got to his feet and reset himself. Reilly fired a changeup, which took so long getting to the plate that it dropped on top of the rubber surface and bounced up in front of Bob Randolph.

"Uh, ball one," intoned the umpire.

Reilly had Tate off-balance, but the Titans' third baseman ran the count full after Deke threw a ball just off the plate that Tate didn't chase. Randolph hustled out to his pitcher.

"Don't walk this guy," said Randolph.

"Thanks, Bob. I'll keep that in mind."

"No. No. Nothing cute. Throw him the screwball. That's it. I'll keep calling for other pitches, and talking to Tate, but just keep throwing the screwball. You'll get him."

"Really? I was wondering what I was doing out here."

"Deke, trust me on this. He doesn't like hitting against you, and it's because of that screwball. Anything else doesn't scare him."

"Just screwballs?"

"Yep."

Randolph ran back before the umpire could complain again about the length of the discourse between the battery mates. Tate stepped in.

Deke whipped a screwball aiming for Tate's belt buckle. It bent away and into the strike zone. Tate reacted late and fouled off the pitch.

"Damn it," said Reilly to his glove.

This scenario played itself out five more times with Tate barely getting a piece of the ball. Deke felt a twinge in his shoulder. He wiped his mouth and dug his chin into the pain.

"Not now."

Deke wound up, but this time delivered a screwball aimed right down the middle of the plate. Tate hitched his bat, pointing the barrel toward the mound and swung.

"Strike three!" the umpire announced. One down. Tate was gone.

But Reilly was done. He raised his gloved hand.

****

"Ah, damn it," said Murtaugh. He trotted out to the mound. In the bullpen, both Slade Maberry and Nate Watson got up and started throwing.

"Make it quick, Brian!" the umpire barked.

Murtaugh grunted.

"How is it, Deke?" asked Murtaugh.

"Not good, but a day off will help."

"Yeah, we'll just hope Grantland can go deep tomorrow."

"Sorry."

Reilly handed the ball to Murtaugh, who signaled for Slade Maberry, the righthander, to face Tanner Smythe, the Titans' first baseman, so far having a quiet Series.

"How ya feelin', Slade?"

"Could use a few more tosses," he acknowledged.

"Take as many as you want."

Randolph and Murtaugh left the mound. Maberry started throwing, but the umpire walked into the left-side batter's box after a half-dozen throws and signaled that he wanted to get going.

Murtaugh sprinted from the dugout, but Maberry waved him off.

"Ready to go, skip," shouted Maberry.

"You'd better be," muttered Murtaugh, as he made his way back to the dugout steps.

Maberry wound up and delivered a pitch that sailed over Smythe's head. Murtaugh smacked himself on the forehead. Jack Slavik, never one to show much emotion or even interest, stood up from his third base position and spat at the bag.

"What the—?"

Maberry got the ball back from Randolph after Randolph chased it down, but the umpire wanted a new one, which he tossed out to Maberry. Randolph called for another fastball.

****

"Be glad Reilly is out of there, boss," said Vallarta. "He was throwing a really nasty screwball."

"He made Tate look like a rookie," said Kentfield. "How could he have fallen for that last pitch? It was a foot outside."

"Kinda the idea of a screwball against a righthanded batter, Harris."

Kentfield had enough.

"You need to leave," he said to Vallarta.

"Thought you'd never ask," replied Vallarta, who grabbed his sport coat and sprinted out of the owner's box.

Kentfield once again found himself alone. As he thrummed his fingers on the narrow counter in front of him, he honed in on Smythe, whose count sat at two balls and no strikes.

"C'mon Smythe," said Kentfield. "I'm signing those big checks."

****

Maberry, behind in the count, shook off Randolph's request for another fastball and delivered a changeup.

Which Smythe sent to intercept Voyager as it passed by Mars. It disappeared over the left field wall so deep that Steve Seacourt didn't even bother to turn around to watch.

5 to 4.

Murtaugh wasted no time. He ran out to the mound and pointed to his left arm. Nate Watson jumped into the Bicentennial Park golf cart and buzzed out to the mound.

Watson arrived to find an argument ensuing.

"I needed more time, skip," said Maberry.

"Yes, well three pitches and we're making a change, Slade," said Murtaugh. "I'm not leaving you out here. You ain't got it tonight."

"One more batter," said Maberry, who gripped the ball tight.

Murtaugh, not accustomed to getting called out by his players, backed up a half step. He put his hands on his hips.

"Slade, don't make this hard on us."

"I got the next two."

"No, you don't," said Murtaugh.

"Coach, let's go!" the umpire shouted out to the mound. "Keep this up and I'm going to have to complain to the League."

"Making a pitching change, Jim!"

"Well, make it and let's get going."

Murtaugh turned back. Maberry still held the ball.

Hector Enriquez sprinted from the dugout. Maberry saw him coming and dropped his glove. He squared up to face Enriquez. Murtaugh got between them. Behind them the three field umpires closed in on the mound.

Jim Thomas, the plate umpire, arrived.

He said nothing, but pointed to Slade Maberry, whose right hand closed even tighter around the game ball. With his left hand, Jim Thomas threw Slade Maberry out of the game.

"You're gone, son," said Thomas. "You don't leave this mound, I will throw you out for the rest of the Series. Got it?"

Maberry slammed the ball into Nate Watson's mitt and stalked into the dugout.

Fifty-thousand respiratory systems exhaled when Duff Mackie, Watson's first batter, flied out to Moses Pendleton, who tucked the ball away with both hands. But the Quakers were still somewhat unsettled. Not ever having gone to the big dance showed as Moses Pendleton fluttered the ball into Omar Clarke. Two outs.

Then Clarke barely got the ball to Watson, who almost dropped it.

Buster Hodges asked for a time-out. He scratched at his mustache as he surveyed the bench. He pointed at Bruce Wells, the long-ball-bashing designated hitter, who'd had a rough 1975 regular season. A surprise, given the southpaw Watson.

Wells, himself a lefthanded batter, hesitated.

"Let's go, Bruce!" Hodges shouted at Wells.

****

In the owner's box, Harris Kentfield pitched a fit. He tossed his coffee mug across the room and swept away what few papers lay in front of him. He grabbed the desk phone and called the dugout.

Hodges answered.

"Not now, Harris!"

"What the hell are you doing, Buster? Wells is a lefty. You've got a lefty on the mound. Don't ya think—"

But Hodges had hung up.

Kentfield pulled the phone jack out of the wall, and sat down so hard that he hurt the bones in his keister. He shoved his considerable behind around in the chair and swore at the pain to go away.

Wells, as surprised as anyone about his choice as pinch-hitter, took a series of practice swings. He pulled on the collar of his Titans' jersey, and sized up Watson.

The light wind in Bicentennial Park ceased. Watson wiped his mouth on his sleeve. The former closer for the Knights had bounced around the Majors for eight years. He'd never been able to duplicate his early seasons with St. Louis, where he had averaged 15 saves a year for four years. Ironically, during this second stint with the Quakers, Watson had cobbled together a decent season as one of the League's first set-up pitchers.

No longer a reliable closer, yet here he stood, one out from victory on his shoulders. The power-hitting Wells squared up. Watson, his signature poker face on display, flipped the ball around inside his glove. Randolph called for a curveball to come in on Wells' hands. Watson shook him off.

Randolph again called for a curveball, but outside the strike zone. Watson signaled agreement and went into the stretch. The pitch flew in and Wells turned on it and drove it deep toward the opposite field, but foul.

Watson exhaled into the glove. He held the ball in his left hand and looked in for the sign. He delivered and just missed the inside corner. He snapped the ball back into his glove when Randolph returned it and called for the curveball one more time.

A sickening crack halfway through Wells' swing signaled a broken bat. The barrel flew down the third base line and over the bag. Wells held onto the handle as the ball drifted out over the left side of the infield and headed for Texas Leaguer territory with all the makings of a bloop single.

Jack Slavik dodged the bat barrel, which set him on a direct course for the ball. He hustled into left field. Ricky Davis also made a straight line for the erstwhile hit. They arrived at the same time.

Both shouted "Mine!" in stereo several times.

The ball dropped out of the black sky, and Slavik reached over with his free right hand and shoved his infield mate to the ground. He snared the ball just before it got beyond his compromised reach.

The roar from the ecstatic crowd drowned out Slavik as he pulled Davis up from the artificial turf.

"What the *hell* were you thinking?" shouted Slavik, below the ongoing din. "That was mine from the start!" He held onto Davis' forearm tighter, and the two came face to face.

Davis broke Slavik's grip and stepped back in disgust.

"I called for it!" Davis defended himself.

"BS," said Slavik, staring at Davis. The crowd's cheers dropped as the drama on the field unfolded. Slavik advanced on Davis. "What is wrong with you? You can't buy a hit! Your fielding looks like Triple-A, and now you forget infield protocol? Get your head in the game, Ricky. It's the World Series. This ain't some—"

Moses Pendleton spotted the confrontation and ran over from center field. He forced himself between the two.

"Hey! We won! Settle this later. We won the game!"

The Quakers had tied the Series at two games apiece.

****

Kentfield tromped out of the owner's box and headed for the visiting team's locker room. When he arrived, he found that Buster Hodges had already departed.

"I know where he hangs out in Philly," said Kentfield to Gus Vallarta, who had the unpleasant task of telling Harris about Buster's escape.

"Harris," whispered Vallarta. "Take it easy. Wells' first swing goes fair, we're still playing. Buster made a good call."

"But not the right one. He's going to hear about it from me."

****

In a luxury box, Max snapped a pen in half, the ink spurting everywhere, but not anywhere near her.

"I see Scizzor decided not to watch the game with me," she said out loud. "He better hope Garvey and Echevarrian perform as badly over the next two games as they did for the first two. I really don't wanna see a seventh game with that lefthanded freak of nature on the mound, Twitchy Paul Skountzos."

Max stomped out of the luxury box, her goons close behind.

CHAPTER TWENTY-FIVE

Cecil Jones and Game Five

"Don't even have a crime scene yet," said the detective.

"Let's just add that on top of no motive, no gambling debts, and a happy marriage. We're exactly where we were when the body was found."

"Anything else?" asked his lieutenant, who covered a yawn. He rubbed two tired eyes.

"Other than the fact that there's no reason this poor guy should be dead? No, there is nothing else."

"That's just great."

****

"And what would you tell the police?" Bobby asked as he dusted his toes with athlete's foot powder and pulled on his socks. He had his back to Chip Dunkirk.

"I don't know."

"Look, Chip, nothing Garrett does surprises me. If his best friend works for the mob, or, now hang on, try this one—" He looked over his shoulder to Chip, "—If you asked me, 'Who in the organization would have a very good friend in the mob,' I'd say, drum roll please, 'Garrett Revenell.'"

"What about Davis' visit? And the car. It belongs to Scizzor McQueen."

Bobby stood, spun around, and placed his right hand on his friend's left shoulder.

"You wanna do something for Cecil?"

"Yes, I do."

"Help us win two more games against the Titans."

****

Grantland Garvey, roughed up in Game One, pitched a quick first and second inning, but in the third, with the game scoreless, gave up consecutive doubles to Duff Mackie and Lex Slattery for the first Titans' run. He walked Titans' starter, Buddy Sieracki.

- 175 -

Murtaugh called time and went to the mound for what the fans saw as about the 100th trip in the Series. They booed.

Murtaugh shrugged.

"Not looking like the regular season again, Grant," said Murtaugh, staring at Garvey through a suspicious right eye.

Garvey avoided Murtaugh's eyes and looked down into the confines of his glove.

"It's just two batters, skip," he said.

"Three. You walked the pitcher, Grant."

"Just missed a few times."

Murtaugh took a half-step back from Garvey. He rubbed his bloodshot nose and signaled to the bullpen. Veteran Sam McGee got up and started throwing. Everett Hayes, a lefthanded spot starter, got up as well.

"Top of the lineup," said Murtaugh, handing the ball back to Garvey. "You're on a short leash. Next time I'm out, you know what the deal is."

"OK, skip."

Garvey took the ball from Murtaugh, who returned to the dugout. Randolph reclaimed his spot behind home plate.

Rafael San Marco stepped to the plate. Garvey checked Sieracki at first and Lex Slattery at second and decided he didn't need to go from the stretch. Garvey went into his windup and San Marco took a ball low. Randolph called for another low fastball in an effort to keep anything out of the power-hitter's wheelhouse.

Garvey wound up and delivered. Randolph winced. From the time the pitch left Garvey's hand he knew it would be up in the strike zone. The only question remaining was what San Marco would do.

Randolph lifted his glove.

San Marco watched as the stitches came into focus.

He jumped on the pitch and drove it into the right field corner. He took off, not even looking at the hit. He sped down the first base line. San Marco turned and went for two. And then for three.

In right field, Bobby Young sprinted into the corner. Two runs scored, but Bobby concentrated on San Marco. The hit was a sure double, but Bobby had his sights set on third base.

He took the ball on a carom off the foul ball side of the right field wall. It dropped into his glove but stayed there only for an instant. San Marco flew by Davis and launched himself into a traditional hook slide. Dirt from the baseline flew up in front of San Marco's right cleats, as Slavik took a bullet from Bobby on one hop and tagged out San Marco.

An unbelievable throw from Bobby Young, but the damage was done. The Titans had given 25-game winner Buddy Sieracki a 3 to 0 lead, which proved to be more than enough as the righthander breezed through the Quakers' lineup for more than seven innings.

Sieracki, who the Titans would have loved to see start a Game Seven if he could get even one extra day of rest, got the hook from Buster Hodges after getting Ricky Davis to ground out to start the Quakers' eighth.

Hodges then handed the ball to Byron Snider, the righthanded Titans' closer. Snider threw a dozen warmup pitches.

Chip Dunkirk stepped out of the on-deck circle as a pinch hitter, his first at-bat in the World Series. He whooped it up as he Irish-jigged his way to the plate, and proceeded to lace a single between Duff Mackie and Tanner Smythe. The dance continued after Chip got to the bag. Smythe growled at Chip.

"You're gonna die here, Chip," said Smythe, making reference to the looming possibility of a double play.

Snider started the next batter, lead-off man Omar Clarke, with an off-speed pitch. Clarke topped the ball, and it shot up in the air directly in front of the plate. Espinosa took no chances with the ball staying fair. He grabbed it bare-handed and threw to first to get Clarke by a step. Dunkirk, though, made it safely to second and motioned to Smythe.

"Hey, Trog!" Chip shouted. "How about another prediction?"

Smythe dropped his head and spat on the ground.

Bobby took his stance on the left side of the plate to face Snider, who worked a full count with a series of pitches barely on the plate. Espinosa called time and ran out to the mound, his trail filled with a waterfall of boos and whistles.

"What do you think?" he asked Snider.

"Whew," said Snider. "Really don't want Slavik making it to the plate. Not this inning."

"Yep. How about coming in on the hands? You been painting the outside part really well, but now he's waiting on it."

"OK, slider in and down."

Espinosa trotted back, pulling his mask down as he went. The crowd quieted.

"Espinosa!" yelled one fan from behind home plate. "Can you wear that mask all the time? You are one ugly mother—"

The crowd drowned out the last part of the taunt as Bobby stepped back in and took a practice swing. Snider whipped a slider, and Bobby stepped out with his right foot and caught the pitch on the barrel. The ball found the alley between San Marco and defensive replacement Gene Dailey. It landed just beyond the grasp of San Marco, but he recovered and got to his feet. The Titans' outfielders raced each other to the ball. Dailey got to it first and came up throwing. Dunkirk scored, and halfway back to the dugout, turned around to watch the rest of the play unfold.

Bobby rounded second and headed for third when he noticed that Dailey had some trouble getting the ball out of his glove. Every fan in Bicentennial Park stood when they saw Bobby continue at the same speed after his foot hit the bag, foregoing the safe double.

Dailey hit the cut-off man, Mackie, on the fly. Mackie, who saw Bobby sprinting right through second base, spun on his left foot and threw a strike to Craig Tate.

Too late. Bobby slid away from the tag to the inside of the bag, something Tate didn't expect. The Titans' third baseman missed Bobby's right leg.

****

In the visiting owner's box, Gus Vallarta didn't hesitate to run out the door and into the safety of the corridor. Behind him, he heard Harris Kentfield shouting and throwing bottles and drink cups around the box.

"The world's oldest rock star," said Vallarta, who waited for the tantrum to subside. He pulled his sport jacket on and walked back inside.

"Maybe you could sign him in free agency," said Vallarta. "Quakers only have him for a year."

Kentfield had his back to the door when Vallarta walked through.

"Don't think I'm not thinking about it," said Kentfield, who grimaced when Slavik lofted a deep fly ball to center. San Marco gathered it in, but Bobby scored from third. "That kid is killing us on both sides, offense and defense. Where the hell did he come from?"

"And only twenty-one years old," said the non-plussed Vallarta. "Nobody seems to know where he's from. Does it matter?"

Kentfield grunted and turned his attention back to the field. He wrapped his feet around the chair legs. The corners of his mouth twitched. 3 to 2.

Two outs, but Rick Nayle and Ike Jackson, both home run threats, were due up next.

****

Espinosa stomped out to the mound again.

"Don't lift that face mask!" some joker shouted. Espinosa ignored the taunt.

"Nothing good," said Espinosa to Snider. "These guys are feeling it."

"Got it, Daddy-O."

Espinosa returned. Rick Nayle, into a groove after a one-for-eight start, stood at the plate. An empty popcorn box bounced behind home. Morty Addams, the veteran umpire, held up a hand, delaying Snider. The Titans' bat boy ran out of the dugout and grabbed the offending piece of paper trash and ran back. The crowd whipped itself back into a standing single-voiced yell, as Snider wound up.

"Strike," yelled Addams. Nayle stepped back and wrapped his hands around the barrel of the bat.

Snider wound up for the next pitch and delivered.

The entire stadium leaned forward as the ball headed toward the right field fence. It slowed as a cool autumn breeze blew in just before it crested the yellow stripe that marked the top of the wall. Left fielder Gerry Sorrell gathered in the ball as he stood about halfway into the warning track, then ran in from the outfield to the Titans' dugout.

A collective sigh escaped the stadium. The Quakers hit the field for the ninth inning.

****

The luxury box that held Max and Scizzor also contained four bodyguards and a few "professional models." The occupants all clapped when the third out was recorded. Clarice, the obligatory platinum blonde in the mix, catwalked to the bar and poured a couple of ounces of tequila into a paper cup.

"Cheers!" She lifted the cup and gestured toward Max and Scizzor, who hadn't moved from their seats.

"Need three more outs, doll," said Scizzor. He hadn't taken a bathroom break since the third inning, and decided, with the Titans at bat, that now might be a good time. He left the box and walked to the private restrooms.

A sign that read, "Please have patience while the crew services your restrooms!" greeted Scizzor. The sound of a rusty razor blade scraping three days of beard, escaped from his throat and he walked by the taped-off entrance to the restrooms. Scizzor took the elevator and went all the way down to the players and staff level.

"Baseball fan bathroom?" he asked himself as the elevator arrived. "Not a chance in hell."

****

"Nature calls," said Dunkirk to the balance of the Quakers in the dugout, when he returned after scoring. "I'll be back for the ninth inning rally."

Chip ran faster out of the dugout than he had between third and home when he notched the Quakers' first run. He accelerated into the clubhouse bathroom.

No toilet paper.

"Aaaarggghhh!" Chip shouted at the ceiling. He was on his feet and out the door.

He shoved open the swinging door to the bathroom on the players' level and settled into the stall closest to the door.

"Ten minutes, Chip," he mumbled to the toilet paper roll.

****

Scizzor found the bathroom, which was not more than a slight upgrade from the ones on the fan level—bad lighting due to a broken bulb or two, sinks neglected, and a depressing lack of lockable stalls. His heels clacked on the floor. The sound echoed into the sanctuary of Chip Dunkirk. He sat on the porcelain throne, not ten feet from Scizzor McQueen.

Through the space between the stall door and the stall wall, Chip saw a flash of houndstooth fabric.

McQueen. What is it about bathrooms in this stadium?

Scizzor finished his business and headed to the sink. The door opened again.

One of the bodyguards walked in.

"What gives, Trip?" asked Scizzor, who did not look up from the sink.

"Boss sent me after you."

"Really. And why is that, Trip?"

"Wants to make sure you're back for the end of the game. Didn't like you not showing for the last one."

"She made that clear."

Trip, stuffed into a polyester suit, crossed his hands in front of him at belt buckle level.

"You 'bout ready?"

"What's the hurry?"

"C'mon Scizzor," said Trip, rocking back and forth, and from side to side. "You know what she's like."

"Yeah," said Scizzor as he washed his hands. "But she's going to be a lot easier to deal with once that bet on the Titans pays off. Garvey and Echevarrian held up their part, at least so far they have, and their turn in the rotation is coming up next. Davis has also. And haven't really seen that oddball relief pitcher in any situation where he'd have to lay down."

Scizzor dried his hands. In his stall, Dunkirk's cleats slipped and skidded on a tile.

"Let's go. I hope to see Davis make the last out," said Scizzor, ignoring the sound.

Trip said nothing but raised a finger to his lips. Scizzor's hand went to his jacket pocket and he pulled out enough of the gun to show the handle.

The bodyguard moved down the line of stalls. He stopped at the first one with a closed door, and caught a glimpse of someone inside. Scizzor pulled the gun out and pointed it in the direction of the stall.

****

The Quakers, down to their last three outs and still trailing by a run, watched Snider take his last warmup throw.

"Fastball's movin', Ike," said Murtaugh to the first batter, Ike Jackson.

"Yeah, I see that."

Ike Jackson dropped his 40-ounce bat and picked up the lighter 38-ounce version. He headed for the plate.

Murtaugh scanned the dugout.

"Where's Goofy Dunkirk?"

"You pinch-hit him last inning, skip," said Moses Pendleton incidentally passing by on his way to the on-deck circle. "He scored, and then headed to the john."

"Been gone a while," said Murtaugh. "Phil!"

Phil Ostrowski, down the dugout rail from Murtaugh, leaned back so the coach could see him.

"Go check on Dunkirk. Make sure he didn't get lost."

"Will do."

Ostrowski slogged by the bench through the empty clubhouse and down the corridor to the locker room.

"Man, by the time Phil gets there, if Chip ain't done with his business . . ."

Omar Clarke's offhand remark drew some laughs as Ike Jackson ran the count to two balls and two strikes.

****

Trip lifted his right leg to kick in the door to the stall, but the handle flipped over, and a surprised-looking Chip Dunkirk sat inside. The men looked at each other.

"This ain't good, Scizzor. It's one of the Quakers."

"No, that ain't good. Get him out here."

"Hey!" demanded Trip. "Out here! Now!"

Scizzor lifted the gun in Chip's direction. Chip stumbled to his feet, pulling his pants up past his sternum. He lowered them to the appropriate height, but remained rigid inside the stall, his head down.

Scizzor put away his gun. The bodyguard reached in to grab Dunkirk. Chip lifted his head and held up one finger, which stopped Trip's hand about a foot from his throat.

Chip reached into his ears and pulled out two significant amounts of toilet paper, each wadded into a tight ball.

"Sorry, I wear these when I'm hitting. Didn't hear you two come in."

Trip dropped his arm and motioned to Scizzor.

"Cuts down on crowd noise. Didja see me score? I gotta get back because it's the ninth, but I really had *to go*. I don't recognize you two. What do you do for the Quakers? You look like investors. Didn't know the Revenells had investors. Are you from another club? Maybe the Titans. Yeah, that would explain the clothes."

Chip would have continued babbling to cover his nerves, but Trip cut him off.

"We aren't investors. Just enjoying da game."

Dunkirk walked over to the sink and washed his hands.

"Enjoy the rest of the game, guys!"

He exited. Phil Ostrowski met him in the corridor. Chip grabbed the ancient-looking Quakers' coach by the shoulders.

"Get me back into the locker room," panted Chip, his breath coming in short bursts.

****

Ike Jackson returned to the dugout after popping out. Moses Pendleton took Snider's first pitch and drilled a double down the third-base line. Buster Hodges held a brief conference at the mound.

"Short leash, Byron," said Hodges.

Bob Randolph moved Pendleton to third when he sent a slow roller toward second. Duff Mackie barehanded it and threw Randolph out at first. Only 90 feet separated Moses Pendleton and the Quakers from a tie game, with Ricky Davis due up next.

Davis left the on-deck circle. Chip Dunkirk and Ostrowski made it back to the dugout. Murtaugh caught a glimpse of Chip as he dropped down on the dugout bench. Chip did not look well. Already light-skinned, he looked even paler than usual. Beads of sweat rolled from his forehead and he appeared to be hyperventilating.

"Chip?"

"Can't let Davis bat," whispered Dunkirk, who leaned over, puked—and passed out.

Bobby Young walked the length of the dugout and with the help of Ostrowski, took Chip into the trainer's room. They propped him up on one of the tables.

The team trainer rushed in. He hooked up a saline bag to hydrate Chip and placed an oxygen mask over his nose and mouth.

"His breathing has slowed," said Dominick, a man as wide as he was tall. "He'll be OK. Wonder what caused him to hyperventilate so badly?"

"He kept muttering something about Ricky Davis," said Ostrowski.

A collective groan from the stadium filled the trainer's room.

Dominick looked at Bobby.

"Guess we gotta win two at Titan Stadium."

CHAPTER TWENTY-SIX

Elizabeth Leonard

"Scizzor," Max began. "I've decided I am not taking any chances with this. Have you seen Bobby Young's stats for this Series?"

"Yes," Scizzor replied, his tone reticent and weak.

"He's hitting over .500 and has at least one home run in every game since the opener at Titan Stadium. He's chased down a lot of sure hits in the outfield and thrown out more runners in five games than anyone has ever done in seven."

In the living room of Maxine's fashionable Chestnut Hill home, Scizzor reached for his cigarettes.

"Grab the little girl," said Max. "No smoking in the house."

"We're up three games to two, and we're going back to Titan Stadium," said Scizzor, who was jonesing for a cigarette. "And you still want me to snatch a five-year-old girl on the off-chance that she's related to our mystery player? I'm sorry I ever suggested it. It ain't worth it, chief."

"This one was your idea," said Max, outfitted in another gray, form-fitting suit. "Now hang on. *Only* if the Quakers take it to a Game Seven do I want you to do this."

Scizzor pulled a single cigarette out by deftly removing it from its pack. He lifted it up in front of his face and showed it to Max with a pleading look.

"Oh, go ahead, Scizzor," said Max, waving a hand. "One cig in the house ain't gonna be hard to get rid of. But just one."

Scizzor lit the cigarette and took a calming pull. He held the smoke and walked over to the casement window at the back of the kitchen. He exhaled.

"Like I said, sorry I suggested it," said Scizzor. "And the least you can do is let me smoke. See? Fresh air. No problem with the smoke."

"It sticks to the furniture. The smell."

"I'll exhale out the window."

"Doesn't matter."

"You smoke. Why are you so darned peculiar about your house?"

"Just enjoy your cigarette and shut up for a minute. You're starting to bug me."

Scizzor did just that. The cigarette-in-the-house-conversation ended.

"Give me the particulars, Scizzor."

Scizzor took another long pull on the cigarette, exhaled, and held his cigarette out the window.

"Little Betty gets home from kindergarten around one p.m. She stays with the neighbors until around three-thirty. Mom comes home from working at Campbell's Soup not long after that. We have a narrow window to grab the kid, but Mom won't be a problem if she walks in."

"And what about Dad?"

"He's not usually back from his produce stand in Philly until four. I wouldn't worry about Dad. He's about a hundred and fifty pounds in winter clothes."

Max grabbed the cigarette out of Scizzor's hand, and stuck it in her mouth. She motioned for Scizzor to light another one. Both leaned on the window sill and smoked.

"Dad's been known to slap Mom around once in a while," said Scizzor. "So maybe I let Trip stick around and give him what for."

Max took another drag. The cool October weather sent another light breeze into the house and pushed the smoke inside.

"But only if I can watch," said Scizzor.

They laughed.

****

Garrett Revenell, his right leg shaking underneath his desk, looked across it at Chip Dunkirk and Bobby Young. The players had come to him with the story of mobsters, an all-star shortstop in the middle of a scandalous throwing of the World Series, and a request for the manager of the ball club that he could not possibly fulfill. Brian

Murtaugh, head bowed from stress and bad posture, stood next to the desk on Garrett's side.

"You are not serious," said Murtaugh.

Dunkirk, the blood still not bringing any color to his face, lifted his gaze to Murtaugh.

"Serious as a heart attack, skip. Can't put two and two together any better than this and it always comes up four."

"English, Goofy," said Murtaugh.

"Eddie Cicotte and Lefty Williams from the Black Sox of 1919. Same as Garvey and Echevarrian," said Dunkirk. "Can't give away four games for sure without two starting pitchers guaranteeing two starts apiece."

"Wait a minute," said Garrett. "How do you go from some chance meeting in a bathroom to involving three players, including one of the best shortstops in the game?"

Dunkirk, Bobby's hand on his shoulder for support, addressed Garrett.

"Garvey's blown up *twice*. He never had two bad starts in a row the entire season. Jose Echevarrian was clutch all the way down the stretch and through the Series with Cincinnati, and then he tanks? Something wrong here."

"They can't take the pressure," said Garrett.

"You know that ain't true," interjected Murtaugh, but was quick to add, "I am not buying Chip's full story, but something is off, especially with Garvey."

Garrett yelped and slapped his hands down on the desk. Everyone shifted at the sound.

"Who do we pitch, then?" he asked.

Murtaugh, whose eyes hadn't left the floor, lifted them and focused on Bobby and Chip.

"Tony Edwards," said Murtaugh. "If I believe this, which I do not."

"I'm very glad to hear that, Brian," said Garrett, "though I might have gone with Escondido."

"The only chance we'd have is with a complete misdirection, and Tony is lefthanded. And he had a much better season than Everett Hayes."

Garrett's leg continued its own personal foxtrot. The two players fidgeted in their seats and eyed the door. Murtaugh shifted his gaze back and forth from Chip to Bobby.

"You been awful quiet, Flash," said Murtaugh.

"I wasn't there with Chip."

"You believe him."

"Yep."

Garrett barked out a laugh.

"Really? Can we go over this again? I mean, humor me with this fiction."

Bobby stood and banged his fist on the desk. Garrett's paper clip holder jumped, as did Garrett.

"We should have swept the Titans by now! They've got one really good pitcher who we could have taken in Games One and Five, but for Garvey laying down. Their lineup includes a converted outfielder playing shortstop, a Cleveland Rocker, and a guy in the outfield who looks like he should be drinking beer and watching the game at home."

"Now hold on, Mister Philly Phenom —"

"Let's go, Chip," said Bobby. "And coach, put Edwards in. Your instincts are right. Titans won't be expecting a lefty. Not even a little."

The players left the room. Garrett waited until the door shut.

"You are pitching Echevarrian tonight."

"I haven't decided," said Murtaugh. "You know he's had arm trouble all year, and he looked it in Game Two."

"You're joking. He won twenty-one games this year. Only Skountzos won more."

"I know that, and I wish I could count on him. I'm going down to watch him throw in the bullpen." Murtaugh paused. "And I'm going to watch Edwards throw in the inside batting cage, the one next to *our* clubhouse. Don't want to tip off the Titans if we're going with Tony."

"Brian, don't even think about that."

"Garrett, I'm getting us to a Game Seven. I am. Jose Echevarrian might not be my best option tonight," said Murtaugh, his voice rising toward the end. "And why are you so damned interested in what I might do to *win* a game? You should at least have called the Philadelphia Police about Scizzor McQueen. He's been involved in a lot of sports gambling over the years."

"Sports gambling," said Garrett. "Not throwing the World Series."

"Forget it, Garrett. Have you at least told your uncle?"

"Wouldn't bother him with something as silly as this."

"Tell your uncle, Garrett. He'd want to know."

Murtaugh walked out of the owner's box.

Garrett waited what he thought was long enough for Murtaugh to get to the elevator and be on his way to the locker room. He walked across the hall and into an empty administrative office. He paced the room for fifteen minutes before snatching a desk phone out of its cradle and dialing a number.

"You ready for tonight?"

Garrett waited silently until the voice on the line finished.

"Just want you to be prepared," said Garrett. "Murtaugh is thinking about using Tony Edwards instead of Echevarrian."

The voice on the line got louder.

"I did," said Garrett. "I did try to make that clear, but he's watching both of them throw right now, so maybe you could get that information to the right person.

"Buster Hodges ain't gonna care about any of that stuff. There is no way anyone associated with the Titans is gonna get dirty on this. This deal was struck with the Quakers. They lose this. It doesn't involve the Titans. You know that.

"It's the best I can do for now. Edwards is lefthanded and no one on the Titans is expecting that."

Garrett jerked his head away from the phone as the person on the other end of the line slammed the phone down.

CHAPTER TWENTY-SEVEN

Game Six and the Extortion Gambit

"Who's the mole, Buster?" asked Murtaugh at home plate, as he and Buster Hodges exchanged lineup cards.

"Just some last-minute changes," said Hodges. "I saw Edwards throwing out there in the bullpen. Looked him up. Good season for a rookie. I'd check your own backyard for a mole."

"So you're benching Smythe, Tate, and Wells?" Murtaugh's voice rose. "Smart move, but you ain't that smart."

Buster Hodges shifted his body and leaned across the plate. The home plate umpire, Keith Tesoro, shoved his considerable body between them.

"What the hell are you saying, Murtaugh?"

Brian pushed himself at Tesoro, but the portly umpire didn't budge. Behind them, camera flashes went off.

"Come on. You haven't played Ralph Barrett in a month. And Crash Warren ain't an upgrade, so don't pat yourself on the back too hard. Who's dishin' it to ya?"

Tesoro grabbed both lineup cards and signed them.

"Let's go, gentleman."

"Kiss my—"

"Brian, don't force me to toss you before we get started," said Tesoro, showing Murtaugh a thumb that had been broken more than once during his tenure in the Major Leagues.

"I'll figure this out, and both of you will be in front of the commissioner after we win Game Seven." Murtaugh wagged his forefinger in front of Hodges and Tesoro.

Hodges laughed. Tesoro growled. Murtaugh took back the lineup card.

****

At the top of the fourth inning, Bobby doubled Omar Clarke home after the second baseman drew a walk off Ross Kerwin. Kerwin settled down and retired Slavik, Nayle, and Jackson to end the threat. Bobby never got past second base. Crash Warren, the DH in place of Bruce Wells, belted a home run at the bottom of the fourth inning. Up to that point, Tony Edwards had set the Titans down in order.

Up in the owner's box, Harris Kentfield had cleared the room when Bobby's double landed between Rafael San Marco and Jorge Ferro. Hodges had also benched Gerry Sorrell to save him for a defensive or pitching change in the late innings. This turned out to be a mistake because Sorrell would have run Bobby's hit down. Ferro, a good hitter, ran so slowly that "he actually goes back in time" a former teammate had joked.

At the top of the fifth inning with the game still tied at 1 to 1, Moses Pendleton led off with a single and stole second when Bob Randolph struck out. Davis ran the count full before taking a called third strike.

"What the hell?" asked Omar Clarke, who jumped off the bench. "Right down the middle. Get the bat off your shoulder!"

Before Davis could get back to the dugout, Chip and Bobby pulled Omar back.

"That's not helping, Omar," said Dunkirk. Clarke sat down but let his disgust show when he barked out, "He's about half here and half somewhere else."

Murtaugh called time and walked to the on-deck circle to talk to Edwards.

"Feeling good?"

"Yep."

"I ain't pulling you for a pinch-hitter if you tell me not to."

"Don't. I got these guys."

"We'll get you some runs."

Edwards looked down the bench at Bobby and grinned.

"Yes, we will. Keep me in, skip," he said.

Murtaugh left. Edwards approached the plate and dug in. He looked down at Moses Pendleton and rubbed the bottom of the bat, and waited for Ross Kerwin's offering.

Moses took off for third, which surprised Danny Espinosa. The Titans' catcher had called for a curveball and the ball took just enough time getting to the plate that Espinosa's throw to Ralph Barrett was late, and off line. The ball skittered into the outfield. The speedy Pendleton scored on the error. 2 to 1, Quakers.

Titan Stadium sounded like Bicentennial Park, as the boos rained down on Espinosa, who was hitting .500 for the Series and had tied the record for most assists by a catcher in a World Series. It was Danny's first error since a passed ball in July.

And the Titans' fans let him know about it.

"Quit readin' the *Daily News!* You ain't Oscar!"

"You suck, Espinosa!"

"Nice throw!"

Ross Kerwin received the ball from Espinosa, and under a noise blanket, managed to strike out Tony Edwards.

Edwards then set down the Titans in order in the bottom of the fifth, which only increased the volume of boos, and when the Titans took the field in the top of the sixth inning, they were still down a run.

Omar Clarke again worked Kerwin for a walk, with Bobby Young due up next. Buster Hodges headed to the mound. Espinosa trotted out, which brought on another round of turbulence from the stands.

"I got Vlad throwing, Ross, but he'd be wasted on Bobby, who will just switch sides," said Hodges referring to Vladimir Dellacorte, the off-season pickup from Baltimore. "I'd rather save him for the rest of the lineup, if I have to. You got this rookie?"

"He got lucky last time. Just found a seam."

"I know that, but he's on a tear. He's the only player outhitting Danny. I gotta know if your arm is still OK. It's the sixth."

"Arm's good."

"We're having this chat again when your at-bat comes up. You need some support, Ross, but I need you to keep us within a run."

"I'm ready to go, skip."

"Then get this kid out, preferably with a double play."

Buster jogged back to the dugout with his hands in his midnight-blue Titans jacket. As soon as he got back, and before Ross Kerwin could deliver a pitch to Bobby, Hodges called the bullpen.

"Keep Dellacorte throwing as long as he likes. I'm pulling Kerwin for a pinch-hitter no matter who's on base and how many outs there are."

Hodges hung up. The clunk of the handset coincided with the crack of the bat, as a baseball made its way into the upper deck of right field at Titan Stadium.

It was a home run that reminded the older fans of Mickey Mantle. About 55,000 people stood slack-jawed in admiration and respect as Bobby circled the bases behind an ecstatic Omar Clarke.

As Bobby passed Ralph Barrett at third, he lifted his head and waved to the visitor's dugout. His teammates jammed the rail to watch the third and fourth runs score.

But in the owner's box and on camera, Kentfield sat expressionless.

On the mound, Ross Kerwin didn't even bother to get another ball from Danny Espinosa or the umpire. His pitching stint over, the veteran southpaw walked, head weighed down by the boos, in a Walk of Shame to the Titans' dugout before Dellacorte arrived from the bullpen.

Buster Hodges took the baseball from Espinosa and handed it to Dellacorte.

"Stop the bleeding, Vlad," said Buster.

"Guess I ain't starting tomorrow?" Dellacorte said with a smile. A terse squint greeted Vlad's comments. He kicked the pitching rubber and took his warmup throws.

Slavik greeted Dellacorte with a single, and the Titans' bleeding continued when Rick Nayle powered another home run over the center field fence. The rout was on.

Hodges kept Dellacorte in, since he would now pitch Connor Anderson in Game Seven, a game no one anticipated.

Final score: Quakers 11, Titans 1.

****

Kentfield, true to form, stormed out of the owner's box and headed to the locker room to berate Buster Hodges, or to catch him before the Titans' manager escaped to a Bronx watering hole or two.

****

In the visitor's locker room, a quiet and subdued confidence. Ike Jackson shared a laugh with Omar Clarke. Rick Nayle did an Elvis imitation.

Brian Murtaugh made a brief statement to them.

"Good game, Quakers. Just need one more."

They had to win another game in Titan Stadium. Their ace, Cy Young Award-winner for the 1972 season, Paul Skountzos, would start Game Seven. They felt good about their chances.

Phil Ostrowski came into the not-so-boisterous locker room and walked over to Jose Echevarrian's area. The righthander stood up from his bench and the two talked for several minutes.

Dunkirk saw this and walked over to Bobby.

"You seeing this?" he asked.

"Yep," replied Bobby.

"What do you think?"

"You know Phil. He's got to be trying to get Jose to buck up since he was denied the start. Can't imagine what else it could be."

"They're heading to the visiting team's offices," said Dunkirk, who picked up a towel and headed in the same direction as Echevarrian and Ostrowski.

"Where do you think you're going?"

"Nowhere."

"Goofy," said Bobby. "Leave it be. Do not try one of your espionage acts. I think we know what Brian is up to."

"Just wanna make sure."

Dunkirk wrapped the towel around himself and headed off to eavesdrop on Murtaugh, Ostrowski, and Echevarrian. He waddled down the walkway and found the Quakers' lone traveling security guard standing just outside the visiting coach's office.

"What's up, Oddjob?" asked Dunkirk, a broad grin crossing his face.

Miles Johnson, nicknamed Oddjob after the James Bond hitman due to his heavyset frame and bald head, rolled his right hand into a fist and covered it with his left.

"Mister Murtaugh said that no one, including management, was to interrupt him."

"Oh, come on," said Dunkirk. "Just wanna have a little listen."

Miles Johnson said nothing, but advanced a few steps until the top of his shiny pate sat just below Chip's chin. He looked up at the grinning ballplayer.

"No one."

"Got it."

Chip retreated back to the Quakers' locker room.

****

Kentfield, still apoplectic after the thrashing, caught up to a hustling Buster Hodges in the VIP parking lot.

"Buster!"

Hodges kept running to his car, buried at the back of the lot. He stopped short and sighed. There would be no escape from the boss tonight.

"Damn it, Buster! Stay right where you are!" Kentfield, sweating from exertion and emotion, descended on Hodges. His red face pressed into Buster's. The manager backed up a foot. They squared off for at least the tenth time that season.

"Eleven to one! Are you insane!? In Titan Stadium? In *our* backyard?"

Buster, who'd heard it all before whether directed at him or not, folded his arms over his chest and rocked on his cleats. He hadn't changed out of his game uniform. All he wanted to do was get out of the lot and away from Titan Stadium for a couple of hours. Several beers at D'Oro's Grill wouldn't hurt.

"Well?"

"Harris, that's a good team we're playing," said Buster. "It ain't the Double-A Waves."

Kentfield, who had been leaning into Buster, eased back. He wiped his moist forehead and upper lip with a black-and-white handkerchief. Buster, thinking he might be off the hook, looked over his shoulder at his car, then scanned the parking lot for an attendant.

"Did you have to leave Dellacorte in there that long? It looked like batting practice."

Hodges cut off his search for the attendant.

"Not wasting another arm," he said to Kentfield. "The Quakers had our number tonight and I could not come up with any reason to throw anyone else out there. Anderson goes tomorrow night, and he's as good as we got to go against Skountzos. Matched up pretty well against him in Game Three."

Kentfield, who had relaxed his posture, leaned in closer.

"What? We lost, Buster. Remember? We lost Game Three, and it wasn't exactly a squeaker. I think at one point, and correct me if I'm wrong, we were down twelve to two. Now, you sure you wanna pitch Anderson?"

"Give me another option."

"Montgomery."

Now Hodges leaned in.

"Are you insane?" Buster asked, jabbing a finger in Kentfield's significant gut. "He's lefthanded, boss. The Quakers lineup, except for Slocumbe, is all righthanded. Are you serious?"

"Yes," replied Kentfield, swatting at Hodges' finger. "The Quakers won't be expecting it."

"Expecting it? You think it matters to the Quakers? They'll unload on Montgomery, unless he does a great Howard Ehmke imitation."

"Howard—"

"Look it up, boss. Ehmke held the record for strikeouts in a World Series for decades. Piled up thirteen in a Game One win against the Senators in 1929."

"Game One!?" Kentfield shouted, which brought security and the parking lot attendant out to the garage. "What's your point?"

Kentfield repeatedly jabbed his finger into Hodges' chest, who allowed the boss to jackhammer his ribcage with the digit. Buster finally stopped it by crossing his arms. He lifted one hand to wave off security.

"My point," he said, "is that Ehmke was a veteran. Had already played about a dozen seasons and wouldn't be thrown by the crowds and the noise and, well, *the fact that it's the World Series,* boss! Montgomery is a spot starter, and this ain't the spot."

The impulsive Kentfield threw a jab with his left hand, which caught Buster by surprise. Hodges, no stranger to brawling, spun out of the punch and squared up in a boxing stance, ready to take on the Titans' owner.

Kentfield backed away. Buster relaxed his posture.

"We're fine, Buster," said Kentfield. "Just a little disagreement. Right?"

"Yep," he replied. "We'll figure it out."

The security guard, not completely satisfied, walked away, but not very far.

"OK, Harris," said Buster. "Here's what I can do. I'll talk to Montgomery *and* to Anderson and see how they feel about this. They're both gonna want to go, but I think a talk will reveal a lot. *If* Montgomery is the right choice, and remember the Quakers' only true lefthanded hitter is Javier Slocumbe, who's starting only because of Skountzos. Too much righthanded damage in that Philly lineup." Buster paused and looked Kentfield in the eye. "OK, Skountzos swings from the left side of the plate, but I ain't basing a pitching decision on whether the opposition's hurler bats right or left."

"Montgomery looked very good down the stretch," offered Kentfield.

"Yes, he did, and that was a real boost to us, but there is a big difference between a September contest and Game Seven. Remember, I've played in a few of them. And you haven't."

"Don't push it, Buster."

"Lineup card is still mine, Harris."

"Then make it a winner."

CHAPTER TWENTY-EIGHT

Back to Audubon, New Jersey
Friday, October 31, 1975

Scizzor and Trip took another pass by the house at 118 East Pine Street. The child hadn't gone to the neighbor's house by 1 p.m. as usual. Three o'clock had come and gone. Their window of opportunity grew shorter—the mother would be home soon from her shift at Campbell's Soup, and the father's workday might have him back soon after that.

"Should we call it off?" asked Trip.

"Nah," said Scizzor, smoking. "Got at least another half hour. She's thirty pounds at best. We'll be in and out in five minutes."

Thirty minutes later, they spotted Betty Leonard. She walked from the opposite direction of the neighbor's house.

"Maybe she stayed at the school playground?" asked Trip.

"Who cares?" Scizzor snapped back. "Get ready."

She let herself in, as Trip parked the car. The parents, who had weathered World War II, had no issue with a five-year-old returning home from school and entering through an unlocked door in the safe neighborhood in which they had lived the last ten years.

"Wanna grab her now?" asked Trip.

"What are you, an idiot?" asked Scizzor, stubbing out his cigarette in the car's ashtray. It now occupied the same space with at least a dozen other butts. "Be good to do it before Mom and Dad get home, don't you think?" replied Scizzor. "Let's go."

"What are you gonna do with her?"

"I'm not gonna hurt her unless Bobby and the Quakers won't lay down tonight," said Scizzor. "We'll get her into Titan Stadium, and I will sit with her and Max during the game."

"But—"

"Look, the next thing we have to do after we snatch the kid is get hold of Brady, Max's second-in-command, and he'll get a message to Bobby."

"How?"

"Don't know, Trip. Brady says he knows how to get something to the locker room, and I believe him. He'll pass Bobby a note with our instructions."

Trip rubbed his nose and sniffed. Scizzor exhaled.

"Like I said, let's go."

Trip and Scizzor stepped out of the car onto East Pine Street. In addition to the eponymous tree, oak and maple filled the yards of many of the homes. The colors glowed, sharp and robust in the October sunshine.

The trees, planted just after the turn of the 19th century, had grown to heights which towered over most of the two-story homes. The smell of autumn filled the yards in Audubon, New Jersey.

The neighborhood remained quiet despite school being done for the day. Parents not at work kept busy with housekeeping or shopping. No one had any idea that an innocent little girl was about to disappear.

Trip looked up and down the block.

"Nothing," he said to himself. "Let's make this quick."

Scizzor, already across the street, glanced in both directions from the sidewalk. No pedestrians. No cars. He hustled inside the house with Trip right behind.

Betty Leonard had not locked the door behind her.

Trip stepped through the front door, a combination of small, morticed windows from top to bottom. His feet hit the braided area rug in the entranceway, surrounded by a matching collection of Victorian furniture—two chairs, a couch, and an ottoman. Scizzor knelt in front of Betty Leonard. The child sat on the ottoman, frozen in place.

"Who are you?" she asked, her brown eyes suspicious. Betty's eyelids half-closed, and her brows formed a V-shape of accusation.

"I'm a good friend of your daddy, and so is this man behind me."

"No," she said. Betty clutched a hardback copy of L. Frank Baum's *Ozma of Oz* in front of her plaid jumper.

"Yes, we are, and we've come to take you to the zoo."

"No!" She shouted this time, shaking her head, which brushed her black hair across her face. The book dropped to the ground. Scizzor picked it up and handed it to her.

Betty spun on her feet and ran from Scizzor, who missed while grabbing her. He hustled across the floor, boards creaking under his feet. Trip followed, his bulk making such an impression on the old wood that a collapse sounded imminent. Betty sped past the dining room table and toward the kitchen. Just as she reached the saloon-style swinging doors, Scizzor caught her, and the two slid across the linoleum floor.

Trip pulled up short of the dining room table when he saw Scizzor catch Betty. He launched himself forward, though, as the two skidded into the kitchen. The book skittered away from her, but Betty snatched it off the floor. She headed for the steps that led down to the backyard after she pulled herself free from Scizzor's grip.

Scizzor caught her again before she got to the back door. He emerged from the kitchen with Betty in tow, his left hand over her mouth, his right arm wrapped around her tiny body. She hung just below his chest, unable to scream, still clutching *Ozma of Oz*. Trip stood just inside the dining room, now no more than a few feet away from Scizzor and Betty.

A shape appeared from a side hallway. It dropped to the ground under the head-of-the-table chair and emerged. Quickly.

"Who the hell are you?" she shouted. "You let go of my daughter, you creep!"

Kathryn Leonard, who had been laid up in bed with a migraine, slammed an iron skillet into Scizzor's shocked face. He staggered back and dropped Betty to the floor. Trip reached forward before Kathryn could deliver another blow to his boss. He grabbed her arm, and yanked it back, freeing the pan. It clunked to the floor.

Scizzor, his nose broken and a welt already forming on his right cheekbone, kept his feet, reached out, and put his hand on Kathryn's throat. She gagged taking a breath and coughed out her exhale.

"Scizzor! Let me tie up the old lady."

"No," he shouted. "I'm going to kill this treacherous bitch!"

Scizzor continued to choke Kathryn. Betty, freed from his grip, screamed a little girl's ear-piercing scream. Trip snatched her and covered her mouth.

And Wendell Leonard, fresh from another street fight, ran into the melee in his dining room. Already bloodied from the daily street brawl with the gang at his produce stand, the man took on an offensive posture. Trip turned around, still holding Betty.

"Drop my daughter, you fat pig!"

Trip smiled until Wendell fired two quick left jabs into the thug's face. He backpedaled, dropping Betty, who ran to the far side of the dining room. Trip recovered and swung a haymaker, which the wiry man ducked. Wendell delivered an uppercut to the bigger man's solar plexus. The wind flew out of Trip and he crashed onto the threadbare Victorian rug. Floorboards cracked under his bulk.

Behind the two combatants, Scizzor let go of Kathryn and reached into his jacket pocket.

****

Buster Hodges, his cleats in front of him on top of the desk, dropped both feet to the ground when Connor "The Scholar" Anderson and Mouse Montgomery walked into the manager's office. Buster slammed both hands in front of him, causing the lineup card to jump on the blotter.

"Don't tell me Kentfield sent you."

"Kentfield sent *us*," replied Anderson. "What gives, Buster?"

"What do you think?" Hodges' eyes went from Anderson to Montgomery to Anderson.

"I think The Scholar's pitching tonight, skip," said Montgomery, the Titans' southpaw.

"Yes, he is," said Hodges, picking up the phone and shouting into it. A minute later, Harris Kentfield blew into the office.

Hodges dropped the phone into its cradle and put his feet back on the desk. Kentfield put his left hand on the right shoulder of Anderson and his right hand on the left shoulder of Montgomery. He and Buster engaged in a Who Blinks First contest.

Buster won.

"Anderson starts, Harris."

"You said you would discuss the issue with both of them."

"Just did."

"Buster."

"I am not changing this lineup card," said Hodges, picking up the 4" x 8" paper and waving it at Kentfield.

"Is it a winner?"

"Yes, it is."

"It better be, or you're gone after tonight."

"Hey," said Hodges, his old-lady cackle breaking the tension, or adding to it. "Don't threaten me with a good time."

"Buster."

Hodges ignored Kentfield, a grumble coming from the Titans' owner's throat.

"Hey, Scholar," said Hodges. "Get down to the training table and let Mike take one more look at you. I'll let you decide when you want to start throwing." He paused and switched his attention to Montgomery. "Mouse, get yourself out to the bullpen around seven o'clock."

The pitchers walked out of Buster's office, brushing by Kentfield as they exited to the hallway. The Titans' boss waited until they were well down the hallway.

"You embarrass me in front of the players again and I don't care if we win tonight, you are still gone."

"Like I said," snapped Hodges, "don't threaten me with a good time. Now get the hell out of my office, Harris. Go sit in the owner's box and root for the Titans. I've still got some work to do. The weak spot in their lineup looks like Davis, even though he hit over .300 this year. He's not even hitting his weight in the Series, but everybody else? Tough eight to get out, including Skountzos."

Hodges pulled out a scouting binder on the Quakers and paged through it. Kentfield stood in front of him for a solid five minutes before leaving.

"Just win the game, Buster, and all will be forgiven."

Hodges picked up the binder and continued skimming through it for ten minutes before rising and walking to an aluminum, four-drawer filing cabinet. He pulled open one compartment and yanked out a bottle of clear liquor.

A couple of pulls later, he sat down. He eyed the bottle, which he placed at his feet for the duration of his study of the binder. He took another shot every five to ten minutes. After 45 minutes, a toasted Buster Hodges lifted the half-empty vessel and pointed it skyward.

"Here's to you, Harris Kentfield," he laughed. "You are going to drive me to drink."

Hodges' toast reached its crescendo and echoed down the hallway to the Titans' locker room. A handful of players performed various pre-game rituals such as wrapping injuries, meditating, pulling off warmup jackets, and playing cards.

Duff Mackie turned toward the manager's office.

"That stuff is going to kill that guy," he said.

Hodges' laughter continued, and finally chased the players out of the locker room and into the dugout. Just another game at Titan Stadium.

****

Betty, tossed aside like a sack of rice when Wendell punched Trip, tumbled past the dining room table near the head chair. She lifted her gaze and saw the man in the funny suit throw her mother to the floor. *Ozma of Oz* lay next to her. She picked it up.

Scizzor pointed the gun at Wendell.

Mom's next.

Betty, with both hands, threw *Ozma of Oz* at Scizzor's knees. The gun went off, silenced but still lethal in the close quarters. Betty's meager toss threw off the shot and it caught Trip, who had just gotten up, in the shoulder. The big man stumbled forward. He shoved Wendell out of the way and crashed through the front door, shattering most of the windows. He fell down the steps and staggered toward the car, his face, hands, and part of his suit a blood-soaked mess.

Wendell remained on his feet and ran at Scizzor, who couldn't get the gun in front of him in time to ward off the charging man. They landed in the kitchen. Grunting, Scizzor stood up and pistol-whipped Wendell, but only once.

The man, more sinew than anything else, landed a series of blows that forced Scizzor to escape out the back door. He sprinted around the house and back to the street, holding onto the gun. Scizzor yelled and flagged down Trip, who had gunned the car and was a half-block away.

Trip backed up. Scizzor jumped in.

"Titan Stadium. *Go!*"

CHAPTER TWENTY-NINE

Game Seven

Fifty-thousand Titans fans shoved each other through the security areas. Their zeal to take part in yet another signature Game Seven in the iconic stadium turned every one of them into rush hour subway commuters on a clear Thursday evening. Dusk enveloped the Bronx, the air still, 70-degree temperature, low humidity.

Hunter Hatfield, the Golden Voice of the Titans for more than 30 years, would have intoned his usual, "It's a beautiful day for a ballgame."

And it was. As night approached the Bronx, the air gave way to an occasional fresh autumn breeze, but one that hadn't picked up any of the Hudson or Harlem River aromas. Outside Titan Stadium, the shadows of the few trees still alive in the Bronx lengthened. The sienna leaves laying at their roots mixed with a variety of trash strewn about the sidewalks and streets that rimmed the ballpark.

The fans streamed into their seats and began the obligatory New York City catcalls toward the Quakers, who had hunkered down in their dugout prior to the top of the first inning.

"Might as well hit the turnpike now!"

"Exit three!"

"Game Seven in Titan Stadium! We know how those turn out!"

Bobby looked out from his seat in the dugout at Paul Skountzos, who was on the sideline pitching mound throwing to Javier Slocumbe. Skountzos' signature nose twitched in full game mode.

The 1975 World Series finale, five minutes away.

Bobby ground his teeth every time he looked out past Skountzos and Slocumbe at Ricky Davis. Ricky took some infield grounders from Ike Jackson just to pass the time, or perhaps to get a better feel for the grass in Titan Stadium.

"Why does he want to throw it all away?" Bobby whispered to himself.

"What's that, Flash in the Pan?" asked Gonzales.

"Nothing, Viejo," said Bobby. "Just nerves."

"Doesn't sound like nerves." Davey Gonzales stood from his dugout seat and approached.

Bobby crumpled up a piece of paper, the note from Scizzor, as Gonzales nudged him into the clubhouse.

"You got something to say?"

"Not a thing," replied Bobby. "Just that we're going to beat those lousy Titans, aren't we?"

"We better, or calling them the Dreaded Titans will hang on you like—"

"Don't say it, Viejo. Just don't say that year," admonished Bobby, his lips drawn into a straight line across his face. "Let's play ball."

Davis and Ike Jackson trotted off the hometown diamond. The Titans took the field under a blanket of cheers from their fans. Their shouts and screams reached lunatic level, and the stadium rocked with energy.

****

Sounds of Titans' fanaticism erupted throughout the stadium even as the Quakers pushed a run across in the first inning.

Omar Clarke singled to lead off and stole second base. It did nothing to quiet a crowd that had screwed itself into the ground over the possibility of the return of Titans' prominence. Eleven long years out of the World Series spotlight, and now a Game Seven gave the fans a sense of baseball harmony.

Bobby failed to move Clarke along. He struck out on three fastballs by Connor Anderson, who reinvigorated the crowd by silencing the stellar rookie's bat. But when he tried the same combination with Jack Slavik, the Quakers' slugger drilled a double down the right field line on the second fastball and Clarke scored easily.

Anderson, looking every bit the medical school student he'd been before the Titans drafted him, stood stock still on the mound, but then slammed his glove down on the ground when Slavik called a time-out to dust himself off. Anderson's fit almost backfired as Rick Nayle vaporized the first pitch — but right at Duff Mackie — who easily doubled up Jack Slavik. Inning over.

The Titans had dodged a bullet, yet trailed 1 to 0.

****

In the owner's box, Harris Kentfield's round face took on the color of a stop sign, and the other occupants braced themselves.

"Montgomery!" he shouted to his staff. "Buster should have started Montgomery! I knew it."

In the broadcast booth, the Quakers' announcer, Oscar Markley, nudged Skeeter Thompson, and covered the microphone with his hand.

"Kentfield got an early start on his tantrum."

"Yes, he did."

Markley uncovered the mic.

"Stepping in to face Greek is Rafael San Marco, who's having a great Series."

****

Skountzos and Anderson breezed through the initial five innings, save for the Quakers' lone run in the first. Between the two pitchers, the Titans and the Quakers gave up a grand total of three hits leading up to the sixth frame. The home team hadn't gotten a runner past first base. Both the singles collected by New York were wiped out by double plays.

Skountzos had faced the minimum number of batters, fifteen, through the fifth frame. Anderson had only seen two more than that.

Paul Skountzos led off the top of the sixth. The game remained 1 to 0, Quakers. Greek, a good hitter for a pitcher, worked the count full, then slapped a single to left field with an inside-out swing. Anderson faced the top of the lineup with a man on.

The crowd's wrath at Anderson for giving up a hit to the pitcher descended on the field with a depressing thud. A beer bottle, launched from the upper deck in right field, bounced in front of Jorge Ferro.

"Hey, Jorge!" shouted a fan. "Still some left in the bottle!"

The second base umpire called time as Ferro picked up the bottle and handed it to one of the bullpen attendants. The boos continued.

"PLAY BALL!" shouted the home plate umpire. Anderson threw from the windup.

On a two-and-two count, Omar Clarke smacked a sharp ground ball to shortstop Lex Slattery's right. The converted outfielder snared it, but was so deep in the hole that his only play was to get the speedy Clarke at first. Skountzos slid hard into second.

And felt a twinge in his hamstring.

He covered for it when he stood up and dusted himself off.

The boos resumed as Buster Hodges made his way to the mound. The Titans' manager raised his left arm and Mouse Montgomery began warming up in the bullpen.

"Short leash, Doc," said Buster, wiping the ball.

"You ain't pulling me."

"Nope, but you don't get Bobby Young out, and I will," said Hodges, eyeing the young switch-hitter as he slapped the ball back into the pitcher's glove.

Anderson worked around Bobby, who he'd struck out twice, but Hodges' admonishment took just enough heart out of The Scholar that on a two-and-one count, Anderson hung a slider and watched it disappear over the center field wall.

The Titans' fans choked in mid-cheer as Bobby circled the bases. Ahead of him, Skountzos—who walked to third given the luxury of the home run—managed to trot to home just ahead of the jubilant rookie.

The Quakers now led 3 to 0.

****

Buster didn't hesitate. He sprinted out of the dugout, waving his left arm. Montgomery threw a couple more times and rode the golf cart out to the mound. Anderson didn't wait for the handoff; he headed to the dugout under an operatic assault of unhappy Titans fans.

Montgomery received the ball.

"No more runs. Got it?"

"I'll keep us in this one," said Montgomery.

****

"I don't see Kentfield," said Thompson, stifling a laugh.

"Me neither," replied Markley. "Maybe he had to use the restroom."

****

Montgomery got out of the inning when both Slavik and Nayle went deep, but not quite deep enough to generate anything more than two long outs.

Skountzos returned to the mound at the top of the next frame although the ache in his hamstring felt worse. He had easy sixth and seventh innings and cruised right into the eighth, but something had clearly bothered him when he went down very easily during his own at-bat in the bottom of the seventh frame. The bat never left his shoulder.

"Greek," said Slocumbe, pulling his longtime battery mate aside. "You OK?"

"Fine. Why?"

"Because you're not OK, and I'm going to have Brian ask Deke to warm up."

Skountzos poked a finger in Slocumbe's chest.

"I'm finishing this game."

"Four, five, and six hitters coming up, Greek," said Slocumbe. "What's the problem? It's not your arm."

"Hamstring," said Skountzos. "Right leg. I don't have to push off it to pitch, but I do have to land on it."

Back on the field, the Quakers had something going with two outs, and the Titans fans seemed to be booed out. The silence of defeat, unfamiliar in Titan Stadium, drifted down from the upper decks and settled over Montgomery. He'd gotten Clarke on a grounder to first for out number two, but Bobby Young doubled down the left field line and stood on second with the fourth Quakers' run if Slavik could deliver.

Montgomery worked Slavik to a full count. The Philly third baseman then fouled off four straight pitches before scalding one toward the wall in right-center field. Ferro trundled in the direction of the ball, but Rafael San Marco took off at a sprint when he spotted the ball out of the right side of his field of vision. San Marco realized he had overrun it if he meant to snag it with his gloved hand out to his right side, and the ball passed over San Marco's head.

He dropped his glove back toward his left shoulder and before crashing into the wall, caught it, Willie Mays-style, with his back to the plate.

Out number three.

"Damn, that San Marco is spectacular," said Clarke, picking up his glove. "Too bad he's a Titan."

Skountzos worked his way through the bottom of the Titans' lineup in the eighth, but when Montgomery came up to bat, Hodges pulled him for Bruce Wells, the team's, and Major League Baseball's, first designated hitter. Skountzos needed one more out.

The pain in his right hamstring, quiet in the dugout, returned. Greek bit his tongue, drawing blood, and wound up. He delivered a slider to Wells. As he landed on the right leg, a spasm dropped Skountzos to the ground. He attempted to make it look like he tripped, but Murtaugh spotted the injury, and phoned the bullpen.

Wells held off as the ball skipped by Slocumbe, well out of the strike zone.

Skountzos attempted to stand, but another spasm shot through him. He lay on the ground. Murtaugh sprinted, as best as Murtaugh could, to the mound. The Quakers' chubby trainer, Dominick, loped behind.

"Torn hammie, Brian," said Dominick.

"Damn it."

****

Deke Reilly stretched in the bullpen. Bob Randolph, the usual catcher except when Skountzos started, took his position. Both of Reilly's first offerings sailed over his head.

"Sit down, Deke," said Randolph, heading to the bullpen phone. "You ain't been right for a few games."

Reilly stood on top of the bullpen mound.

"Stick around, Randolph," said Reilly, his grin splitting his face. "Got a great screwball coming. You don't wanna miss this one."

Randolph returned to his catcher's stance. Reilly wound up and fired a perfect screwball that tailed away from the right side of the plate at the last instant, as it should have.

Reilly threw several more. Randolph called the dugout.

"Anytime."

Skountzos limped from the mound, supported by the much shorter Dominick. The Titans' crowd cheered, but more out of contempt for the lefthander than appreciation for his world-class performance. Skountzos waved anyway.

More hollow cheers followed at Reilly's appearance. The fans, after watching Reilly depart in his previous appearance, smelled a shark's dinner in the water.

Deke tossed a few warmups and Wells greeted his first weak fastball with a smooth swing and a gapper that landed the oversized DH on second base. Sal Giambri went in to run for him, and the Titans' fickle faithful erupted.

Slocumbe walked the ball out to Deke.

"What in *hell* was that?"

"Changeup," replied Deke.

"I called for a fastball," snapped Slocumbe. "And Wells waited for it, I think, for an hour. You're lucky that ball isn't still heading for Brooklyn."

"New Rochelle," said Deke.

"What the—?"

"Based on the position of Titan Stadium—"

"Shut up, Deke," said Slocumbe. "You throw one more pitch like that and we're going to have another change on the mound. Got it?"

Deke didn't reply and swept some imaginary dirt off the rubber. He spun the ball in his hand and talked to it.

"This is it," he said. "Make sure you do what you're supposed to do."

Deke threw the next batter, lead-off man Rafael San Marco, nothing but exceptional screwballs and worked the count to one and two. Sal Giambri took a huge lead off second. Deke faked a throwback there.

"Get the batter, Reilly," said Slocumbe behind his mask. "What are you doing bothering with the runner when we have two outs?"

Deke went into the stretch and threw yet another exquisite screwball, but San Marco knew it was coming and sent the ball toward New Rochelle.

The Quakers' lead now stood at just one run. Murtaugh, his stomach flipping over several times, called down to the bullpen. Maberry and Nate Watson got up. The team was out of lefthanders. Edwards had pitched the day before, Hayes had been awful for months, and now Skountzos was out. Reilly was on his way to the showers.

****

"That's the oddball we paid for," said Mad Max to the escort service blonde seated next to her.

"What's that?" she asked.

"Nothing," said Max. "Let's see what happens now."

Murtaugh signaled for Nate Watson. The reliever trotted in and received the ball from Slocumbe, who remained in the game. Murtaugh would have a backup catcher in Bob Randolph if the game went into extra innings.

****

A disgusted Mad Max tossed an unlit cigarette across the floor. "Damn it!"

"Max, honey, calm down," said the blonde. "Anything I can do?"

Max leaned forward and said nothing.

****

Watson set down Duff Mackie on two pitches as the second baseman lofted a weak pop-up to shallow right field. Bobby gathered in the last out of the bottom of the eighth inning. The Quakers were three outs from their first World Series title in the history of the ballclub.

Titans' reliever Rufus Finn had no trouble with Ike Jackson, Moses Pendleton, or Javier Slocumbe. Three batters. Three outs. The Titans came to bat with what might be the last inning of the 1975 season.

A lone cheer echoed through cavernous Titan Stadium.

"Let's go Ti-tans!" It reverberated around the outfield walls and settled, but the crowd caught the chant and delivered it in waves as Nate Watson threw the last of his warmups.

Crash Warren took a few swings, and Watson dispatched him with one pitch on a routine fly ball to Bobby.

Up stepped Danny Espinosa, batting over .500 for the Series. Watson threw off the plate to give the Titans' catcher nothing to hit, but Espinosa connected on a two-ball, no-strike fastball about six inches outside, and just missed a home run when the ball caromed off the top of the right field wall. Espinosa managed to waddle to second base.

Titans' fans were apoplectic at the near-home run, but salvo after salvo of cheers greeted the next batter, Gerry Sorrell.

Sorrell, the left fielder, drew a walk from the shaken Watson. Murtaugh decided he'd seen enough and called the bullpen for Slade Maberry.

****

"There we go," purred Max, reclining in her chair.

The blonde, who had retreated from Max's side after having her romantic overtures ignored for the entire game, picked up her money from the bar and walked out. Max sat alone, ignoring the dramatic departure, which included a clumsy snatch of the money, a hands-on-hips huff, and the door-slamming finale.

"There we go," Max said again.

Maberry came in and threw several warmup pitches. The umpire called for play. Hector Enriquez joined Brian on the dugout steps.

"You're a brave man, Brian," said Enriquez, his stare fixed on Slade Maberry. "Smythe, next up, is a lefty, and Maberry . . . "

"Best I got right now."

"Maybe."

The righthanded Ferro hit three screaming line drives but all into foul territory, on Maberry's first three pitches. Slade had the Titan at no balls and two strikes, but Ferro had Maberry in his sights. The Philly reliever served up a hanging curveball. It fooled Ferro and his solid hit lost enough steam for Omar Clarke to knock it down and throw the plodding Titans' outfielder out at first.

Murtaugh stepped onto the field, but his options of Chris Escondido or Everett Hayes were not as good as Maberry. He dropped back into the dugout, his face a roadmap of lines, the color gone.

Both runners advanced on a fielder's choice. Espinosa now at third, Sorrell at second.

In the Titans' dugout, Buster Hodges stood with one foot on field level and rubbed his eyebrows. He looked out over the crowd, one filled with bandwagon-jumping Titans' fans, preparing for another ride. *Should I put in a pinch-runner for Espinosa or leave the red-hot catcher in for extra innings?*

With two out and the slow Titans' catcher on third, the possibility of a sacrifice fly was zero, as was any thought of a suicide squeeze bunt.

Buster stuck with Espinosa. Tanner Smythe, who hit over .300 during the season and .400 in the month of September, walked to the plate. The Titans' manager went all in for the win, as the speedy Gerry Sorrell at second would score on anything Smythe could get safely out of the infield.

The noise in Titan Stadium reached airport take-off levels. Chip Dunkirk, along with every other Quaker, stood at the rail, ready to charge the mound at the last out, or perhaps to walk dejectedly back into the dugout. One pitch could do either.

Under a decibel hurricane, Brian Murtaugh walked out to Maberry, said a few words, and then returned to the dugout from the mound. The conference was over. Maberry would pitch to Smythe, no intentional walk. Craig Tate waited in the on-deck circle.

Smythe dug in and sent Maberry's first pitch screaming down the right field line, but foul by several feet. The decibel level went from a thousand to zero and back to a thousand as Maberry prepared to pitch again. He went from the windup as he recognized the slow-footed Espinosa would only be able to score on a hit.

Maberry's next pitch was off the plate, as was his third offering. He could not afford to be careless and load the bases. The next Titans' hitter was the dangerous Craig Tate, also lefthanded.

Smythe crushed the next pitch, but like the first one, it found foul territory. The count stood at two balls and two strikes.

Smythe stepped out. The Major League Baseball season teetered on one swing.

****

"TIME!" Bobby screamed out the request for the first time this season, as he was too far away from any of the umpires to get their attention with his signature gesture. "TIME! TIME!"

"TIME!" The plate umpire waved off the pitch.

Bobby sprinted in from right field. He arrived on the mound to confront Slade Maberry. Smythe stepped out of the batter's box with the count two and two. Sorrell returned to second from a wide lead. Espinosa grumbled, and put both feet on third.

TIME, working its way around the planet, heard something, and found its way to the source, Titan Stadium.

Something was not right.

"This is it, Slade," Bobby said, staring into Maberry's eyes. "I never figured you for the fourth culprit."

"Get off my mound, rookie," said Maberry, whose 6'6" frame shadowed Bobby.

"You got limited options, here," replied Bobby, who stepped even closer. "You close this game out and you're part of baseball history, or you take the money and you're just another player who took the money."

"Get off my mound."

"And you will get caught, because I will turn you and the others in."

Ricky Davis headed toward the mound. Bobby and Maberry waved him off.

"Just who the hell do you think you are?"

TIME spotted something out of place. Everything appeared to be moving too slowly, too silently, except in the middle of the diamond shape over which *TIME* now passed. Two figures in sharp focus, one in particular. One of the figures out of place. Its surroundings blurred.

"I'm just a Quakers fan who wants to win a World Series. I want to blow away the ghosts of 1964. That's all I am. Who the hell do you think *you* are?"

Bobby turned and jogged back to right field, as *TIME* closed the distance between the mound and right field. *TIME* now saw only one object in focus. Moving. Animated. This figure did not belong here.

Maberry looked at Davis, who averted his eyes.

Smythe stepped back in. Maberry wound up and unleashed a changeup, which dropped just below the Titan first baseman's knees. Smythe swung. The swing that would change everything.

****

The noise level of Titan Stadium vibrated up and through the building. Every single fan lent their voice as Smythe connected solidly with Maberry's offering, an off-speed pitch. Maberry's part was to throw nothing but fastballs and right down the middle.

****

The noise increased as the ball leaped off Smythe's bat and headed for the gap between third base and shortstop. Espinosa "sprinted" for home to at least a tie game, and most likely the win, since Gerry Sorrell was off at the crack of the bat.

****

Scizzor McQueen, his right cheek still bleeding from the split skin earned by the efforts of the fruit-cutting knife-hand of Wendell Leonard, fell out of the VIP elevator onto the floor of the luxury box level. His blood-covered gloved fingers held onto his Beretta as he crab-walked along the concrete to the private room he hoped still held Maxine Hughes. Scizzor didn't want to kill any of her bodyguards, but would if they tried to stop him.

"It's me or Max at this point, if the Titans lose," he croaked to himself.

Scizzor climbed to his feet. He negotiated the bend in the hallway and saw one of Mad Max's goons standing in front of the door. Scizzor looked at the gun in his bloody hand. He raised it.

The goon reached for the door. Scizzor fired and dropped the bodyguard.

Inside the room, Mad Max watched Espinosa run down the third-base line and screamed at the bay window. If Max heard the report of the gun, she ignored it.

"Run! Run! You fat SOB! Run!"

The ball rocketed toward left field. Jack Slavik dove as the ball short-hopped an inch beyond his glove. Behind him, moving to the third baseman's left, he saw Ricky Davis, his bare hand outstretched, snatch the ball on a bounce.

Slavik dove to the ground to clear Davis' vision for the throw to first base. Espinosa closed in on home. Smythe tore down the first base line.

Gerry Sorrell covered the distance to third and headed toward home with the winning run. Espinosa continued his Sumo-wrestler run.

Scizzor slammed himself against the door to the luxury box. Mad Max stopped urging Espinosa to home and turned to see the blood-covered Scizzor McQueen and the black hole of the Beretta.

The first bullet caught Max in the throat.

"Scizzor," she choked. "What the—?"

The second bullet buried itself in Max's skull.

The third and fourth bullets shattered enough of the bay window glass to allow Scizzor a clear view of right field and Bobby Young, grandson of the two people who had nearly ended Scizzor's life.

He dragged himself to a chair and sat down, steadying his elbow on the sash of the broken window.

Scizzor fired three shots in succession . . .

. . . just as *TIME* blinked and pushed Bobby through the continuum and into right field in Titan Stadium in 2020. The mysterious Bobby Young, who had appeared from nowhere had vanished again, but no one saw it happen. They were watching the last play of the 1975 World Series unfold in front of them. Every camera. Every network turned their coverage to the drama on the field, switching from Slade Maberry to Danny Espinosa to Tanner Smythe to Jack Slavik to Ricky Davis.

Another bullet fired, but this one from the gun of a member of the New York Police Department, and was only meant to incapacitate Scizzor, who twisted in his chair to return fire. But before he could, the officer's partner buried a bullet in Scizzor McQueen's forehead, ending the thug's life.

****

Davis had grabbed the ball in mid-air. He would recall the play in an interview with the Sports Network on the 25th anniversary of the Series.

"I never threw a ball harder, or with more control, for the rest of my career."

His throw to home plate stunned every fan crammed into Titan Stadium, all the players on the field and in their respective dugouts, and everyone watching at home. Espinosa, not expecting the play to be at the plate, stepped forward with his right foot and attempted a slide too late. His momentum, though, was plenty to level an NFL-quality tackle on Javier Slocumbe just as the ball arrived from Davis. The umpire stood directly over the play and watched as Slocumbe caught the ball and Espinosa at the exact same moment.

The two catchers toppled over with Espinosa's momentum carrying him onto Slocumbe. The Quakers' catcher bear-hugged his Titan counterpart and the ball, clutched securely in his glove, pressed against Espinosa's back.

Espinosa never touched home plate, his right foot missing "a tie, by an inch" before he sprawled out over Slocumbe.

"Out!" screamed the home plate umpire, his voice inaudible but his thumb clearly in the air. Slocumbe showed the deflated but still raucous crowd the ball in his mitt.

The 1975 World Series was over.

Buster Hodges, as usual, charged out of the dugout to protest the call, but before he got within 25 feet of the first-base umpire, he was run over by several of the Philly bench players.

Chip Dunkirk led the charge out of the dugout, sprinting to get to his best friend in right field, but before he did, he noticed Hodges.

"That jerkweed ain't rainin' on this parade," he said to Jamie Wright, who ran alongside him.

The two were joined by an ecstatic Davey Gonzales and Ike Jackson. The quartet knocked Hodges at least ten feet back toward the Titans' dugout.

Slocumbe, who had suffered through the longest inning of his career, arrived at the mound first. He embraced Slade Maberry, who found himself under a pile that included the two members of the 1964 Quakers, Ike Jackson and Davey Gonzales. Omar Clarke piled on, along with Phil Ostrowski, Moses Pendleton, and Steve Seacourt.

And then the balance of the bench players.

Still out on the field, Jack Slavik and Ricky Davis lay stretched out on the ground, unsure of the final call. But when they saw the celebration on the mound, they got to their feet faster than ninjas and joined the rugby scrum.

Brian Murtaugh, his usual nonplussed self, watched the celebration from the dugout with Hector Enriquez. He shook hands with his Director of Scouting.

"Helluva game," said Murtaugh.

"Helluva Series," replied Enriquez. "Game Seven. Last out on a spectacul—"

Enriquez stopped and looked out at the mound, as the players un-piled and headed for a locker room filled with champagne and a lot of noise.

"I don't see Bobby Young."

Chip Dunkirk also stopped running, but not talking. He shouted for Bobby. Chip stood out in right field just beyond the infield dirt. He placed both hands on his hips and searched right field, then center field, then the foul ball area. He looked back to the mound, where the celebration had ended and the players streamed into the clubhouse.

Chip could see the backs of every player's uniform. Nowhere did he see number 17.

He spun around to the outfield for one more check and ran back in toward the dugout. Hector Enriquez approached from the other side.

"Is Bobby in the clubhouse?" asked Chip. "That is one fast ballplayer if he is."

"No," said Hector, his lips set in a straight line across his handsome features.

Game Seven had ended. The Quakers had won their first World Series in team history.

And Bobby Young was nowhere in sight.

****

The field went black in front of him after Slade Maberry had delivered the last pitch. When Bobby heard the crack of the bat, all the details of Titan Stadium darkened until nothing remained. Not a shape. Not a sound. He crouched in the ready position. One more out. That's all. One more out and the Quakers would be world champs.

The muddy outfield grass appeared before him as his eyes adjusted to the blackness.

"Lights have gone out," he said to himself. "Hey, Moses! What happened?"

No response from Moses Pendleton in center field.

"Moses!"

Nothing.

Bobby's eyes adjusted. Moses Pendleton was not in center field. Ike Jackson wasn't standing at first base.

And there wasn't a soul in the stands at Titan Stadium. He crumpled to the ground. He lay there for a few minutes. He might have remained there for a while but for the jangling of keys and the squawk of a walkie-talkie.

"Outfield grass, right. Looks like a teenager." A pause. "Yes, come on out and help. Call local PD to meet at security."

Bobby picked himself up off the grass.

An emaciated man in a black jacket with a security guard patch trotted toward him. Behind the man hustled another guard with not much more girth. They flanked Bobby.

"Young fella," said the ad for anorexia. "Whatcha doon out here? How'd ya get in?"

Bobby stretched, which caused both security guards to back away. He laughed.

"I'll try to explain everything. All I want to know is today's date—and please include the year."

"October thirty-first. Halloween," said the second guard, "and the year of perfect vision, which you have to know."

2020! Bobby thought.

"I'm back. I'm *home?*" he said aloud.

"Not yet, you ain't," said Anorexia. "Let's go."

"Hold on," said Bobby, after they'd gone a few steps. "October thirty-first was the date of Game Seven of the 1975 World Series. Who won the 1975 Series?"

Both guards glanced at Bobby's uniform.

"Oh, so you're a smart guy, too," replied the second guard. "You trying to rub it in? Is that why you're here? The forty-fifth anniversary of Near-miss Espinosa? Man, I'm glad they traded him after that to Saint Louis. Shoulda started that lousy slide of his earlier."

"Uh, the Quakers?" And despite the chill, Bobby removed his uniform jersey and turned it inside out. The guards were too distracted to ask him why.

"Shut up," said Anorexia. "The police will be here soon."

****

"And your friends dropped you, unconscious, and left you out in right field while they fled the scene, carrying the body bag into which they shoved you?"

"Yes, officer," said Bobby. "I'm very sorry."

One of the police officers turned to the security guards.

"Didn't find a body bag out there?"

"Nope."

"Mister Young. You have no ID."

"That's how I roll," said Bobby trying to draw out a laugh. When none came, he coughed and continued. "My friends must have stolen it."

"Of course they did."

The policeman stood over Bobby, who wrapped the New York Titans blanket the guards gave him over his shoulders to obscure the name and numbers on his uniform, reversed though they were.

"We called your parents," said the officer. "Your mother fainted for some reason. Your father got very emotional. Sounds like your brother is coming to get you."

"George!" His eyes lit up.

"Yes. He's on his way."

"From Oakland, or Manhattan, or—?"

"Nah. Happened to be in New Jersey for a visit. Take a coupla hours."

The officer picked up his cap and prepared to walk out, but he stopped.

"You know, you have the same name as that ballplayer that disappeared so long ago. He was never found."

Bobby allowed himself a smile.

"My parents were huge Quakers fans," he said to the officer. "So were my grandparents, though my dad's dad was a die-hard Philadelphia Lions fan, too, even after they moved to Oakland."

Anorexia, still in the security room, thought about that for a minute, then walked over and handed Bobby a bottle of water.

"Weird, huh? I think he played right field, you know, where your friends dumped you tonight."

"Yeah, weird."

The officer headed to the door but spun around at the last minute. "You can go, Mister Young, when your brother gets here. But look, if you want to come to a Titans game, either buy a ticket, make the club, or play for someone else in the League. Got it?"

"Yes, sir, I do."

****

Two hours later, the phone in the security office rang. Anorexia answered it. His voice woke Bobby out of a deep sleep.

"Yep," said Anorexia. "Send him back."

He hung up the phone.

"Your brother will be here in a couple of minutes."

Bobby straightened up and slapped himself in the face. His brother walked through the door.

George, dressed in workout gear, stopped just inside the door of the security office. He swallowed and ran at Bobby. George hugged him with a ferocious clench and he cried openly, burying his head in Bobby's right shoulder. He wouldn't let go, and didn't, until Anorexia got out of his chair and jangled his keys. George pulled back but kept his hands on his brother's shoulders. He shook Bobby, whose face was wet with his brother's, and his own, tears.

"Where the *hell* have you been these past six months? Where?"

Bobby forced a smile, but it dissolved and he grabbed George even harder and held on through a body-wracking sob.

"Two hours to home?" he asked George.

"Yeah, two hours, give or take New York City traffic. So?"

"That should cover it."

They made their way out into the parking lot. George exhaled, as the two climbed into his own powder blue, vintage 1965 Mustang Fastback.

****

"That was the last thing that I remember," said Bobby, finishing up. "I confronted Slade Maberry. According to the security guard with the eating disorder, Maberry threw Smythe a changeup on a two-two count. And a good one. If I hadn't gotten to him, he might have grooved Tanner a fastball, because that's what Maberry had been told to do by the mob, and that would have been that, but I can't be sure. And that was that, or so I've been told."

"That was that all right," said George. "I've seen the play a hundred times on the Sports Network." He paused. "Near-miss Espinosa. Titans traded him to Saint Louis. He had the last laugh, though, as the Knights won the Series in 1982, 1985, and 1987, and

Danny was a big part of all three. Davis made a great play, though why throw home? Guess he . . . I don't know."

"Yes, I think his conscience got to him."

"You know there were no cameras on right field at the end of the game? Every one of them concentrated on that play."

"Photos?"

"Yes, but only just before the last play, and not after."

"No cellphones during that time. That was hard to get used to," said Bobby.

"And no Sports Network coverage for four more years."

"Had to be regular network coverage."

"Sure, but every camera was on that play, like I said. Every one of them went into closeup on the throw to Javier Slocumbe, who could not have blocked the plate better. Still don't know how he held onto the ball. Espinosa leveled him. Broke Javier's left arm. Though he didn't realize it until later."

They had arrived at Exit 4 on the New Jersey Turnpike. George got off and headed over to Route 295 and the last few miles to Stratford.

George laughed.

"God, I missed that. You still laugh like a hyena that had its tail stepped on," Bobby said as they entered the development. "And just what is so funny?"

"Before I ask you something that just made me laugh," said George, "you should know the rest of the 1975 almost-Black Sox scandal."

"Shoot."

"Murtaugh got Echevarrian into his office after Game Six."

"I remember that," said Bobby, interrupting. "Goofy and I saw Phil Ostrowski take Echevarrian out of the locker room and walk down to Murtaugh's visiting coach's office. They were in there a long time."

"The rumor, legend, myth, is that he got Echevarrian to confess, and then during the celebration in the locker room after Game Seven, he did the same thing with Davis, Garvey, and Maberry."

Bobby sat silently as they negotiated the turns into Laurel Mill Farms and then to his parents' house.

"OK, this is coming back now. There were all these surprise off-season moves, right?" Bobby asked George. "Maberry and Echevarrian retired."

"Echevarrian had arm trouble, which was true, but he played several more years in Japan. Davis was traded to the Senators, which was purgatory at the time. Maberry did retire, and Garvey went over to the American League, to the—wait for it—the effing Titans!"

They both laughed, the sound echoing against the windows of the Mustang.

"The Titans! Oh, man, I forgot about that. I guess he didn't have much of a career there."

The car turned onto Hillcrest.

"Hey, what happened to the mobsters?"

George hit the brakes.

"Are you joking?"

"No. Remember I was gone just before the last out."

He pulled the car over in front of the DeMuro's house, two doors away. He drummed his fingers against the steering wheel.

"What is it?"

"Glad you're sitting down."

"OK. Come on. It can't be that bad."

"They took a shot at you. It was covered up by the crowd noise, but the guy, Scizzor McQueen, got three rounds off from a luxury box before the police broke in and killed him. They also found the dead body of his boss, Maxine Hughes, there. McQueen had killed her, and they think it had a lot to do with the Quakers winning the World Series and the failed kidnapping of a little girl in Audubon."

"Mom."

"What was that?"

"Mom," said Bobby. "They tried to kidnap Mom. They got a note to me in the locker room that they were holding her hostage. We never believed Pop-Pop's story of the break-in and the huge guy Mam-Mom clubbed nearly unconscious with a cast iron frying pan."

"The one she used on Pop-Pop more than once."

"Yes."

"So, it's true?"

Bobby shifted in the seat and leaned back.

"The envelope with the note contained some of her black hair and a picture from her kindergarten class. If I didn't help lose Game Seven, they were going to kill her. I wasn't sure who she was, but—"

"But what?"

"The problem was that some of my memories of the past were erased during my time in 1975. One of them was the family, especially of anyone not you, Kathi, Mom or Dad. Wendell and Kathryn Leonard of Audubon's little girl, Elizabeth? When I read the note, I knew it meant something, but I didn't make that kind of connection. Not at all. I couldn't remember anything after a time. Not even my own family."

"Elizabeth Leonard," started George, the words coming out slowly, one at a time. "That was Mom's name, but everyone called her Betty."

"I know. I know." Bobby clenched the sides of the leather seat. "But I only remembered her as Betty Young. Thank God nothing happened to her."

"God, and that ten-thousand-pound iron skillet."

"Oh, man, that sucker was heavy."

They both laughed. George put the car back into drive for the last part of the trip, but before he stepped on the gas, he turned to Bobby.

"OK, Mister Philadelphia Phenom, what are you going to do for an encore now that you've changed the fortunes of a Major League franchise, averted another scandal like the Black Sox, and saved baseball for the youth of America?"

Bobby laughed.

"Speaking of hyenas."

"Yeah. Yeah. OK. Must be genetic."

"Well?"

"I guess I'll show up unannounced at spring training, catch on with the club, and finish up what was obviously a future Hall of Fame career."

"Good plan. Anything else?"

"Yes, is the team still called the Quakers?" asked Bobby.

"What?"

"Is the Philadelphia franchise still called the Quakers?"

"What else would they be?"

"I don't know. Didn't they have a nickname at one point?"

"Yeah, but it was stupid. What gives?"

"Never mind," said Bobby. "Oh, one more thing."

"What's that?"

"Don't ever let me play in that charity game against the Lions."

"Yeah," said George. "I could see where that might cause some problems."

They pulled up in front of nine Hillcrest Road. Their parents' Oldsmobile occupied the driveway.

"Mom and Dad are home," said George.

"Me too."

George W. Young

Bio

George W. Young started his professional life as a dancer in New York City in 1979, where he worked in summer stock and way-off-Broadway in musical theater, and he performed in some of the earliest music videos with Diana Ross, The Pointer Sisters, and Louise Robey.

He switched over to the other side of the camera in New York City in 1984, where he worked on national and international TV commercials for Fortune 500 companies. Directors on his credit sheet include Bob Giraldi, Joe Pytka, and Steve Steigman. He moved to California in 1988.

George spent the next 30 years working on a variety of projects including feature films such as *The Nightmare Before Christmas, Junior, Serendipity,* and *The Internship.* He also produced three video games for George Lucas based on the *Star Wars* canon, *Rebel Assault, Jedi Knight,* and *Force Commander.*

He worked with Larry Page at Google on several projects including the launch of Google+. He collaborated with Steve Jobs at Apple on many of the company's advertising campaigns, and the introduction of QuickTime as the standard for computer-based digital video.

In 2017 he turned his attention to writing novels including *DracuLAND,* the story of a New York City real estate mogul who purchases Dracula's Castle and finds no vampires, but plenty of other undead inconveniences; *The Google Earth Murders,* a serial killer reboot; and the nonfiction, *Try Not to Annoy the Kangaroo, A lifetime of putting up with creative people in the film industry.*

Other publications from Celestial Echo Press

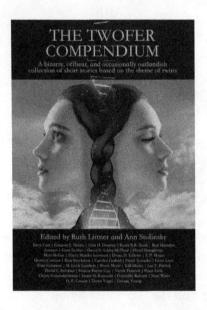

"Twins are said to share special bonds, understand each other's unspoken communication, speak their own languages, even possess powers of ESP. Their double-ness continues to fascinate the rest of us. Adored or abhorred, sheltered or shunned, twins have universally and perpetually aroused attention and curiosity. It was that fascination that inspired this collection of twin-themed stories. In them, you'll find all matter of twins: the good, the bad, the fantastic, the fearsome, the magical, the envious, the secretive, the devious, and more. Being a twin. Fun, right? Think about it. *What could go wrong?*"

–Merry Jones, from the Foreword

The Twofer Compendium is available at Barnes & Noble and other fine bookshops, and online at Amazon.com.

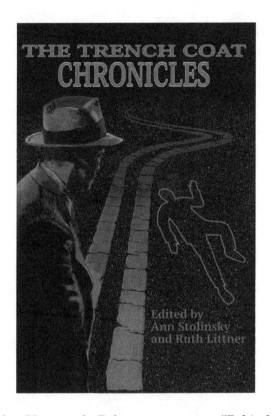

French novelist Honore de Balzac once wrote, "Behind every great fortune lies a great crime." And we believe him. Some of the stories you will read in this anthology include criminals motivated by riches and fortune. Some of the stories have perpetrators with more pure agendas. But as Jacques Barzun quipped, "The danger that may really threaten crime fiction is that soon there will be more writers than readers." We don't believe him. We know you, along with millions of other book lovers, will continue to enjoy reading stories throughout the ages. It's because crime stories evoke the "bad boy" in all of us, the hidden, mysterious desire to vicariously commit the crime—and get away with it. And we love to read about those criminals. "We don't give our criminals much punishment, but we sure give 'em plenty of publicity." Thanks, Will Rogers. We agree, and we promote. This murder mystery anthology is dedicated to Sam Spade, Hercule Poirot, and Dick Tracy, as well as to all the writers of hard-boiled detective stories of years past, many of whom formed the basis for the crime mysteries we read today. Enjoy this wide variety of storylines, each of which include criminals, victims—and trench coats.

The Trench Coat Chronicles is available at Barnes & Noble and other fine bookshops, and online at Amazon.com.

CPSIA information can be obtained
at www.ICGtesting.com
Printed in the USA
JSHW020258081221
21070JS00001B/42